THE BODY IN THE MOONLIGHT

It's October in Aleford, Massachusetts. Minister's wife Faith Fairchild is excited about catering her church's Murder Mystery benefit dinner. But the event, a restoration campaign kickoff at historic Ballou House, is marred by real murder. A young woman dies moments after finishing dessert, and Faith is in serious trouble. Not only is her catering business jeopardised, but she's also the victim of Aleford's wagging tongues. The gossip suggests that Faith herself had laced the goodies with cyanide. Never before have Faith's amateur sleuthing skills been more crucial, especially when another body is found carrying the unmistakeable warning — you're next!

Books by Katherine Hall Page
Published by The House of Ulverscroft:

THE BODY IN THE KELP
THE BODY IN THE VESTIBULE
THE BODY IN THE BOOKCASE
THE BODY IN THE BIG APPLE
THE BODY IN THE SNOWDRIFT
THE BODY IN THE BONFIRE
THE BODY IN THE MARSH

Katherine Hall Page is the author of several previous Faith Fairchild mysteries. She lives with her husband and son in Massachusetts.

KATHERINE HALL PAGE

THE BODY IN THE MOONLIGHT

Complete and Unabridged

ULVERSCROFT
Leicester

First published in Great Britain in 2009 by
Robert Hale Limited
London

First Large Print Edition
published 2010
by arrangement with
Robert Hale Limited
London

British Library CIP Data

Page, Katherine Hall.
The body in the moonlight.
1. Fairchild, Faith Sibley (Fictitious character)- -Fiction.
2. Women in the food industry- -Massachusetts- -Fiction.
3. Caterers and catering- -Massachusetts- -Fiction.
4. Detective and mystery stories. 5. Large type books.
I. Title
813.5'4–dc22

 ISBN 978–1–44480–332–7

Published by
F. A. Thorpe (Publishing)
Anstey, Leicestershire

Set by Words & Graphics Ltd.
Anstey, Leicestershire
Printed and bound in Great Britain by
T. J. International Ltd., Padstow, Cornwall

This book is printed on acid-free paper

To Ginny and David Fine,
who knew what's important in life —
a good sense of humor, chocolate,
and true friendship

Acknowledgements

I would like to thank Dr. Robert DeMartino for his continued help on medical details; Kyra Alex, Lily's Cafe, Stonington, Maine, and Elizabeth Bledsoe for treasured recipes; the Lizzie Borden ladies: Barbara Boiden Morrissey and JoAnne Giovino; my editor, Jennifer Sawyer Fisher, on this first voyage together; and, as always, my friend and agent, Faith Hamlin.

'There's no use trying,' she said: 'One can't believe impossible things.'

'I daresay you haven't had much practice,' said the Queen, 'When I was your age, I always did it for half-an-hour a day. Why, sometimes I've believed as many as six impossible things before breakfast.'

— LEWIS CARROLL.
Through the Looking Glass

Prologue

'Tell me about the voices.'

'Not voices, a voice. My voice, I think. But that's not how it starts. When I hear words in my head — the voice — I know what to do. I know it will be over soon.'

'How does it start?'

'I wake up at night — very suddenly. I'm terrified and I don't know where I am. Then, during the following day, it seems as if people are talking to me from far away. They sound as if they're at the end of a tunnel. Even people I know. Especially people I know.'

'This must be very frightening.'

'It is. Frightening. More than frightening. But it's not the worst part.'

'What's the worst part?'

'The panic. The terror. My heart races. Usually when I'm driving. I can't think. I can't breathe. I have an impulse to steer off the road — or straight into the oncoming traffic. I pull over and my fingers are numb from gripping the wheel. I'm sweating and nauseous. The roof feels like it's pressing down on top of my head. When I close my eyes, it gets worse. A bright light starts to pulsate.

Flesh-colored — round and shiny. It feels hot, and if I don't open my eyes immediately, it will explode. When I start to drive again, I tell myself I only have to make it to the next exit or the next stoplight. Whatever I can see ahead of me. That's how I make it home.'

'When did this all begin?'

'I can't remember. Last spring? Maybe last winter. But it's always the same. Then I hear the words. I know what I have to do and everything stops. I can function. I can sleep. It stops sometimes for a long time, but not for good.'

'What you need — '

'No! I've told you. One person — that's enough. And you can't repeat it to anyone else. Not a living soul.'

'You're right. I can't . . . Now tell me again what the voices tell you to do.'

1

'Patsy, sorry to wake you. It's Faith.'

Fully awake, even though it was only 6:30, Patsy Avery got out of bed and walked into the hall, away from her sleeping husband.

'What's wrong? I can hear it in your voice. What's happened?'

'I think I may need you; that is, I think I may need a lawyer.'

'Don't say another word. I'm on a cell phone. Get over here — or do you want me to come to you?'

'I'll come, but I'll have to leave in time to get ready for church.'

'Heavens above,' Patsy said mockingly, 'I certainly wouldn't want to be responsible for the minister's wife missing the service.'

Faith said good-bye without either laughing or responding to the quip with one of her own.

Things must be very bad.

Patsy pulled a dressing gown over her large frame and debated whether to awaken Will. He was a lawyer, too. She'd wait and ask Faith.

She went downstairs to the kitchen,

pausing at the thermostat to hike it up several degrees. It was October, and she knew that by New England standards she shouldn't even have the heat on until the first snowstorm forced a grudging acknowledgment that it could be a mite nippy out. She went back and flicked it again, hearing the furnace respond with a satisfying rumble. She was from New Orleans, and as far as she was concerned, it started getting cold up north just about the time you thought summer might finally have arrived. Damn cold.

The days were getting shorter and by the end of the month daylight saving time would end. It would be dark when they got home from work. It was dark now, but an early-morning dark already starting to thin to gray. The birds were up and creating their usual bedlam. Traffic noise didn't bother her, yet when they'd left the city for bucolic Aleford, it had taken months for Patsy to learn to sleep through this avian chorus.

Her eye fell on the calendar hanging near the phone. There would be a full moon tonight. The house gave an appropriate groan. Just the wood expanding and contracting, the Realtor had hastened to explain when a bansheelike wail accompanied their ascent up the attic stairs. Patsy didn't believe in ghosts, especially northern ghosts. She

4

chuckled to herself, remembering her mother's comment: 'Don't worry, honey, from what I've heard, those old Yankees don't like giving space to tenants who don't pay any rent.'

Patsy had spent most of the fall traveling back and forth to the Midwest on a case, returning from the latest trip only on Friday. She and Will had spent the day before getting reacquainted — and that did not include a trip to the market — but she knew Will would never let them run out of coffee beans, and their freezer was always full of food. She quickly brewed a large pot, then dug around for some of the sticky buns her mother-in-law regularly sent up, along with vats of gumbo and the occasional sweet-potato pie. Faith Fairchild wasn't just the minister's wife but also a successful caterer. Besides a whole lot of other things in common, she and Patsy shared the sincere belief that food was an antidote to misfortune, easing the pain as well as loosening the tongue.

Why on earth would Faith need a lawyer? A criminal lawyer? Patsy worked mostly with juveniles, but she kept her hand in with a few adult cases now and then. She put the rolls in the microwave to defrost and poured herself a cup of coffee. Despite the urgency in Faith's voice, Patsy knew it would take her awhile to get to the house, although they lived within walking distance. The parsonage was one of the white clapboard houses tidily arranged around the Aleford village green, a hop, skip, and a jump through the old burying ground to the First Parish Church, where the Reverend Thomas Fairchild held forth. The Averys' move from Boston's South End last year had taken them to one of Aleford's 'modern' architectural offerings, a large Victorian on a side street off the green. But Faith wouldn't be able simply to walk out the door. She was a woman with responsibilities.

Patsy stood at the kitchen window, holding the oversized cup in both hands, bringing the fragrant steaming liquid to her mouth. Still too hot to drink. She turned off the overhead light she'd switched on when she'd entered the room and looked outdoors. The tomato plants, blackened in late September by an unusually early frost, and other horticultural detritus filled a rectangular plot in the back corner of the yard. Neither Will nor she had had time to put the garden to sleep, as they whimsically expressed it in these parts. Patsy hadn't even had a chance to harvest the green tomatoes. Dipped in cornmeal and fried, they were one of Will's favorite vegetables. How did the man stay as thin as a rail? She smiled reminiscently, savoring the day before. He didn't want a skinny woman, thank God. Next year, she'd make sure she harvested the tomatoes or, if she had to be away, leave a reminder for Will. It had obviously slipped his mind. He was even busier than she was. No, she wouldn't wake her husband unless there was a very good reason.

It was almost day now, and she had a sudden impulse to go outside and sit on the bench next to the bluestone path that wound its way through the yard. Will had given her a fountain for her birthday, turned off now. The grasses surrounding it, bleached out, dry, and swaying ever so slightly in the morning air, looked beautiful. But Faith would be here soon, and besides, there was the cold.

There weren't any swing sets, sandboxes, bicycles left out — evidence of younger Averys. But there would be someday. That's why they'd moved to white-bread land, 'moving-on-up' land. 'Schools and safety, baby,' Will had argued. 'We owe our kids that.' Driving down Aleford's Main Street Friday on her way home from the airport, Patsy had seen three middle-aged women sprawled motionless on a bench, waiting for the train — bronze statues, weariness etched deep on each face. Their hands were clutching the bags that held their work clothes — and maybe an old tired-out shirt or pair of scuffed-up shoes, gifts from a charitable employer. They weren't even talking to one another. Bone-weary. Their long day was ending as it had begun, with a long ride, a welcome ride, coming and going, before the work started up all over again. She felt ashamed for the whole world and, catching her own reflection in the rearview mirror, saw her own guilt. She was tired, too, but like it or not, she was home.

'Schools and safety' uh-huh — and here was the minister's wife needing a lawyer.

★ ★ ★

Thirty minutes later, Faith arrived, breathless. 'Had to feed the kids, then popped good old *Blue's Clues* in the VCR and Amy in her playpen.' Benjamin Fairchild was five and viewed his sister, Amy, at two, as a cross between an amusing sort of pet and total moron, incapable even of intelligible speech. 'Tom is frantically rewriting his sermon, as usual.'

Patsy nodded. Part of her yearned for motherhood with an intensity that often surprised her. Part of her flinched in abject terror at the thought of no deposit, no return.

She poured Faith a cup of coffee and placed the plate of warm rolls on the table.

'Sit down and tell me all about it. You haven't been arrested?'

Faith shook her head, 'Not yet.' She took a deep breath. Where to start? Coming to talk to Patsy was exactly the right thing to do, but now that she was here, she didn't know where or how to begin. Last night? Last month? Last summer? Her childhood?

'Begin at the beginning.' Patsy had sensed her quandary. 'I'm not going anywhere. Do you want Will to hear all this?'

Faith shook her head. Too distracting to look from one sympathetic face to the other — and besides, Patsy was a woman, and there were some things Faith didn't want to talk about with a man, any man, not even her husband. Last night couldn't have been her fault. She knew that for certain. Yet the agitation and the thoughts that had followed were her responsibility alone. She grabbed her pocket-book and took out a dollar bill, shoving it across the table.

'You're on retainer. It's all privileged information now, right? You can't repeat it to anyone else. Not a living soul.'

Patsy took the money and put it in her pocket. 'All right. I'm on retainer.' Whatever Faith wanted.

On the way to the house, Faith had thought about her choice of confidante. Pix Miller, who lived next door to the parsonage, was her closest friend and they had been through a great deal together. Patsy was a new friend and didn't really know the Fairchilds that well, but it was what Faith wanted now. Legal advice and someone who wasn't enmeshed in their lives. Tom and Faith's life. Someone who wasn't a member of the congregation.

Patsy Avery was used to clients who had trouble getting to the point. With kids, it sometimes took weeks. Sometimes, it never happened. Faith was picking at the sticky bun and Patsy kept quiet. The hum of the refrigerator sounded unnaturally loud.

'I don't mean to be so melodramatic and I *will* start at the beginning, but you have to know where we're going. I was catering an event last night and someone died. Someone died after eating one of my desserts. The police are calling it a homicide.'

'Holy shit!' Patsy said, shocked from her normal calm. She paused a moment to place her warm, smooth hand over Faith's, then reached for the pad and pencil she'd taken from her study. 'Okay, let's go.'

2

The beginning. Faith let her gaze soften as she cast back in her mind — far back, months ago.

The First Parish Church of Aleford, Massachusetts, had no intention of letting the congregation's 250th anniversary slip by them without proper notice. It coincided with the upcoming year, 2000, which was noted with varying degrees of interest. There had been a handful of dreary sticklers insisting that it wouldn't really be the millennium until January 1, 2001, and the vestry had reached a swift, rare, unanimous decision to concentrate on the event of *real* importance. That decided, how, in fact, should the church mark the occasion?

A committee was formed, and after several interminable and increasingly rancorous meetings during the summer, it reached a stalemate. Half the members wanted to restore the steeple, the other half the crypt. When ex officio member Tom Fairchild returned home to tell his wife the news, she was sure he'd made it up.

'No, really, darling, you can't be serious. It's too perfect. Steeple or crypt — diametrically opposed proposals. The paint in the sanctuary is starting to peel and the organ could use overhauling, yet no one's pushing them. It's pique, that's what it is. You want the steeple, then I'll take the crypt.' She put a cool mug of Killian's Red ale in his hand and set a plate with a sandwich within reach on the coffee table. As usual, Tom had had no time for much of a dinner. Most of the clergy Faith knew had adopted grazing as an eating habit born of necessity long before it became fashionable.

They were sitting on the couch, which Faith had moved from in front of the fireplace to a spot perpendicular to it. During the summer, she'd gotten tired of looking into an unlighted hearth and decided she'd rather face the cemetery and church through the wavy glass of the windowpanes instead. Besides, from the marks on the floor, she was sure a couch had always been in front of the fireplace, and she was feeling uppity. Virtually every parishioner entering the room since had remarked on her avant-garde decorating. She had never heard four words — 'You've moved the couch' — uttered so many different ways. Tom was slumped comfortably against its deep cushioned back. He was the only person who had not commented — unless one counted a slightly raised eyebrow.

'Unfortunately, it's not a joke. I hate this

kind of thing. It's a side to the congregation I'd rather not know anything about.'

'Like your parents having sex.'

'Worse. Like your children having sex.'

Faith thought of Ben and Amy mushrooming into adolescence and adulthood. Hair growing in new places. Hormones. Muffled sounds from behind closed doors. Tom was right. It wasn't something you wanted to consider — this leap from Little Tikes to Trojans.

'What do you think the church should do? Are you for the heavens or the bowels of the earth?' There were so many ways to express the dilemma — and Faith was sure she'd be treated to them all in the months to come.

'I'm not supposed to have an opinion and I'm sticking to that. Much safer — and saner.'

'Come on, I know you've wanted to use the crypt for Tenebrae and other services. You can tell me. I promise not a word will cross my lips, even if the entire vestry shows up en masse and threatens to toss the new pew cushions into the Charles River.'

The old cushions, consisting after many years of two worn pieces of fabric with a thoroughly compressed millimeter of stuffing and thereby unworthy of the name, had finally been replaced the previous summer when a sudden and dramatic infestation of moths had rendered them holey. Suspicion had briefly fallen on Faith, who had made no secret of her pious discomfort, and mutterings of 'Just like the gypsy moth that escaped from that scientist's house in Cambridge' were heard. But the cushions had been replaced, to Faith's delight — and surprise. Talking with friend and fellow parishioner Pix Miller, she'd voiced her fears that the congregation would opt for the hard, unadorned wood as more conducive to penitence. But First Parish had had pew cushions for as long as anyone could remember, so, with a bow to tradition, pew cushions it had been.

'You're right. I would like the crypt to be restored — not only for services but also because the memorial stones need cleaning. They're a significant part of the church's history, and if we don't take care of them, they'll disintegrate. The steeple is certainly more visible and it does need repair and new paint, but it can wait.'

'So, what's going to happen?'

'This is an incredible sandwich. What's in it, anyway?' Tom had inhaled it in a few bites, and the beer was almost gone, too.

'Chèvre, roasted peppers and red onion. I'll make you another, but I don't have any more of that bread. It will have to be focaccia.'

'My tough luck.' Tom grinned. He was feeling better, much better. He followed his wife into the kitchen.

'To answer your question. I have no idea. It could go either way, but they're going to start the fund drive immediately.'

Faith nodded. This was the maddening thing about the congregation — and probably about any congregation. They could be at each other tooth and nail, irrevocably divided one minute, then in complete accord the next. They'd conduct the campaign in total equanimity while thrashing out the object of the effort behind closed doors.

'What's the plan? Or is it another committee?'

'A subcommittee. Specifically to plan a kickoff event for sometime in October, raise a moderate bundle that way, then pledge cards in the mail the next morning, before the rosy glow of a good time had by all has had a chance to wear off.'

'That doesn't give them much time. Do they have any idea what this event is going to be?'

'Paula Pringle proposed one of those mystery dinners — as in solving a crime, not what's being served. She wants to hold it at Ballou House, very 'swish,' with 'luscious food' — her words — and 'fun people.' Again — '

'Her words,' Faith interjected, finishing the sentence for her husband, then handing him another sandwich. 'Are you sure that's her real name? 'Paula Pringle Parties' has such a made-up ring to it.'

'I don't know how she started out, but she is definitely married to a Mr Pringle, although I have never met the man. He's 'not a spiritual being.' Again . . . '

Neither of them bothered to finish.

Faith laughed. 'Oh dear, this wasn't what you signed on for, was it? Was there ever a time when you believed you would be simply practicing theology with a pastoral call or two?'

'Some nasty types at the Div School used to spread it about that all was not to be loaves and fishes, but I didn't listen. Such is youth.'

'Well, Paula Pringle is a professional party planner — I'll bet you can't say that six times — so you won't have to be involved in this part at any rate.'

★ ★ ★

The phone rang the next morning precisely as Faith closed the front door, having put her son on the kindergarten bus and waved goodbye to her husband and daughter, who were setting off for a morning of work and

16

day care at the church.

'Mrs Fairchild — Faith dear — it's Paula. Paula Pringle from church.'

A deep sense of foreboding swept over Faith.

'Yes?' Then hastily remembering her manners, she added, 'How are you?'

'Fine, and you, too, I hope?' The woman had not called to waste time in exchanging pleasantries. 'Perhaps Reverend Fairchild told you about our plan of action for the Anniversary Campaign?'

It had a distinctly militaristic ring to it phrased that way, Faith realized — and Paula Pringle was definitely the one to marshal the forces.

'He mentioned you'd formed a subcommittee to do some fund-raising for a commemorative project,' Faith said cautiously, mindful of the word *crypt* and nervous at the possible intent of the call. Her ministerial spousal radar system was bleeping loud and clear. Paula Pringle wanted her to volunteer.

'I know how busy you are . . . '

Here it comes, thought Faith.

'Your business is soooo successful. Everywhere I go, people only want Have Faith to cater their events.'

In which case, Faith wondered, why is it

that I've never worked at one of your functions?

'After the meeting last night, a few of us got together at my place and sketched out some rough ideas for a really fabulous fund-raising kickoff party.'

Don't these people sleep — or work? It had been after eleven by the time Tom came home.

'And this morning, I was lucky enough to reach Mattie Hawthorne, who manages Ballou House, and we have a date.'

Up with the chickens as you both were. Faith was fatalistic, possibly resigned. Whatever was coming, she was no match for this woman.

'Have you ever catered at Ballou, Faith? Such a treasure, and right here in our own Aleford.'

Faith *had* catered several weddings at Ballou House. It was an extraordinary eighteenth-century country estate built in the Georgian manner by Increase Ballou as a forty-acre retreat from his Beacon Hill mansion. True to his name, he had taken the modest shipping company founded by his father and made a fortune, staggering at that time — or any time. Ballou House had a large ballroom, punctuated by the classic columns beloved by the Georgians. At one end, French

18

doors, a later addition, opened on to a patio overlooking Italianate gardens. At the other end of the room, an architectural wall, complete with pediment and more columns, surrounded a huge fireplace with a gray-veined marble mantel wide enough to display the shiploads of Chinese export porcelain Increase's ships had used for ballast. The cargo was an example of the perfect marriage between pragmatism and aestheticism that characterized so much of New England, even up to the present day.

Subsequent generations had added wings and outbuildings to Ballou House, making it still more of a grand mixture. The furniture that had not been given to the Museum of Fine Arts, along with Copley's portrait of Increase, was a hodgepodge of Queen Anne, Chippendale, Gothic, Victoriana, and Arts and Crafts. The original Chinese wallpaper graced the drawing room, protected by glass, and a grand Palladian window above the front door had also happily been left alone.

Besides Ballou House, there were several other 'rustic' retreats tucked away in Aleford. During those long-ago summers, the town's sturdy populace, mostly farmers descended from its first settlers, was outnumbered by these wealthy landowners and their servants — from Ireland, the Maritime Provinces, and

Italy — all essential to maintain their masters' way of life. Eventually, many of these employees and their descendants became year-round residents, distinctions supposedly blurred as the twentieth century brought dramatic changes to the rural character of the town. Typically, however, Aleford was slower than most to embrace any newfangled notions, actually voting to keep their streetlights filled with kerosene until 1910 — long after neighboring towns had electrified.

The Ballous had continued to prosper, at least financially, and when Increase's last direct descendant died childless sometime in the forties, he left Ballou House to the town and an ample trust fund to keep it in good repair. The thrifty town fathers and mothers promptly began to rent it out for weddings and 'other appropriate functions,' while using it themselves for the yearly Patriots' Day Ball, the reception following the close of Town Meeting, Milk Punch with the selectmen at New Year's, and other joyous occasions. A manager was installed in the former coach house, and it was his daughter who had the job now. Ballou House was an inspired choice for First Parish's kickoff campaign. Aleford residents received a reduced rate, and if the whole idea was to inspire a sense of worth and well-being, there was no other place like it.

'Yes,' said Faith, reluctantly abandoning her reverie to answer Paula's question, 'I've done a number of events there.'

'Marvelous! Now, I know how busy you are, but you are our absolute first choice and we are so hoping you can do the dinner.'

Faith knew what she had to say — and in truth, she really didn't mind. It wasn't as if she was being asked to take on the church school's Christmas pageant.

'I'd be happy to help. And of course I'll do it at cost.'

'I knew you would,' Paula said appreciatively, letting the words sink in, then added briskly, 'Now, we haven't got a moment to spare. When can we meet? You don't need to worry about a thing. I'm going to be with you every step of the way. Such fun! We'll do it in tandem!'

That's what Faith had been afraid of — a yoke.

★ ★ ★

By the end of the first week in October, Faith was ready to kill Paula Pringle — especially Paula Pringle, Party Planner. The menu was set; the menu was changed. The color scheme

21

and table decorations were set; they were changed.

'If she would only let me do my job and stick to planning the entertainment, I might, just might, get through next week,' Faith fumed to Niki Constantine, her assistant.

'That's supposed to be puff pastry, remember?' Niki commented as Faith pressed the slab of buttery dough with the intensity of a laundress attacking an intransigent wrinkle.

'I never was very good at sharing,' Faith muttered. 'Poor Mother. It must have been mortifying. 'Faith needs to work on her sharing skills.' My first kindergarten report. Apparently, I wouldn't pass the guinea pig on to the next child for a turn. But Eleanor — that was her name (the animal, not the child) was happy with me, and who would want to be handed around like that anyway, being squeezed too hard? Tommy Martin almost strangled her.'

'Faith! Get a grip! What's going on?' Niki meant it. This wasn't like her boss. And Faith *was* good at sharing — especially food.

'I don't know,' Faith said slowly, matching the tempo of rolling the dough to her words. It suddenly seemed like an enormous effort. Most things did lately. She got up tired and she went to bed tired. Tom and she passed, nodded, and went on their appointed rounds.

She thought back. The last time they'd sat down for any length of time together had been that Sunday night when the whole steeple/crypt fund-raiser had first come up. Since then, she'd been working, he had, or they'd both had to be out together — and not at the movies. When was it they'd taken to leaving each other notes on the kitchen table? Last spring, she thought. Not love notes, but 'Put dinner in oven at 350 degrees' notes and 'Home late — hope not too late' notes.

'We've worked with plenty of difficult clients. In fact, difficult clients are the norm. That's why you need never worry your pretty little blond head about my wanting my own business. You know me and 'tact' — gives me hives. Think about what the Bullocks were like. This can't be worse than Stephanie's wedding!'

'True,' Faith admitted as she sat down to let the pastry rest. 'It's me or, rather, 'It's I,' but that sounds terribly affected.'

'Have you noticed you seem to be going off on tangents lately — conversationally, that is? Not that hearing about Eleanor the guinea pig or proper grammar isn't truly fascinating, but why don't we focus on the here and now for the moment? Starting with the Pringle caper. God, I can't wait to meet her. Big smile, right? And really, really sincere. Party planners are like that.'

Paula did have a big smile and sparkling teeth, perhaps a bit too pointed in the bicuspid department, but lipstick always in place, no matter how many cups of coffee she drank. As for the rest of her, the image that came to Faith's mind was of an Afghan hound crossed with one of the Bloomsbury females. If not Virginia Woolf herself, then perhaps Lady Ottoline Morrell. Paula Pringle: long of face and tall in stature. There wasn't an ounce of extra flesh to be seen on her body — not that much flesh was ever revealed. Paula favored Eileen Fisher skirts that grazed the anklebone with matching Jersey tops and cardigans. She loped about with a certain amount of grace, head and shoulders above the hoi polloi.

'You saw the invitations. They went out right away. I'm sure Paula had sent them to the printer even before the meeting.'

Niki nodded her head. '*Très* clever: 'A Murder Is Announced.''

'And she put 'Tickets Limited' in boldface at the bottom. There's nothing like trying to beat out your neighbor. You'd think they were season's passes to the Fleet Center, the way the town has responded. We're sold out and there's a waiting list.'

'It was also a clever idea to invite those

24

mystery writers. People like to rub shoulders — or, in this case, break bread — with celebs.'

The Boston area was particularly rich in talented authors mining veins of suspense, horror, terror, and fright to supply the voracious need readers have to try to outsmart them and guess who done it — or, as one writer had told Faith, to provide reassurance in what at times seemed like an increasingly wicked and capricious world. 'In my books,' she said, 'evil *never* goes unpunished.' Paula had had little trouble finding four 'honored guests.' Few writers are loath — or in a position — to turn down a free meal and a chance to sell some books. Paula had also promptly enlisted Kate Mattes, famed mystery bookseller of Murder Under Cover: Kate's Mystery Books in Cambridge, to come with plenty of wares. Kate was donating a portion of the proceeds to the campaign and, much to Faith's delight, had expressed the wish that they go to the crypt. Since the store's street number was engraved on a headstone in its front yard, this was no surprise.

'The *Boston Globe* covered it in their 'Names and Faces' column with a list of the writers attending. Very impressive. And how did our Ms Pringle get Anson L. Scott? He never does anything like this. Doesn't have to.'

'He lives in town. Didn't you know that?' Faith said. 'But you're right. Even with this, I was surprised he agreed. He's not a member of the church and he's not active in town, but apparently she was able to play on his sentimental attachment to Ballou House. Several generations ago, some ancestor was a parlor maid. I'm sure being lionized in the very same room where great-grandmother cleaned out the fireplace ashes must appeal to him.'

'I read everything he wrote when I was a teenager — and couldn't get to sleep many nights because of it. The man never gives you a chance to breathe. Just one totally terrifying moment after another, one mutilated corpse after another, one totally psychotic killer after another.' Niki smiled reminiscently. 'That scene when the woman opens the trunk of her car . . . '

Faith recalled reading some of the books, too, but only vaguely, and she didn't want any more details. 'Don't remind me.' Real life had provided too many scenes straight from a Scott book since then.

'I haven't read one in a long time. But I guess he's still very hot stuff. I'll have to pick up the latest.'

They worked together in companionable

silence for a while. Tonight's job was a dessert table for a bridal shower. Niki loved to make desserts and had increased her repertoire with courses, besides reading every new dessert cookbook on the market. The puff pastry was for hazelnut mille-feuilles. There would also be chocolate brioche bread pudding with whipped cream, fresh berries with crème anglaise, a white-chocolate mousse cake, champagne sorbet, pumpkin cheesecake, warm apple crisp — these last as a nod to the season — and plenty of mini-pastries and cookies.

'I'll have to run over to the church and get Amy soon,' Faith said. When she had opened the business, she'd had to remodel the existing catering facility slightly and had added a play area for the kids. 'Ben is staying for extended day. I don't know whether to be happy or sad that he doesn't want to come here or go home.' This had been a recurrent theme throughout the fall, ever since Benjamin Fairchild had walked into his kindergarten classroom with merely the briefest of backward glances at his stricken mother. She was proud of his independence and immediate, self-confident adjustment to the rigors of block corner, storytime, snack, and recess, but some slight reluctance, some small sign of separation anxiety, would not have gone amiss, so far as she was concerned.

Instead, from day one, it had been a cheery 'See ya!' and he was off into the arms of another woman. Faith liked the teacher, Mrs Black, a straightforward yet clearly nurturant lady, who was doing a fine job of setting her son's feet on that long and twisted path known as 'school.'

Back to School Night had been an eye-opener. Perched on a tiny chair, Faith had watched Mrs Black field questions with aplomb. She was bombarded with queries about college entrance requirements, spelling tutors, and whether particularly creative Giant of the Week presentations would be noted on a child's permanent record. Apparently, it was all old hat to her. It was new to the Fairchilds, though, and they were shell-shocked. At least they had been prepped on Giant of the Week. Ben was counting the days until his turn. You got to sit in the special Giant chair and wear a paper Giant hat. This was apparently the only effort required of the child. The parents, on the other hand, had to prepare an 'All About Me' poster, complete with family photos from birth to the present, 'attractively arranged with meaningful captions,' supply a favorite — nutritional — family snack for the class, and 'enhance our students' learning experience' with a 'cognitively challenging' presentation about 'what Mommy and Daddy do all day.'

The current Giant's father, a doctor, had come dressed for surgery, and he had brought those little blue paper booties and things that looked like shower caps for each child. The mom had baked cookies in stylized shapes — stethoscopes, lungs, hearts, and brains — and they'd hired a graphic designer to do the poster *and* a video.

Faith had promptly called Pix. There were three Miller children, not counting the dogs. Danny, the youngest, was in middle school, Samantha was a freshman in college, and Mark, the oldest, a college junior. Pix had been there and done that. Faith had a feeling she'd be calling her frequently about the mysteries of education in years to come. 'Nobody told me kindergarten was going to be so much work!' Faith had wailed. 'And what are we going to do? Tom can't pass out surplices and Communion wafers.'

'You'll cook something with the children. And if Tom's free, he can help or read a story. It doesn't matter what you do, so long as you do something. All the kids care about is sitting in the chair. It's the parents who are out of control — and if you join them, you might as well close Have Faith, because you'll be too busy sewing costumes for the all-school musical or running the book fair,' Pix had cautioned.

Just as Faith had been about to let her breath out, Pix had added, 'You do need to be an active presence at school, though. Otherwise, you won't know what's going on, and in Aleford, that often means some unpleasant surprises. I remember when Samantha was in third grade, a very nasty group of parents had it in for the teacher. It was her first year and they didn't think she was 'seasoned' enough.'

'And little Ignatz might not get into Harvard because of it?' Faith had immediately flashed on the group of intense adults at parent night.

'Exactly. George handled it beautifully, but a great deal of damage was done. It was insidious — the way they undermined her self-confidence. George got some of us to volunteer in the classroom, and eventually we were able to get her to see what a marvelous teacher she was. She's still at Winthrop, and now parents complain if they don't get her.'

George Hammond was the principal of Aleford's Winthrop Elementary School and had been for so long that he now had students in the school whose parents he'd had. A widower, he was a member of First Parish, and Faith was glad Ben was starting school with such a kind, patient man at the helm.

'Faith! Where are you?' Niki had seen Faith distracted, distraught even, but these abrupt, deep withdrawals into the world of her own thoughts was something new — like the meandering conversational tangents.

Faith managed a smile. 'Sorry. Thinking about Ben at school got me thinking . . . well, about Ben at school.'

'But I thought it was all going fine.' Niki was fond of the little Fairchilds, especially Ben, who could hold up his end of a conversation. She hoped he wasn't flipping out and becoming a biter, say — or, worse, a whiner.

'Everything *is* fine. We now have 'The Sayings of Mrs Black' as our guide to life, and it's hard not to laugh when Ben solemnly tells us that keeping things in place makes it easier to find them again or 'Cross words trip us.'' She paused and looked at her assistant. 'I know I've been kind of out of it lately. It's not the kids; it's me. Maybe it's winter coming. All those cold, dark days. Maybe it's the parish party. I don't know — but no big deal.'

'A touch of weltschmerz,' Niki said, noting Faith had omitted any mention of Tom. 'Or, as some people call it, the blues.'

This time, Faith smiled for real.

'You got it, baby.'

★　★　★

31

Paula Pringle called the meeting to order.

'People, people. I don't need to remind you that we have less than a week before our party, and this is the last chance we'll all have to get together.'

Faith glanced longingly out the window at the parsonage. The late-afternoon sun had turned the leaves of the big oak in the backyard to Midas gold. The foliage had peaked, according to the *Farmer's Almanac*, except no one had told the trees, which continued to cling to their leaves, hues from a child's paint box against the deep blue skies of autumn. But nothing gold can stay — the Robert Frost lines came back to her: 'So dawn goes down to day. Nothing gold can stay.' Until next year. There was always next year.

The various subcommittee heads were giving their reports, and Faith grudgingly admitted to herself that Paula had whipped the benefit into shape in an amazingly short period of time. In addition to the revenue from the ticket prices, Paula had scoured the area for silent-auction items. She planned to run it all evening, confiding to Faith that as people imbibed, they'd up their bids.

'That sounds wonderful, dear,' she said, congratulating the woman who had done the seating. Faith would be in the kitchen, so she hadn't been paying much attention to the table arrangements. Paula didn't intend to be seated, either. She and her husband, Sydney, would be roving about the room, making sure everyone was at approximately the same point in the game.

Faith wanted to get the timing down. Paula had coordinated the courses to coincide with the unraveling of the whodunit.

'Could you give me a final timetable? I know you want drinks and hors d'oeuvres before everyone sits down and starts playing.'

'That's right. In the foyer, but the ballroom will be open so people can check out the auction items on the tables by the windows and start making bids. And they'll be introducing themselves, both in character and out.'

Faith hadn't read the script, yet she had a general idea of what would be happening. Paula had sent each ticket holder the name of his or her character, a description, and genial encouragement to dress up and bring props. The mystery was set on a large Long Island Gatsby-like estate during the twenties. Tom planned to borrow his father's black-and-orange-striped Princeton blazer and had himself, somewhere along the line, acquired a straw boater. His name was Willoughby Forbes III. Each round table seated eight and, accordingly, there were eight suspects. The 'crime' had already occurred — the murder of Willoughby's grandfather Willoughby Forbes — a crusty but likable curmudgeon with no known enemies. Paula had asked one of the mystery writers, a former actress, to read the description of the scene of the crime; then everyone was to do his or her best to fool everyone else while unmasking the 'real' killer. Paula had obtained elaborate scripts for each player, including facts about themselves or the others that could be revealed in answer to questions and facts about themselves that could be concealed — things like so-and-so was overheard arguing fiercely with the old man the night before he died, and various relevant hobbies, such as the study of plant poisons. It sounded rather complicated to Faith and the plot was not exactly Conan Doyle, but Paula had assured her that everyone would love it.

The notion of combining a game, any game, with the kind of dinner Faith had planned was an alien one. Each course was meant to be savored, and conversation, possibly witty, the only accompaniment required. She seriously doubted whether anyone would notice that the game hens had been smoked with apple wood or that Niki's *panna cotta* dessert — that luscious Italian cream — had home-made crushed amaretti biscuits on top. Faith was tempted to tell Niki to use imported Lazzaroni biscuits instead, but *they'd* know. Maybe they should have some of them on the table anyway with the other cookies and small pastries that would accompany coffee at the end of the meal to sweeten the denouement. They were so pretty, wrapped in brightly colored tissue paper. After eating the cookies, you flattened the paper, rolled it into a tube, set it upright on a saucer, and gently lighted the top. In a darkened room, watching it rise, glowing, toward the ceiling was lovely. If they wanted a game, this should be sufficient. Then Faith thought of possible fire code violations and nixed the idea.

'Soup at eight,' Paula instructed. 'They'll have had an hour to arrive, drink some champagne, chat, and bid before sitting down. Then the main course at eight-thirty, dessert at nine-thirty?'

'I'd planned on serving a salad course after the main course,' Faith remarked.

Paula wrinkled her brow. 'We're giving them soup *and* salad?' She made it sound like 'caviar *and* foie gras.'

'Yes,' Faith said firmly. The tickets weren't cheap, and besides, Paula's timetable would have them eating dessert before ten o'clock. It was Aleford, but even so, the guests wouldn't be ready to leave that early. Suitably, a combo would be playing twenties music and people would be dancing as well as sleuthing. Of course, each course would inevitably stretch out longer than planned. Faith hated events where plates were whisked from the table before you had a chance to finish, or if you had, the next was arriving while you were still full.

'Then salad it is. Our salad days! But surely after the soup and before the main course.'

Faith sighed. 'If everyone insists, but I like to serve it after the main course. It refreshes the palate for dessert — light, you can always eat salad.'

The party planner brayed her distinctive laugh and cried, 'We bow to the expert, of course. It's going to be a madcap night, so why not have salad then? I'm sure you know best, dear.'

The next day, she called to change the table decorations one 'absolutely last time.' It was revenge — a reminder to 'dear' of who was really in charge. Faith had already sprayed the gourds she'd selected to use with gold paint and decided to let them come as a surprise to Paula the night of the party. She planned to group them around the center-pieces, clear glass globes filled with crushed

36

colored tissue that bled beautifully when wet. The flowers themselves would be simple — snowball dahlias, tiny late sunflowers, burgundy astilbe, and sprigs of boxwood lightly touched with the same gold as the gourds.

★ ★ ★

At last, the night of the First Parish 250th Anniversary Campaign Kickoff arrived. Faith and Niki were at Ballou House, getting ready. The sun had set in a glory of roses and magentas streaked with molten rays, but the evening was still warm, especially for October 23. At breakfast, Ben had informed the family that today was the day the swallows left Capistrano. More lore from Chairman Black? Faith hoped he wasn't becoming precocious. This yearly event was something she had never given much thought to, but now a host of questions crowded into her mind. How did the birds know when to leave? Where did they go, anyway? Why did they always come back to the same place? She could imagine a group of birds challenging the leader: Can't we go someplace new for a change? Just because you like it so much doesn't mean we all do.

When she'd tuned back into the conversation, Ben had been posing the same queries, except for the bird conversation part. She'd felt relieved. He wasn't ready for *Jeopardy* yet.

A bird flew by Ballou House's kitchen window. Niki looked up from the bread she was cutting. Faith had combined the salad with a cheese course by serving mixed greens in a vinaigrette topped with warm chèvre on a lightly toasted round of thin *ficelle*.

'What a place! Can you imagine the staff they must have had to keep everything running?'

Faith nodded. She'd brought plenty of staff tonight herself. It was a big party and, so far, a great party. Her spirits had been lifting steadily since she'd arrived.

The kitchen door swung open and Tricia Phelan, who worked for Faith part-time, came through with an empty tray. 'Nobody wants to sit down. Lots of people are out on the veranda watching the moon rise. It's almost full and I need another tray of hors d'oeuvres.' Her words rushed together and she was slightly flushed. The party mood was infectious. 'We're also pouring champagne like there's no tomorrow. You could almost believe it *is* the twenties, the way people are acting. Hubba, hubba! I never knew your husband was such a good dancer, Faith. He's doing the Charleston with some babe in a beaded dress, and they are moving!'

Faith knew Tom was a good dancer, but he'd kept his Charleston act a secret. She took the tray out herself to get a look.

Most of the guests were in costume, and from the slight smell of mothballs as she passed some of the older people in attendance, she guessed that their raccoon coats or fringed silk chemises had been father's or mother's — stowed in the attic along with all the other generational accumulation that just might come in handy someday.

She spotted Tom on the dance floor and winked. He waved and motioned her over, but she shook her head. She had to get back to the kitchen. He was dancing with Gwen Lord, a striking brunette who was engaged to Jared Gabriel, First Parish's choirmaster and music maven in residence. Jed had composed some music for the church and was working on the 'Anniversary Chorale.' Gwen's beaded turquoise dress shimmered as she shimmied. She worked in a gallery on Boston's Newbury Street and her stylish, sleek haircut fit both eras. Faith didn't know her that well, but this was only the second time she'd ever seen Gwen in an outfit that wasn't black or gray and Armani.

Someone grabbed Faith's elbow, neatly

tipping the tray sideways. The last of the coconut shrimp toppled to the floor. The parquet had been covered by a thick Aubusson carpet in Increase Ballou's day, a symbol of his taste and success, but it had been removed and sold by his heirs. Too French.

'No harm done,' Faith said, pulling a cloth from her pocket and turning with a smile to reassure the party-goer. Except it wasn't a partygoer, but a party planner, and she never needed any reassurance.

'We have got to get people to sit down, or we'll be here until the wee hours of the morning!' Paula wailed. She was wearing a vintage beaded black flapper dress. A black velvet band encircled her brow, complete with feather trim sprouting straight up above her eyes. She looked like something you'd rather not see circling in the desert sky.

'The wee hours of the morning wouldn't be so bad,' Faith couldn't help teasing her. 'People are having fun.' But Paula was right. It was time to start serving — and start the game.

'Have the mystery writer (what's her name? — Veronica Brookside — and is that really her name?) invite everyone to be seated and give the combo a break. We'll stop pouring wine. That should do it.'

As Faith offered the solution, she wondered why Paula was in such a state. The woman did parties all the time and must have encountered this problem before. Paula had been mildly crazed all evening and had not said a word about the table decorations. What was the woman so worried about? The silent-auction bids were already higher than they'd projected for final bids and Kate Mattes was running out of books to sell. The mystery writers were circulating, happily signing their books and greeting fans. Even Anson Scott was smiling. As Faith passed him on her way back to the kitchen, he stopped her.

'From your attire, I surmise you are the chef. My compliments. If those toothsome vegetable fritters and scallop seviche are portents of what is to come, we are in for a sublime gastronomic experience.' Faith had rented twenties servant's attire for the wait staff, but she was wearing her usual checked chef's trousers and white jacket.

'Thank you,' she said. Did he always speak this way, or was it a result of the ambience and what he'd been drinking?

'My good lady, that was not an idle compliment. Food is a passion with me and I fancy myself a knowledgeable connoisseur. Do not let me leave without one of your cards.'

A kindred spirit. 'There are cards on the table in the hall, and if you don't pick one up, the name of my firm is easy to remember, Have Faith. My name is Faith, Faith Fairchild.'

'Clever, very clever. I believe I will be sitting with your husband at dinner — if the Reverend Thomas Fairchild is that man.'

'He is, and I'm sure he'll be delighted.'

'Well, I mustn't keep you from what awaits. Have Faith. Yes, an inspired choice. And do you?'

'Have faith?'

'Yes.' He fixed his gaze directly on her. His deep-set brown eyes invested the question with mock gravity. Anson Scott was a mountain of a man, whose girth was keeping pace with his height. He'd dressed for the occasion in a well-cut shawl-collared tuxedo. Instead of a boutonniere, he sported a tiny silver dagger in his buttonhole, dripping ruby droplets of blood. He was clean-shaven, but his hair reached his collar in back, a mass of tight curls, more gray than black. He wore a large signet ring on his right hand, nothing on the left.

'Quite a bit,' she answered, judging it neither the time nor place to describe her somewhat pantheistic beliefs, which still managed to fall under First Parish's rubric.

He'd be a fun dinner guest, so long as he didn't talk shop, regaling them with his villains' modus operandi. He traveled a great deal and was never seen about town, but she was sure she could lure him to her table with the promise of something like a risotto with lobster and wild mushrooms or an herb-encrusted rack of lamb.

'Welcome to the party of the century,' Faith heard as she pushed open the kitchen door. The room almost immediately quieted. What a voice! Low, rich, incredibly sultry. It was Veronica Brookside. Veronica wrote a hard-boiled series that featured a foul-mouthed female former librarian turned private detective who could hit a knothole at seventy-five feet while quoting the ruder parts of the *Canterbury Tales*. But what am I thinking of? Faith chided herself. They had to get the soup out! Ginger squash — and it had to be served hot.

By the time they'd cleared the main course and started to serve the salad, Veronica's declaration was well on the way to becoming a reality. Aleford was uncharacteristically letting its hair down to Rapunzel length. Faith had been drawn out of the kitchen several times, ostensibly to check up on things, yet really to watch the fun. The mystery game was an uproarious success.

People were switching tables and sharing clues — and from what Faith gleaned, the floor should be awash with red herrings before the night was over. Paula and Sydney Pringle had completely given up trying to organize the game. Faith took pity on them and squeezed in two more places at Tom's table. Besides Anson Scott, there were Janice Mulholland, a parishioner and single mother with an elementary-school-aged daughter; Jared and Gwen; Nick Gabriel, Jared's cousin and owner of the gallery where Gwen worked; and Pix and her mother, Ursula Rowe. Sam Miller was out of town. Faith had advised Paula to reserve spots for the two of them, but Ms Pringle had been adamant that they would not have a moment to sit down. She continued to pop up and flit about the room, adding to the confusion. Sydney didn't budge, devoting himself to the food and devouring the entire contents of the bread basket Faith had replenished.

The combo had returned and was playing Gershwin and Cole Porter. Looking through the glass of the French doors, Faith could see couples dancing on the veranda in the moonlight. She half-expected a pool filled with shrieking flappers to appear on the sloping lawn beyond. The moon, almost full, illuminated the scene with what appeared to be artificial light. The Hunter's Moon. It was so clear, the canals and craters stood out, but not like Roquefort cheese, Faith's usual thought. No, tonight there did seem to be a man in the moon, armed or not. The pattern was a face, a face with a slight smile — indulgent or sardonic, Faith wasn't sure which.

It had been impossible to link the courses to the game — some tables were still happily mired in part one — but she thought she'd try to see how close Tom's table was to the solution and serve dessert based on that. With Anson Scott close at hand, they definitely had an advantage, and Ursula had kept them all on track, moving things right along. Pix's family, like Tom's, were inveterate game players and considered a night without Scrabble while on vacation in Maine or Nantucket much worse than a day without sunshine. Fog or rain was natural. The inability or disinclination to pit one's wits against all comers was not. Faith fell into this category, much to her friends and family's bewilderment. 'Not even the dictionary game?' 'Not even tiddlywinks,' she'd asserted. She did play a mean game of poker, however.

'I believe you are secretly engaged to Willoughby Forbes the Third, Miss Pretty-man, and his grandfather had objected strongly to the match on the grounds that you were nothing more than a gold digger. Pray tell us what you have been hiding.' Ursula fixed her daughter with a gimlet eye.

'Well, if it comes to that,' Pix retorted smartly, 'I believe you have been blackmailing the old man for years, Mrs Hardcastle. Your position as housekeeper made you privy to certain family secrets.'

'But,' Anson pointed out in a reasonable tone of voice, 'why would she want to kill off her goose? Let's get back to the question she addressed to you, missy.'

Everyone laughed at Pix's discomfort. 'That's supposed to be concealed information, Mother. How did you find out? I'm sure it's not in your script.'

'No, it isn't, but there's always a secret engagement in this kind of story, and rich grandfathers always object. Jealous, probably.'

'Have you ever thought of writing a book, my dear? You have the formula down perfectly.' Anson raised his glass to Mrs Rowe and then to Faith, with a nod at the wine — an excellent, full-bodied Hawk Crest merlot.

Ursula demurred. 'At my age, it's quite enough to read one through to the end.'

Jed Gabriel jumped in. 'Now, Mrs Rowe, you can't get away with that. We all saw you kayaking your way past everyone else during the retreat last spring.'

Pix met Faith's eyes. They were used to the way Ursula became the focal point without so much as pointing a finger toward herself.

Paula, however, wasn't. 'Are you ready to make an accusation?' she asked Anson.

'Accusation?' he asked, puzzled. 'Oh, you mean do I want to guess who the guilty party might be? Gracious no, we're having too much fun. Besides, I've known since the soup. Excellent, by the way. Just a touch of Jamaican ginger, if I'm not mistaken.'

Faith nodded and smiled. The man certainly knew his ingredients. She leaned over to Pix. 'Where's Tom?'

'I think he's dancing with Gwen.'

'I have *got* to take lessons before the wedding.' Jed sighed. 'I've always been hopelessly clumsy. Good of Tom to do this. Gwen adores dancing.'

Faith was surprised at the admission. Jared was a slender, compact man, neither too tall nor too short. He moved with a great deal of grace, and when she watched him conduct the choir, she was always struck by how balletic he was. His normal expression was calm and relaxed — with a touch of humor. When he was conducting, his face became plastic, moving swiftly from grimace to grin.

47

She would have thought him a natural dancer.

She went back to the kitchen by way of the dance floor and soon picked out Tom and Gwen. They were a perfect match, effortlessly weaving their way in between the other dancers, matching their steps to 'Cheek to Cheek.' Gwen, like Ginger Rogers, seemed to have no trouble tripping the light fantastic backward and in heels. Faith tried to catch Tom's eye to wave, but he didn't see her. He was looking through lowered lids at Gwen. His lips were moving slightly and she was sure he was singing softly. The song was one of his — one of their — favorites.

Faith slipped into the kitchen and surveyed the scene. The dessert was ready to go as soon as the salad plates were cleared and the tables crumbed. Trays of Niki's confection — the *panna cotta* with the crushed amaretti topping, surrounded by a raspberry coulis — sat on the counter. Niki herself must have gone to the bathroom or out to watch the goings-on — the party, that is. The rest of the staff was either in the large butler's pantry, now equipped with sink and dishwasher, starting to clean up, or out waiting on the guests. She was alone for a moment in the empty room. She sat on one of the high stools and leaned her elbows on the table, resting her face in her hands. She was getting tired. Tom would be tired, too. Good that he was having such a nice time. He hadn't expected to and had been dreading the event. He'd been sure that both the steeple contingent and the crypt group would try to corner him. With all the joie de vivre in the air, Faith thought it would be the perfect time to get one group to give in. Take a quick vote. But no, that would instantly destroy the mood. It would be back to business with a vengeance.

Yes, she was happy that Tom was happy. Except it was, she admitted to herself, a little like Ben and school. Just as a tiny bit of regret on Ben's part would not go amiss; she wouldn't mind if Tom's steps were not in such perfect synchrony with Gwen's. If an occasional toe got stepped on. She didn't expect him to dance with her. She was working, after all, and it was important to keep professional and personal lives separate, but, damn it, did he have to be having *such* a good time?

The kitchen door swung open violently and Paula burst in. 'I've decided to change the schedule and close the silent auction during the dessert course. Some of the tables have solved the mystery already and they might leave right after dessert. You never know with people.'

This was certainly an understatement, but Faith agreed that closing the auction sooner rather than later was a good idea. Aleford might look like it was in for an all-nighter at the moment, but old habits die hard and once dessert was over, they, like lemmings, might all rush to the sea of their bedchambers in a single reflex. It was way after ten o'clock.

'I'll have Bill Brown make the announcement,' Paula declared.

'Let me get the desserts on the table first to avoid any collisions. You know how people are with silent auctions. They'll be running back and forth until the last second to check their bids. It won't take long. Everything's ready to go. We'll wait and serve the coffee afterward.'

Paula nodded and left. Niki returned and the room filled up with staff. Faith was suddenly too busy to dwell on Tom's dancing partners.

Dessert out, she signaled Paula and told the band to take a break. She had food for them in the kitchen.

Bill Brown wrote a series featuring an ex-rabbi, ex-homicide detective, ex-gambler who ran an unorthodox private detective agency when he wasn't hang gliding, sailing, or fishing — Hemingway-type fishing, not Thoreau. Brown himself was a small man, solid — brush haircut, nothing extra, nothing wasted. His character was a six-footer with hands like mutton chops and the ability to slice them through bricks, stacks of cord-wood, and the like. Brown announced the impending close of the auction. He had a surprisingly mellow, blurred Southern accent — like Shelby Foote's, incredibly charming and incredibly sexy. Had Paula Pringle selected the writers on the basis of their voices? Certainly Veronica and Bill were star turns.

For the next ten minutes, everyone concentrated on the tables by the windows. The combo returned and Brown led them in a dramatic countdown. Paula shrieked her thanks, but, cannily she did not announce the total raised — 'If it sounds too good, they won't pledge enough,' she'd confided to Faith earlier — then told everyone, 'Keep on dancing.'

They started serving coffee and plates of small confections. Niki walked over to Faith.

'Give me five! This was a good one.'

Faith raised her hand. She had to agree. The aggravation of the last few weeks was already receding and soon would be a distant memory, just as all her other work-related woes tended to be.

'It's partly the place. I love working here. All the ghosts of sumptuous repasts past. The courses, the silver, the china, the flowers . . . '

'I get it, boss.' Niki laughed. 'Except in those days, I think I would much rather have been a guest than in the kitchen.'

'You're right, but I could see myself here as an American version of the British chef Rosa Lewis, Duchess of Duke Street — style. Nothing else. Which reminds me — I never asked Anson Scott about what his ancestor did.'

'You don't think he's touchy about it?'

'I think all the rumors about how difficult he is have been vastly inflated. He's been charming all evening. He's signed books, even just given autographs. It must be hard to have people always wanting things from you, trying to invade your privacy.'

'I thought that was how you describe your life.'

Faith punched her assistant lightly on the arm and tried not to think how apt the comment had been. Living in a parsonage wasn't simply like living in a fishbowl; it was like living in a fishbowl online.

'I'm going to see when Tom plans on leaving. Danny Miller has been baby-sitting for us now that Samantha is at Wellesley, and this is his first really late night. I told him to go to sleep, but I bet he won't.'

Faith got to the table as Tom was pushing

in Gwen's chair. He caught his wife's eye.

'A last dance,' he said quickly.

Gwen looked up at him. Their eyes met.

'And a perfect ending to a perfect evening.'

Then she smiled brightly at the table. 'But I wouldn't have wanted to miss dessert and the end of the game. Then we must all go out and look at the moon. It's incredible tonight. So, who's the murderer?' She took a large spoonful of the almond cookie-crusted *panna cotta* and continued to eat with relish. The conversation at the table had turned to suspects and Faith lingered to hear the possibilities. Gwen joined in, offering her own theory that the old man had probably killed himself to spite everyone. She looked into her empty dish.

'This was absolutely fabulous. I've been trying to eat slowly to make it last, but I couldn't. Jed knows what a sweet tooth I have.' Her voice slurred over the words. She swallowed the last bite, and the spoon dropped from her hand, clattering against the bowl. She clutched her throat and began gasping for air. Jared and Faith were the first to react, offering water.

'Honey, are you okay? What's wrong!'

Gwen slumped into his arms and Faith sprinted for the phone to call 911.

As she passed the band, she screamed, 'See

if there's a doctor in the house. Table twelve. Gwen Lord. Hurry!' What could be wrong? There was nothing in the dessert large enough to block Gwen's airway.

Faith wasn't gone more than a few minutes, but by the time she made her way through the hushed, frightened crowd, Gwendolyn Lord, a bloody froth at her mouth, one hand twisted in the folds of her beaded silk dress, was past all human help and Tom was bending over his dancing partner, saying a prayer.

It may have been a perfect evening; it hadn't been a perfect ending.

3

Faith put her head down on Patsy's wooden table. It felt good — cool and hard. She wanted to cry. She thought she should be crying. But not a single tear had leaked from her eyes since she'd stared in horror at Gwen's sightless face. She wanted to scream. She hadn't done that, either. After a moment, she raised her head and looked at Patsy, who had stopped taking notes.

'Don't tell me I shouldn't be worried.'

'I'm not going to tell you that, but I am a bit confused about why you think you might be arrested. The police can't possibly think you're a suspect. You scarcely knew the woman.'

'Niki made the desserts, but didn't have time to finish them. I put the crumb topping on — the amaretti topping.'

Patsy's face was calm. 'It's too soon for any lab reports. It could have been any number of things.'

Faith shook her head. 'Gwen was fine until she took a bite of her dessert. Over the years, I've learned a few things about poisons and the way they work. All her symptoms — ' Faith's voice shook. There it was again. The picture of Gwen, bloody mouth, her body contorted in an agonizing struggle with death. A battle lost. Lost quickly. The picture had been appearing over and over again — a crime-scene photo, with all the flashbulbs going off at once — in a part of Faith's mind that she could not shut down. Her voice steadied. 'All her symptoms point to cyanide poisoning.'

'Very Agatha Christie — the smell of bitter almonds.' Patsy reached for Faith's hand. 'Have Faith can't possibly be held responsible. We can check with a civil attorney. Maybe even brief someone, just in case her family takes it into their heads to sue for negligence. People will do anything for money — even take advantage of the death of a loved one.'

'She didn't have any family,' Faith said dully. She hadn't thought of a civil suit. She'd been too busy thinking of other things — things like word of mouth. Caterers had watched their businesses go down the tubes after a single case of mild food poisoning — chicken salad left out too long.

'No one at all?'

'An only of onlies, and both her parents are dead. She and Jed have that in common — or almost. He has a second cousin, Nick Gabriel, older than he is. Gwen works for him; that's how she met Jed.'

Patsy thought of her family, and Will's. At times, she had fantasized about being an only child, the sole focus of her parents' and grandparents' affections, but she knew she'd miss the loving, teasing, noisy whirlwind of her brothers and sisters — one that scooped her up into that particular club whenever she was home. Will's was similar.

She looked down at her pad. She'd scribbled a few questions.

'Okay, let's say it was cyanide poisoning and it was in the dessert topping. How did it get there?'

Faith had been over this already in her own thoughts. 'Obviously when I was putting it together from the amaretti cookies Niki had made, which means I'm the killer, but how would I know which dessert was going to be Gwen's?'

'And why would you want to kill her?'

Faith ignored the question and continued. 'At the event, again I was the one who unpacked the desserts and set them out on the trays.'

'Was there ever a time when no one was in the kitchen and the desserts were on those trays, ready to be served?'

'No, it was a big party. My staff was around all the time.' Faith stopped herself suddenly, remembering the empty kitchen she'd walked into shortly before the desserts were served. She told Patsy.

'So anyone could have walked in and poisoned Gwen's portion.'

'Yes, theoretically, but how could he or she be sure Gwen would get the right dessert?'

'Forget the kitchen. How about after the desserts were served? Could it have been done then?'

'That's what I think happened. It's the only thing that makes any sense. There was mass confusion. Paula Pringle, the party organizer, decided to close the silent-auction bids, because she was afraid people would leave and not make that mad dash to up their bids at the last moment. We served the desserts, because I didn't want people knocking into the wait staff as they took them around. Gwen was dancing, and her dessert sat at her place at the table for some time. The killer could have passed by and put the poison on top. It would have been very risky, but everyone was getting up and down, so perhaps not as risky as it sounds. Although I don't think Ursula would have moved about much, so there probably was always someone at the table.'

Patsy nodded. 'But it wouldn't have taken long.'

'I'll talk to Charley about it. He's dropping by the house this afternoon.'

Charley MacIsaac, Aleford's venerable police chief, had been the first law-enforcement officer on the scene, because he'd been at the party. Faith had been surprised. A mystery dinner party game didn't seem to be Charley's thing. He got enough of crime in his everyday life, but then she remembered that Mattie Hawthorne, the manager of Ballou House, was an old friend of Charley and his late wife's. He must have gone to the event to lend Mattie some moral support.

'Do you want me to be there with you?' Patsy asked.

Faith shook her head. 'No, I just like knowing that you could have been.'

'Have you had enough? We can talk some more later.' Outside, the bright morning mocked them.

'I should get home.' Faith stood up. 'What else is there to go over?'

'I need to know what happened afterward. What you can remember about various people's reactions, especially the people at the table.'

'Yes, they're the ones who were closest — opportunity. And we know the means, or at least think we do. But motive? That's what's missing here.'

'Call me when you have some spare time. I know, I know, it's an oxymoron. But call me and we'll go over the rest of the night — and anything else you want to tell me.'

Faith was fumbling with her coat. She put it on and Patsy walked her to the front door. She pulled Faith to her in a tight hug and said good-bye. She watched Faith walk down the path to the sidewalk. Patsy knew Faith hadn't told her everything — and it wasn't just what she'd observed after Gwen's death. No, it was something else. Faith was holding back — but what, and why?

★　★　★

Faith walked quickly back to the parsonage, her feet rustling the fallen leaves, ankle-deep on the ground. She still had to change and get the children dressed. She'd been right to go to Patsy, and the total panic she'd been feeling earlier had lessened. But not disappeared. In the end, she hadn't been able to tell her friend everything she was thinking, everything she was fearing. Putting her amorphous fears into words would have made them real — and they weren't. They couldn't be. She was sure of it, yet . . .

Tom and Gwen. It was crazy. Except she

couldn't forget the way he'd been looking at her when they'd danced. Couldn't forget the way he had been holding her. Or the rhythm of their bodies swaying together so familiarly, as if each already knew the way the other moved. Had known for a long time. She couldn't tell Patsy this.

She also couldn't tell her about seeing Gwen leave their house by the back door two weeks ago. Faith had been cutting across the cemetery on her way home from the library. She watched Gwen stand absolutely still for a moment, then saw her look about before darting across the driveway into the Millers' yard. Faith ran in that direction, in time to see the young woman cut into the field beyond her neighbors' garage. She'd walked into the kitchen. Tom was drying a mug. She'd planned to tease him, but something in his face had stopped her. She'd merely said, 'I see you've had a visitor.'

'A visitor?'

She didn't want to hear him deny it, and feeling chilled to the bone, left the room to get a sweater.

She also couldn't tell Patsy about the way Tom had been behaving since he rose from Gwen's side, his face a mask of grief. During the commotion that followed, he'd been completely silent and had withdrawn. If he'd

61

been aware Faith was by his side, he'd given no indication. Everything she'd thought of to say sounded completely banal: 'Tom, are you all right?' Words to that effect. Obviously, he wasn't. She wasn't. They weren't.

As she walked home, she was hit by a wall of fatigue. She didn't want to talk over the whole thing with Patsy — or Charley MacIsaac. Living through it had been enough. And she had been reliving it in her mind ever since.

When she'd returned to the ballroom after calling 911, Charley had moved everyone away from the body. The music had stopped, but there had been a feverish level of conversation. Upon seeing Faith, Paula Pringle had promptly pointed one long, bony finger at her and screamed: 'It was the food! Something in the dessert! The desserts are poison!' Then equally promptly, she began to laugh hysterically and cry at once. Ursula Rowe stepped over to the woman and coolly slapped her smartly across the face. Paula stopped instantly and returned to what was, for her, normal. 'At least we finished the auction,' she said. Her husband took her to the far end of the ballroom and made her sit down and put her head between her knees. At any other time, Faith would have kissed Ursula for executing what Faith herself had yearned to do for several weeks. But just then, she scarcely took the gesture in.

'Things are getting out of hand,' Faith heard Ursula tell Charley. 'You'd better do something quick.'

Charley nodded and took the mike.

'I know I can trust all of you to remain calm. There's been a tragic accident, and it will take a while to sort the whole thing out. We're waiting for a unit from the state police to arrive, and in the meantime, I'd like to ask you all to stay in this room. Since there is a possibility that this could be food-related, I suggest that no one eat or drink anything further.'

That had caused an even more hectic buzz, but at least they'd avoided a repetition of Gwen's death. If it *was* the food, that is.

Faith walked up to her own front door with no recollection of the steps taken between it and the Averys' house. As she stepped into the living room, she heard Tom call from the kitchen.

'Faith, is that you? I have to leave five minutes ago!'

'Go on. I'll see you later.'

She heard the door slam shut and went to get the kids. Ben had dressed himself. He was wearing the navy sweatpants he'd had on the day before, which he must have dug out of the hamper, one of the two dress shirts he owned, and his Superman cape from last Halloween.

'I can't find my sneakers,' he wailed. 'I bet Amy took them again.'

Last month, Amy had lovingly put Ben's favorite sneakers, the ones with Velcro frog fastenings, in the bathtub, where Faith had fortunately discovered them before turning on the tap.

'I'm sure she didn't, but why don't you look there just in case?' Faith decided to let Ben's outfit go. He'd appeared in worse combinations, and it was going to take more than little-boy outfits from Brooks Brothers to win over those in the congregation who thought her mothering skills sadly lax.

Amy was patiently stringing large wooden beads on a long string, unaware that there was no knot on the end. She simply kept on going, retrieving the beads as they fell off, then putting them on the other end. Her breakfast was on the table, practically untouched.

'Sweetheart, you need to eat your breakfast; then we'll get dressed and go see Miss Nancy.' Amy was passionate about Miss Nancy, her Sunday school teacher. Her little face glowed. 'See Miss Nancy?' She laughed and clapped her little hands together. Faith pulled her on to her lap, burying her face in the sweet silk of Amy's hair and soft neck, which smelled like the baby soap Faith still used on her daughter's tender body.

'But first, eat some cereal. It's your goat spoon,' she wheedled.

Amy clamped her mouth shut. 'No.' No explanation, no apologies, no guilt. Just no. This was happening a lot, and Faith's worst nightmare — that she'd give birth to a picky eater — seemed to be coming true.

She dipped the spoon — a silver one with a mountain goat and goatherd on the handle that Pix had brought back from Norway — into the cereal and brought it to Amy's tiny mouth. 'Just three bites.'

The mouth didn't open. Faith sighed. 'All right. Drink your milk.' Amy gleefully picked up her glass and drained it. She had graduated from a spouted beaker and was very proud. Faith was going to have to start concocting power shakes for her recalcitrant daughter and hope the phase passed. She pulled on one of her all-purpose church dresses, a soft gray Calvin Klein knit, ran a comb through her hair, and then, after looking in the mirror, added some blush and lip gloss. She dressed Amy in the latest of the smocked dresses Tom's mother turned out with deceptive ease. This one was buttery yellow, with a cornflower blue tulip design.

'We're going to be late, Mom!' Ben screeched up the stairs. At five, he'd suddenly become extremely aware of social conventions, or perhaps it was kindergarten. Going out the door and across the well-worn path through the cemetery, Faith watched him speed toward church, his cape streaming out behind him. Amy walked at a slower pace, pausing to examine each passing blade of grass, small stone, ant.

'Ben is flying,' she announced without a trace of envy or doubt.

'Apparently,' Faith agreed, keeping a sharp eye on him as he disappeared through the side door on his way to his own class. He wasn't supposed to run ahead. He wasn't supposed to do a lot of things, and the list got longer every day. Some items would get crossed off — the running-ahead part. By the time he was sixteen, he could do that. But other things would be added. Be home before midnight. Call your mother. It was a life's work. She laughed at herself.

'Come on, chickadee, let's get you to Miss Nancy.'

'Chickadee-dee-dee,' Amy chortled. It was a game she never tired of; nor did her mother.

In church, Faith prayed briefly — for strength, for clarity, for forgiveness, for Gwen — then turned to look up at the choir loft.

She was surprised to see Jared. He was there, playing his heart out. Brahms's Requiem, his own arrangement for solo organ.

While the music filled the sanctuary, Faith's thoughts returned to the night before and the scene that had greeted her when she'd returned to the Ballou House ballroom from the phone.

Nick Gabriel had had his arms around his cousin, Jared, turning him away from the sight of his dead fiancée. He was stroking the back of Jared's head and mumbling something in his ear. He was in full view of the corpse himself, however, and he was obviously in shock. His face was deathly pale and Faith could see that his hand was trembling. Jared's full weight was collapsed against his cousin, and from the way his shoulders heaved, Faith could tell he was sobbing. He'd screamed when Gwen fell to the ground, and the sound of his voice, crying, 'Gwen! Gwen! Don't!' had carried above the crowd, following Faith into the kitchen. Gwen. Don't. Don't die. Don't leave me.

Pix and Ursula were standing near the Gabriels, far enough away so as not to intrude on their grief, but close enough to help if help was needed. Anson Scott was with Janice Mulholland. She seemed about to faint. He had distanced her from any sight of

Gwen and was talking to her in an insistent manner, forcing her to focus on him and his words. There were several ornate gold-framed mirrors on the walls, enormous — reaching almost from floor to ceiling and wide enough to reflect any number of bygone ladies in their full-skirted crinolines. Faith saw Anson's and Janice's reflected images mixed with those of the other partygoers. The mirrors gave the illusion of another room, another party, but with the same people. A party where nothing bad had happened. These mirrors had held Anson's relative — how many years ago? Had she helped serve at a ball? Or had she been in the vast room only to clean the floor, dust? Had she looked at herself in these mirrors? Servants started when they were still children in those days. Had she danced a step or two, singing to herself, twirling around?

While Faith watched, Scott pulled out a chair from the nearest table and sat Janice down. She looked limp, in sharp contrast to the mystery writer who now loomed large over her, still talking in an animated fashion, as if to keep her conscious.

Faith went over to them and Anson called out, 'Brandy. That's what everybody needs. Some brandy. No, I'm not asking you for it. Nothing must be touched. But wish I'd thought to put a flask in my pocket.' She had had a fleeting disconnected feeling that she was watching a play — had been for the entire night — and here was Anson Scott playing some role to the hilt.

And Tom, Tom was stage right, standing alone. Immobile. Staring in disbelief.

Tom's voice. The Reverend Thomas Preston Fairchild's voice. It was Sunday morning. Faith was in church.

'Dearly beloved, the Scripture moveth us in sundry places to acknowledge and confess our manifold sins and wickedness . . . ' Gwen Lord had been murdered the night before. Wickedness was afoot.

*　*　*

The last thing Faith Sibley Fairchild had ever wanted to be was a minister's wife. She was the daughter and granddaughter of men of the cloth and had sworn to avoid that particular fabric after growing up a preacher's kid. Her home hadn't been in a moss-covered manse, but a Manhattan duplex. Her mother hadn't been the pillar of the Ladies Aid, but a real estate lawyer. Still, both Faith, and her sister, Hope, one year younger, had felt that the eyes of the congregation were on them — always. The family had had very little time together, except for a two-week vacation in the summer. Her father's busy times had been holidays, not only with the designated services but also with the pastoral calls and crises accompanying these occasions when one is supposed to be feeling great joy. Faith was proud of her father and treasured his ministry, but she'd seen the kind of sacrifices her mother had had to make — the kind they all had. No, she'd decided early on — a godly man, all right, but not a man of God. Then she'd met Tom and fallen hopelessly in love. In what seemed like the blink of an eye, she'd found herself a new bride in Aleford, Massachusetts, a small town west of Boston. Then a year later, a new mother. Three years later, a mother again. Next, she'd revived Have Faith, the highly successful catering company she'd founded in Manhattan ten years earlier. Before going back to work, she'd had moments of acute boredom, acute distress at her distance from the Big Apple — a decent haircut, Balducci's, Barneys, and Bloomies. Now, life was a high-speed juggling act and boredom was a luxury like Petrossian caviar or a Kate Spade pocketbook.

Sundays meant Sunday dinner, and they had just finished the meal and said, 'Good-bye and come again' to the extras invariably invited to round out the table, when the doorbell rang.

'Someone must have forgotten something,' Faith said. 'I'll get it.' Tom grunted from the couch, where he'd stretched out. Amy was napping and Ben was at a friend's house for the afternoon.

She opened the door and saw Charley MacIsaac. Of course. He'd said he was coming. She also saw Detective Lieutenant John Dunne of the Massachusetts State Police. This was a surprise.

'Come in. Good to see you, John.' She could hear Tom leap to his feet. 'Let me take your coat. May I get either of you some coffee?'

'No thanks, Faith,' Dunne said, handing her his top-coat. Joseph Abboud, she noticed, and cashmere. John Dunne was one of the tallest men she knew and one of the homeliest. To offset this, or to add to his unmistakable presence, he dressed as elegantly as a New York stockbroker. Charley was wearing a threadbare Celtics jacket over an equally venerable sports coat.

Dunne and Faith eyed each other warily. Their lives had touched during several other investigations and the friction had produced sparks. When Dunne had heard about this latest case, he hadn't even bothered to ask who the caterer had been. He walked into the living room.

71

'Moved the couch.' It was a statement.

'Yes, we like it better this way,' Faith said defensively.

Dunne nodded and sat in one of the wing chairs. Charley took the other, leaving the Fairchilds the controversial piece of furniture with its view of headstones.

John Dunne hadn't been at Ballou House the night before and Faith had wondered where he was. Instead, another state police officer appeared to be in charge, sealing the kitchen and taking down the names of all the attendees. 'I didn't see you last night,' she said.

'It's my case now,' Dunne said. He had left the Bronx many years ago, yet his voice hadn't. He added wryly, 'Headquarters thought I'd better take over in light of my close connections to the town.' Several corpses and Faith.

'How did she die? Was it cyanide?' Faith asked. She was glad Dunne had taken over. The devil you know . . .

He took a PalmPilot from his pocket and removed the stylus.

'Potassium cyanide. Very nasty stuff. Very painful death.'

Tom coughed and got up. 'I'll be right back,' he said.

Dunne looked sharply at the retreating

figure. Faith pretended not to notice.

'It was in the dessert topping?'

'It was in the dessert topping. And only hers. We're sure of that. All the plates left on the tables were checked, and there were no plates missing. No one had taken a dessert someplace else to eat or dispose of, unless that person put it in a pocket, which seems unlikely, although we can't rule out the possibility. We also checked what was left in the kitchen and the trash. Which means — '

'Which means that I couldn't conceivably have done it, nor could any of my staff,' Faith declared excitedly.

'Which means . . . ' Dunne scowled. He hated being interrupted and was vividly reminded that this was one of Faith's less endearing traits. That and her annoying insistence on sticking her nose — and foot — in his investigations. 'Which means it was done after the desserts were served. By whom, we don't know yet.'

'Isn't cyanide hard to come by?' Faith asked.

'Not if you have access to a lab, especially a research lab, and with all the Harvard and MIT employees in town, that eliminates nobody. It's also in a variety of pesticide products — and darkroom supplies. Not hard at all.'

73

'What we're particularly interested in, Faith, are the times when the desserts were out in the open,' Charley said.

They'd asked her this the night before, but she supposed he had to ask again for Dunne's benefit.

'I unpacked them and set them on the trays to be served. Then the staff put one at each place.' She remembered what she'd told Patsy and now corrected what she'd said to Charley at Ballou House. 'I'd thought there was no time when the kitchen wasn't occupied, but this morning I remembered that when I went in just before the desserts were served, there wasn't anybody around. Either they were clearing or they were in the butler's pantry, where the dishwasher and other sinks are, starting to clean up.'

Dunne was jotting down a few words.

'You knew everyone at the deceased's table. What was each person's relationship to Gwen Lord?'

Faith's throat closed over. The question had caught her completely unawares. Tom. Where was Tom?

'Well, most of them didn't know her, or very slightly. I'm certain the writer Anson Scott hadn't met her before. Nor had Janice Mulholland, unless it was at a church coffee hour. Gwen has come to services several

74

times — last spring and this fall.' Faith realized she'd have to try to get used to the past tense. Came to church. 'She was engaged to Jared Gabriel, the choirmaster and our music director. His cousin, Nick Gabriel, owns the Undique Gallery on Newbury Street. Gwen worked there. Who else was at the table?' She paused as if in thought to give herself some breathing space. 'The Pringles, Paula and Sydney, joined the group late, but again, they hadn't met Gwen before, unless Paula, who's also a church member, had run into her after a service. Sydney isn't a churchgoer. Then there were Pix and Ursula. You know them, of course, and even if they did know her, it would be absurd to think either of them had anything to do with her death.' Faith knew she was beginning to babble. 'Other than the Gabriels, no one had any relationship to her.'

There was a moment of silence. Cops did this — kept quiet, so eventually you'd feel so uneasy, you'd have to fill the empty space yourself. Have to say something. Say anything.

Tom entered, carrying a tray with several mugs of coffee and a plate of molasses sugar-and-spice cookies. Both Dunne and MacIsaac regarded him suspiciously. He might as well have been carrying a bomb

— carrying it with an apron tied around his waist. Faith knew for a fact that John couldn't boil water, let alone make coffee, and Charley ate all his meals at the Minuteman Cafe in the center of Aleford. Besides providing him with the five food groups, leaning heavily toward fats and carbohydrates, it served up everything that was going on in town to and by whom.

'Thank you, honey,' Faith said, reaching for coffee she didn't want. It gave her something to do with her hands.

'We were just discussing any possible links between Gwendolyn Lord and the others at her table last night,' John said, reaching for a cookie.

'Other than her fiancé and his cousin, her employer, I wouldn't imagine there were links to anyone else,' Tom said firmly. 'Jared lives in Cambridge, so she wasn't out here much, except for a few church services and the Spring Choral Recital.'

Faith had forgotten the event. Both the church school choir and the adult choir worked all year on it. Jed had composed a special round for the children, and it had been lovely — ever so slightly off-key, but lovely. The adults had sounded almost professional. It was one of the first times Faith had met Gwen and the first time she'd

76

talked with her at any length. Faith had asked about her job. Newbury Street with DKNY, Ermenegildo Zegna, Pratesi, agnès b., and others was the closest Boston got to Gotham, and Faith assumed it must be a fun place to work.

'I never get out of the gallery,' Gwen had told her. 'And if I did, everything costs the earth. Even a cup of coffee.'

It was something Gwen wouldn't have to worry about once she was married, Faith had reflected at the time. Jed had inherited a fortune when his parents died, one that had started with his grandfather. When she'd asked Tom how large a fortune, he'd said no one ever mentioned a figure. 'That big,' she'd commented.

Gwen had looked very beautiful that day, too. It had been a brilliantly sunny day, not unlike today, but spring sunlight — lighter, less dense than autumn's. Gwen had worn a pale green silk sheath, abandoning her basic blacks. Afterward, Jed was over the moon with the success of the concert and the two stood hand in hand at the reception in the parish hall, looking like a bride and groom.

A bride and groom. They were to have been married on the Saturday before Christmas, the eighteenth. A small wedding — a few friends, Nick, some of the choir.

Earlier this fall, Faith had asked Gwen what her dress was like and Gwen had looked embarrassed. 'I haven't picked one out yet. Everything I try on makes me look like one of those plastic ornaments on top of a wedding cake or so plain that I might as well just wear something I already have.' Faith urged her to go to a dressmaker and get something made, something like the dress she'd worn last spring, but long, in ivory or a soft bisque. 'I know it sounds corny, but you'll treasure the dress for the rest of your life.' Gwen had thanked her somewhat absentmindedly. Faith wondered if she'd gotten a dress, a dress for the rest of her life.

Dunne's next question jolted her from her reverie.

'So, you didn't know her well yourself, Reverend.'

Didn't Dunne usually call him Tom? Faith sat up straight and clutched the mug.

'I'm beginning to think I didn't know her at all,' he answered wearily, which was no answer. 'I know Jared, of course. We both came to First Parish the same year.'

Dunne drained his mug, grabbed another cookie, and said, 'We'll have to close you down for a while, Faith. You knew that, right?'

Faith nodded. They'd told her last night. State inspectors would be going over her work kitchen with a fine-tooth comb. It was a protection for her, really. They wouldn't find anything, and when she received their seal of approval, it might, just might, make people believe that Have Faith had had nothing to do with Gwen Lord's death. Fine-tooth comb. Fleas. Well, they wouldn't find any in her kitchen. She pulled her gaze from the windows and the old cemetery upon which it had settled fixedly as she'd turned these thoughts over and over. She would *have* to get a grip. Have to stop her mind from wandering.

'Did you want to say something, Faith?' Dunne asked, eyeing her quizzically.

'No. I mean, yes. Do you have any idea why somebody would have wanted to kill her?'

'That's just what I was about to ask you,' the detective answered.

* * *

Faith woke up the next morning and went through her Monday-morning motions on automatic pilot. Children up. Children dressed. Children and husband fed. Snack for Amy. Snack for Ben. Frantic search for abandoned bird's nest found by Ben in garden and now absolutely essential for show-and-tell. No clean collars for Tom. Felt

79

sure the Lord would turn a blind eye. Resolved to go to the cleaners, since congregation more observant.

She closed the door and poured herself a cup of coffee and tried to read the paper. They got both the *Boston Globe* and the *New York Times*. Most days, neither got read. All the headlines were as bad as the one in her own head. The murder had occurred too late for Sunday's *Globe*, but it was prominently featured in today's. The picture of Gwen looked like one from a yearbook. She was staring straight at the camera, bold and timid at the same time. All right, world, here I come — am I ready or not? Her hair was much longer, grazing the top of her shoulders. She seemed impossibly young. How long ago had it been taken, and where? Jared was twenty-nine, three years younger than Tom and Faith. Gwen had been younger still. Twenty-four? Twenty-five? She started to read the article but could not get beyond the first sentence. 'While partygoers in the town of Aleford made merry Saturday night, Gwendolyn Lord of Boston sampled her dessert and died in what police are calling a homicide.'

Faith stood up. She couldn't go to work. It was off-limits. She didn't feel like cleaning her house. The day lay stretched out before her — a blank page, and she had writer's block. Be careful what you wish for. She had all the free time she wanted and nothing she cared to do. She called Pix. There was no answer, but she left a message. Pix would suggest something, although it would be something like canoeing on the Sudbury River or taking the dogs for a run in the conservation land. Faith didn't care. She'd even go bird-watching, if that was what Pix was up to today, although she had a vague notion that people did this in the wee hours of the morning. Patsy was at work. They'd spoken briefly late yesterday afternoon. Patsy was going to find out everything she could about the case today, but she'd told Faith not to worry. 'And don't be telling me not to say it. I *mean* it.'

She could call Tom. See what his schedule was like. Usually, he told her, but this morning he'd been in more of a rush than usual. He did say Jared was coming out to discuss Gwen's service and to talk. They'd been on the phone several times the day before. Faith had asked Jed to lunch, but he'd refused. He needed to be alone, he'd told her after church, giving her a quick squeeze.

Jared Gabriel had always been one of Faith's favorites. A New Englander born and bred — his ancestors seemed to form the bulk of the *Mayflower's* passenger list — Jed had gone to school in New York and Paris, kicking over the traces of the bean and the cod. The fact that he had ended up back in Boston was purely accidental. He'd returned to be there for his infirm parents, become involved in the city's rich music world, and then had taken the job at First Parish on a temporary basis. Temporary had become permanent, even after the death of his mother and father six months apart two years ago had freed him to move elsewhere. By then, he'd met Gwen, an art history major, who, after Jared had introduced her to Nick, jumped at the chance to learn about the business of running a gallery. Faith thought about calling Jed, suggesting a long walk, lunch. There had always been an unspoken bond between the two — people who knew what 'away' was like. But she did not want to intrude on his grief. She couldn't imagine coping with both the intense pain of the loss and the horror of how it had occurred.

She went upstairs, made the beds, and shoved Tom's shirts and collars into a large canvas L. L. Bean tote bag. Aleford took recycling very seriously, and appearing at the market without your own assortment of reusable bags was a serious faux pas. The same with anything else you might have to transport. And woe betide the individual who mixed the green glass with the clear in the bins at the dump — the transfer station, to use the official, although never employed, designation.

She walked past Aleford's green — not so green at this time of year, the grass slightly sear, especially after the dry summer. It was another beautiful day. There had been a string of them, interspersed with periods of violent thunderstorms, a reminder from Mother Nature not to get too complacent. Complacent. That was the last thing Faith was feeling.

Millicent Revere McKinley's house was on the left, strategically poised opposite the green with a bird's-eye — and in Millicent's case, the bird was an eagle — view down Main Street. On impulse, Faith crossed over, opened the gate set in Millicent's unblemished white picket fence, walked up the herringbone brick walk, and rang the bell. The door opened immediately, thus confirming Faith's suspicion that Millicent had been watching Faith's every move from the bow window in the front parlor.

Millicent Revere McKinley was descended from Ezekiel Revere, a distant relation of the famous man. Ezekiel's claim to fame was casting the monumental bell that had sounded the alarm on Aleford green that famous day and year. The bell and belfry had been moved to the top of a small hill overlooking the green for reasons no one could recall, and Millicent had been trying for years to get the town to move it back to its rightful place. She had also been campaigning to change the town's name to Haleford, which, she averred, was its real moniker, the handwriting of the time having led to this grave historical error. There was a group sympathetic to the moving of the belfry. It was a long climb for tourists. But Millicent was a party of one on the name change, since it was well documented that the town had been named for an early tavern conveniently situated by the best ford across the Concord River for miles. Mention of this was enough to send Millicent for an ax — a portrait of Carrie Nation occupied a prominent position on the wall of the McKinley dining room, next to those of Millicent's parents. After a Spartan dinner there, Tom had observed that even if Millicent had offered anything alcoholic, the combined gazes of this particular trinity were enough to make a man forswear the grape forever. When asked to grace Millicent's board, most Alefordians had a few shots at home first.

Today, crossing the street to Millicent's was

like crossing the Rubicon. Faith was going to Millicent for whatever information she could pry out of the woman. This act, she admitted to herself, represented a commitment to finding out who had murdered Gwen Lord. There was no choice. She'd known this on some level all along.

'Always lovely to see you, Faith dear. On your way to the cleaner's with poor Tom's shirts? Of course, my mother always did my father's. Monday was washing day; Tuesday, ironing. I can still smell the suds and the starch. You young people today, even with all the labor-saving devices they have now — what would Mother have made of a steam iron, I dasn't think! — don't seem to have time to do such menial chores for your loved ones.'

That was where the 'poor Tom' came from. Apparently, not seeing to his laundry was spousal abuse. Faith had learned not to answer when Millicent made this kind of remark. It was one of those lose/lose situations. Faith had vowed to 'love, honor, and cherish,' but not iron.

She stepped over the threshold into Millicent's hallway and was forced to take a step backward. On either side of the hall, cartons were piled almost to the ceiling. The light was dim, but she could also make out several large sacks of what appeared to be rice and flour.

'What's all this? Are you collecting for a shelter?' Faith was dumbfounded.

'No, dear, although that's a noble thought. This is for me.'

'For you?'

Millicent couldn't weigh more than a hundred pounds and wouldn't consume this much food in a year. Had she discovered Costco and run amok, buying in bulk? Faith had heard of people who returned home from the food warehouse with industrial sizes of everything from mustard to cat food, without the slightest use for any of it.

'Yes, for me.' Millicent was leading the way through the narrow passage she'd left clear, then she opened the door to the parlor. Gallons of water in plastic jugs lined the baseboards. A ham radio was set up where her old gramophone had been formerly, and there was a basket brimming with unopened packages of batteries next to the one with her knitting. Faith started to laugh. She couldn't help it.

'Oh, Millicent, don't tell me you're worried about Y2K?'

'Not Y2K, TEOTWAWKI.'

The end of the world as we know it. Faith stopped laughing.

4

Millicent and Y2K. It actually made sense. Her forebears would have been the ones with plenty of dried jerky and apples, doling out a nibble at a time to fellow needy Pilgrims who hadn't exercised sufficient foresight or self-restraint. Faith could see it all now. She'd be knocking at Millicent's door on New Year's Day, begging an Eveready or a sip of Poland Spring water.

'And you don't even need to depend on batteries for this.' Millicent was waving a flashlight, squeezing the handle like crazy to produce a steady beam of light. 'I've got a radio, too,' she announced proudly.

There was an ancient flintlock over the fireplace and Faith glanced down to the hearth for powder and shot. She had no doubt Millicent would be ready for anything — including the breakdown of law and order. Widespread looting could place not only her family portraits and mourning wreaths of braided tresses from several generations at risk but also Millicent's own life work — the accumulation of Aleford memorabilia. Her earliest treasure was a centennial mug, only slightly chipped. The bicentennial had been a bonanza — mugs, spoons, pens, pencils, even kazoos. This last had been an item distributed on that year's Patriots' Day by Aleford Photo, emblazoned on one side with the date and flag and on the other with their motto — Put Yourself in the Picture — and their name and address. Roughly several thousand were left, and every time the Fairchilds went into the store, Ben was presented with another, much to his delight and awe.

This whole millennium business had been going on for months — or more accurately, years — and Faith had tried to avoid paying much attention to it. Maybe they'd lose power, but that was a frequent occurrence in Aleford. The Fairchild larder was always stocked for a major emergency, and even if they were without electricity for several days, they would survive well on what Faith could cook on the gas stove top. They'd dine quite nicely on pasta, the staff of life, with simple sauces based on canned plum tomatoes; what Faith called 'pantry soups' using last-resort cans of good chicken stock (not her own homemade); and bean dishes, such as one with chickpeas, rosemary, extra virgin olive oil, a dash of balsamic vinegar, and flaked Italian tuna. She'd put up a lot of green-tomato chutney last summer, as well as several kinds of jams and preserves. And she had plenty of garlic. She hadn't purchased any survival grub. Faith would far rather face TEOTWAWKI than eat reconstituted eggs.

New Yorkers, of course, were reacting to Y2K in their own inimitable fashion. She'd heard of one canny gourmet who was stocking up on foie gras to barter. He'd also started laying down champagne well before the recent shortages and astronomical price increases. Faith was skeptical about the champagne crisis, suspecting a plot to fix prices. At this very moment, there were, no doubt, cases and cases of Dom Perignon secreted in dusty warehouses in Hoboken and Jersey City. The parsonage wine cellar in the basement was full — a Fairchild addition — and included several cases of champagne.

Faith looked at Millicent's pile of batteries. These did make sense and she realized they'd better get some. It would be like fans and air conditioners in July. As they inched closer to midnight, December 31, there wouldn't be a pink bunny in sight. Pink elephants, perhaps, but no Energizers.

'Is First Parish *really* Y2K-prepared?' Millicent fixed Faith with a stern look. She'd always seemed to have an uncanny ability to read other people's minds, and Faith suddenly saw all her frivolous thoughts parading across the room, about to be impaled one by one.

'I think so,' she said hesitatingly.

'You think so? I would have thought by now you would know. I'm afraid you may not be taking this seriously enough, Faith. Sit down.'

Faith sat.

'None of this would have happened if computers had never been invented. There wasn't any of this nonsense at the turn of the last century.'

A sudden mischievous urge to ask Millicent for her recollections almost overwhelmed Faith. She bit her tongue. An octogenarian forever sixty-nine, Millicent would not think it was funny. At all.

'But like it or not, we're stuck with them.' Her tone made it plain on which side of the fence she came down. 'They invented them, but they didn't have the brains to think past their own noses — or, rather, own century. The computer identifies the date by the last two digits, so most of them will think it's 1900, not 2000, as of January first. Are you with me so far?'

Of course Faith knew all this, but it was so much fun to hear Millicent that she simply nodded. Besides, she hadn't thought about Saturday night for five whole minutes.

'This may not seem very important to you, but these things — they call them microchips — control everything from our electric lights to missile systems.'

Lights, and gas for cars, food distribution, ATMs, phone lines, water — Faith had thought of all these, but she hadn't thought about missiles, and for the first time, she felt a bit Y2K-uneasy.

There was a stack of millennial books and magazines piled in the dry sink where Millicent normally kept her African violets. Apparently, she had memorized them.

'Here's just one example. You might want to jot it down to tell Tom.' Millicent obviously regarded them both in the same category as those naysayers who'd insisted the world wasn't round when Columbus set sail. 'The average offshore oil rig has ten thousand microchips, some of them set in concrete and below water level. Now, if a single one malfunctions, the rig won't be able to pump oil. And you can imagine what will happen then. It's the domino effect.' Millicent presented the last concept with a triumphant air. She wasn't simply Y2K-compliant; she was Y2K-propelled.

There was no stopping her. 'The average supermarket has roughly a three-day supply of food. How long do you think our Shop and

Save could serve the needs of the Aleford community, particularly since the store will likely lose power? And after January first, how is the food going to make its way from the point of production to the point of distribution? Suppose you are a little coffee bean growing on a tree in Colombia. It might seem simple — get picked, roasted, packed, and shipped.'

This was getting weird.

'But all these operations are controlled by microchips. The chances of that bean getting to your kitchen when this hits are roughly the same as of a camel passing through the eye of a needle.'

Or mine of getting out of here without laughing, Faith thought. Apparently in the dark of night, a microchip had somehow embedded itself in Millicent's head.

Millicent flushed. She was doing the Vulcan mind-meld thing again, Faith noted dismally, and she willed her thoughts to what to have for dinner and how nice Millicent's garden had looked last summer.

'But you didn't come here to talk about all this, I'm sure,' Millicent said with a certain amount of good grace. Faith should have been suspicious. *Good* and *grace* were not words normally associated with Millicent, either paired or singly.

'No,' Faith admitted. It was always better to be straightforward. Millicent was going to tell you what she knew or not, and the approach made little difference. Although, if Faith had appeared with a four-foot cube of dehydrated nutrition, the woman might have been softened up. But who knew?

'No,' Faith continued. 'I'm sure you've heard about what happened Saturday night at the First Parish fund-raiser at Ballou House.' Millicent had not attended. She only left home in the evenings for historical society and DAR meetings.

'Gwendolyn Lord was murdered,' Millicent said matter-of-factly. 'Cyanide in your dessert, apparently.'

'Apparently,' Faith retorted quickly, 'but in *her* dessert and only *her* dessert. Nothing to do with Have Faith.'

'Of course,' Millicent murmured. Either the Y2K soliloquy had loosened her tongue or she wanted to talk about what had happened, because she kept going. 'I only met the girl once myself. After your spring concert. She was with Jared. Quite beautiful, I thought at the time. Perhaps too beautiful.'

Before Faith could ask her what she meant by that, Millicent added, 'I've known Jared since he was a little boy. His parents lived in town, but his grandparents had a house here

93

and he used to come in the summertime. Even after they were gone, the Gabriels kept the place. It burned sometime in the late seventies. It was close to the river. A sad loss. Jared would come with Nicholas — their grandfathers were brothers. It was never a large family. Just those two little boys and now just those two young men. They all seemed to die so young. I believe Nicholas is in the art business, but I doubt it's anything I would be interested in. I saw the Sargent show and I'm afraid it spoiled me for anything modern. Such terrible colors these days, and the subjects!'

Faith didn't want to get sidetracked. She well knew that Monet was as avant-garde as Millicent got, and even that was a stretch. Returning to her own topic, she said, 'The whole thing seems so unlikely. Why would someone want to poison Gwen?'

Millicent shook her head. 'Hard to say what motivates the mind of man to commit evil acts.' Millicent tended to talk in aphoristic sentences. Faith pictured a large bowl of slips of paper with similar sayings that Ms McKinley, or Miss McKinley, as she insisted upon, reached in to memorize each day. 'She didn't have any money, at least not yet. Jared is comfortable. Jealousy?'

Faith knew she was not imagining the

94

emphasis Millicent put on the word, nor the way she peered straight into Faith's eyes and soul.

Millicent went on. 'A man — or a woman. Hell hath no fury like a woman scorned, and Gwendolyn might have snatched someone's beau or someone's something else right from under her nose?' Faith was feeling increasingly uncomfortable. Millicent's Y2K supplies seemed to be closing in on her and the air in the crowded room was stuffy. She felt a little like Alice growing too large for the space — and she hadn't eaten a thing. Not that there wasn't plenty around. Millicent continued to ruminate. 'Or a man. A spurned lover perhaps? What do they call that now — 'stalking'? Someone in her past upset at the prospect of losing her to another?'

This struck Faith as a better idea than the first suggestion, and one that hadn't occurred to her. Both notions pointed to Gwen's past. It was likely that the answer lay there. It usually did.

It was time to go. She had to drop off Tom's shirts and get back to pick up Amy.

'I'll talk to Tom about whether we are sufficiently prepared for the millennium,' Faith promised, hearing words she never dreamed she would ever be saying.

Millicent smiled sweetly. 'I'd say talking to

Tom about any number of things might be a good idea. He knew the dead girl better than most.'

The earlier hint — 'someone's something else' — took on all the subtlety of a sledgehammer. Her willingness to discuss Gwen Lord's death with Faith became sickeningly clear. Faith felt dizzy and leaned against a pile of boxes labeled CANNED GOODS to steady herself, then rapidly threaded her way past Millicent's provisions and opened the front door.

'Good-bye,' she said.

'Good-bye, dear. Drop by any time.' She patted Faith on the shoulder in an overt gesture of affection, or pity — Faith couldn't decide which. All she knew was that she felt as if she'd been to the doctor and the prognosis was grim.

★ ★ ★

On the way home, she addressed herself with brutal honesty. Yes, she'd been jealous of Gwen and, yes, she was disturbed by Tom's behavior since Saturday night, but of course it would have been a shock to see the woman you'd been dancing cheek-to-cheek with moments before lying dead at your feet. That had to have been all it was. This was Tom!

But this was also Aleford and if Millicent was dropping elephantine hints, then everyone else in town would soon be saying, 'Where there's smoke there's fire, and maybe the jealous wife did have something to do with that poor girl's death. She probably just meant to make her a little sick but put too much of whatever it was in the dessert.' Insidious whispers echoed in Faith's thoughts. It wasn't reality. Reality was her good marriage, her children, her job.

It would be winter soon, and shadows were lengthening even in the early afternoon. It was all very wearying.

When she got home, she decided to phone Charley MacIsaac and find out when she could expect to get back into her kitchen. She had several events coming up and wanted to occupy herself with work.

'You know the state, Faith. Nothing happens in a hurry. They said they'd check everything today, but I haven't heard from them yet. I know that John and his crew are finished.'

It had occurred to Faith that Dunne would need to check her premises — on the off chance that Niki or she had left a vial of cyanide lying on the counter. 'Vial?' She didn't even know what the cyanide used looked like. A powder? Liquid? Little granules? To be mixed with the dessert toppings, granules, crystals, made the most sense.

'Can't you light a fire under someone? I need to get back to work,' Faith urged, knowing full well that Charley wouldn't do it and that even if he did, it would have to be a blaze of bonfire proportions.

'I'll call them again,' he promised. 'Enjoy yourself. Take some time off. Most people would be thrilled.'

Faith hung up and then called Have Faith to check her messages. Her throat closed. Thrilled! The word was *panicked*. All but two of the events for the next several weeks had been canceled. Some people tried hard to come up with excuses — 'postponing,' 'illness in the family,' 'sudden cash-flow problem.' Some didn't bother. She was left with a dinner at one of the clubs up on the North Shore, featuring game, and the sixtieth birthday party of one of her most stalwart customers. It was being arranged as a surprise by the woman's husband, and Faith prayed that when the birthday girl walked into her dining room, after all her friends had jumped up from behind the living room furniture, and saw Faith, she wouldn't lose her appetite.

The kitchen door swung open and Tom walked into the hall.

'Oh, Tom . . . ' She reached for those broad shoulders and thought that after she hugged him very hard, she might allow herself a tear or two — anger, frustration, and fear called for no less.

'Have to run, honey. Lucas Prendergast is at Mass General and I promised I'd stop by. There's a book I want to bring him.'

'Then you won't be home for dinner?' It took a good thirty minutes to get to the hospital. Then figuring in parking, the visit, and thirty minutes back, Tom wouldn't be home until the kids' bedtime. Luke had been battling lung cancer since early last spring and was in for another surgery. She knew Tom needed to go, but she needed him, too. She quickly blurted out what had been on Have Faith's answering machine.

'It'll blow over,' Tom said, trying to sound reassuring. She had followed him into his study. He was running his finger over a shelf of volumes, searching for the right title. 'I had it here last week. Marian Wright Edelman's *Lanterns*. Ah, here it is!' He plucked the slender book from its place and started out the door. 'Restaurants, caterers — any business that concerns food is always contending with stuff like this. Remember the problem with your black bean soup when you were doing that *Scarlet Letter* movie shoot?'

Faith did remember. Remembered it all too well.

'But nobody died. It was Ex-Lax added after we'd put the food out. Unpleasant, but not life-threatening.'

He was halfway out the door. 'There's nothing you can do about this, though. You'll just have to accept it.'

This was Tom talking? Talking to the wife he claimed to know so well, he felt as if they were one person — a sweet concept, she'd always thought when he murmured it in her ear, but not one she'd ever fully accepted. Do nothing? Faith?

When her food had been altered on the movie set, she'd had no choice but to find out who did it or risk losing the business that had just started again in its new locale. There was no choice this time, either, if she wanted to retain her good name — and perhaps for some other reasons, as well.

She closed the outside door on the empty space where her husband had been and went upstairs to wake Amy from her nap. Holding her little girl, warm and still muzzy with sleep, Faith stood at the window and watched Tom cross back over to the church, where he'd left his car. Maybe it was her imagination, but he seemed slightly stooped, as if he dared not look up to heaven right now.

* * *

Niki was furious.

It was Tuesday morning. The premises of Have Faith had been given a clean bill of health. Faith had asked Niki to come to work to talk about the situation. To talk about the disastrous situation.

'Assholes. All of them. What do they think? That we pride ourselves on poisoning our customers? State-of-the-art techniques. Strychnine in the Stroganoff, Amanita bisque? Have Faith takes on a whole new meaning. Maybe we should add 'Food Testers Supplied Free of Charge'?'

Faith started to laugh. Niki had the right attitude.

'Look, the game dinner is Saturday night and the birthday party next Monday. We'll use the time to test some new recipes. We're always complaining we serve the same things because we never get a chance to try anything different. Here's our chance.'

Niki wasn't letting go so easily. 'Sure, sure. Wonderful. We'll cook up a storm. Nothing we can do about it.'

Faith was getting tired of hearing this. She didn't reach for the file where she kept notes for new dishes. Instead, she sat down at the counter and tore off a blank sheet of paper from the pad she kept there.

'I keep coming back to motive.'

Niki sat down, too, her eyes sparkling, and passed Faith a pen. 'I might have known you'd decided to solve this thing yourself. Does Tom know what you're up to?'

No — and doesn't care, Faith started to say. 'No — and I don't want him to' was what came out. 'Millicent hinted that Gwen might have jilted someone who then killed her — the old 'If I can't have her, nobody can' rationale.'

'That's good, but don't those guys usually kill themselves afterward, too? And don't they broadcast it all over? Run up with a gun, scream out, 'I love you, baby,' kill the poor woman, then turn it on themselves? That's all you hear about these days. I read about one nutcake in New York recently who waited for his former girlfriend's wedding day, then shot her as she was getting into the limo. Killed himself, too, but not soon enough.'

What Niki said made sense — an abusive ex would have been more noticeably on the scene. Of course, the police might have information they weren't sharing about a stalker/killer, but somehow Faith thought she would have heard about someone like this, possibly from Jared.

'Poison is supposed to be a woman's method. Any possibilities there?' Niki asked.

'I think it's become an equal-opportunity

modus operandi, but Millicent did suggest that Gwen could have been killed by a jealous female.'

'There have to be a bunch of those around,' Niki said, a little too enthusiastically for Faith's current frame of mind. 'The woman was gorgeous. Not flashy, but very, very sexy. On Saturday night, most of the men in the room had their tongues hanging out every time she hit the dance floor, and if looks could kill, she'd have been murdered hours earlier by any number of wives.' Niki chattered on. 'But this was a premeditated crime. You just don't happen to have cyanide in your purse.'

Faith had thought of this. And what about the almond cookies in the dessert? Did the murderer get lucky, or did he or she know the menu in advance? It had been no secret, yet aside from Paula and a few others on the committee, no one outside Faith's own staff was familiar with what would be served. There had been an article in the *Aleford Chronicle* about the party, though.

'Remember the write-up about the event in the paper a couple of weeks ago? Paula wanted to be sure people knew about the auction, and there may have even been a few tickets left for sale then. It mentioned the main course and the dessert.'

'Which means our murderer reads the town paper and must live in Aleford. That narrows the field a bit — at least from the greater Boston area.'

'Although, it would be a pretty safe bet bringing cyanide.' Faith had done some research on the Net and decided it would have been in the form of a white granular powder. 'There was bound to be something it could be sprinkled on. Mixing it into the sugar bowl is one tried-and-true method. Supposedly, Lizzie Borden did this before delivering the forty-plus whacks.'

'That's a relief. Glad to know her parents didn't suffer.'

'But the point is, the murderer could have mixed it into almost anything we served and it would have looked like grains of sugar or salt. I need to find out what it would have tasted like. Bitter, I think, so the dessert made the most sense. To the murderer, that is.'

'I think we'd better split up for a while,' Niki suggested. 'I'll test recipes — no desserts, thanks — and you snoop around. You're better at it and have already been in trouble with the police, while aside from a moving violation or two, I can still look my mother straight in the eye. I think she does suspect I'm not a virgin, though.'

Niki Constantine came from a large

Greek-American family in Waterdown, and the lack of Mrs in front of her daughter's name was a source of constant sorrow and anxiety to her mother. Niki herself had no intention of settling down. Her taste in men was eclectic, and at the moment she was dating a future venture capitalist at the Harvard Business School, a carpenter, and an unemployed musician. She'd repeatedly told Faith that the man of her dreams was a biker who could cook and that she was holding out for him.

'If someone doesn't find out what happened to Gwen, we won't have a business,' Faith said glumly, recognizing the logic of Niki's proposal. 'I have to find out more about Gwen herself. Did you ever see her around town at any of the clubs?'

Niki shook her head. 'I have a friend who's into the art scene, and it seems like there's some important opening every night. That's her social life — and she isn't doing badly. Since Gwen worked at a gallery, it must have been the same for her.'

'And music. Jared has season tickets for everything from the Handel and Haydn Society to the Berklee Performance Center. I know, because he offers them to us when he can't go. Apparently, Gwen was as much of a music lover as he is.'

Faith had been so caught up in the way Gwen's death affected her that she hadn't been giving enough thought to Jared, and she felt a stab of guilt now, a sharp one. The two had been well matched, and he was suffering acutely. She hadn't wanted to intrude, but now she admitted to herself that perhaps this was because she really didn't want to talk about Gwendolyn Lord, not even to comfort Jared, her friend. She'd call and let him know that he could come for dinner, or just drop by to talk anytime.

'I should go to the gallery. Talk to Jared's cousin and anyone else who works there. I can't start quizzing Jared, but I really don't know much about Gwen — where she grew up, how long she's been in Boston. I didn't really read the obit. Maybe there's something between the lines. Other than this, I'm not sure what else to do.'

'I would think it would be obvious, *mon ami*, to anyone with your powerful little gray cells,' Niki said in an atrocious accent. 'You had a roomful of mystery writers. Pros! Find out what they think — and you know that they're all weaving Gwen's death into some sort of plot. For them, life *is* art.'

Faith felt better than she had since Saturday night. 'It is *you* with the mighty brain cells. I'll start right away. With Anson L.

Scott. He's the closest — and certainly a master of devious plots.'

* * *

The mystery writer sounded sincerely delighted to be hearing from Faith, and she made an appointment to see him the following morning. When she promised to bring some doughnut muffins and other treats, he declared himself counting the minutes, which threaten to pass at an agonizingly pedestrian pace.

She called Jared, too, but he was not up to seeing anyone, even Tom and Faith.

'I still can't believe it,' Jared said. 'And the police haven't been able to find out a thing. They keep coming here with more questions. It's like a nightmare. Who were Gwen's friends? What do I know about her past life? They're trying to make it seem like she had something to hide — or that I do. I finally screamed at one of them to get out, so they sent someone else. He's enormous, and at first I was terrified to have him in the room, but at least he's more sensitive. I feel like he really cares about what happened. It's not just a job.'

'I think I know who that is. Detective Lieutenant John Dunne — and he is the best.

You can trust him completely.'

Faith thought John would be amused to hear the recommendation, but it was true. She might not always see eye-to-eye with him, yet she never doubted his sincerity and absolute devotion to a case. It wasn't just a job. His hair would be less gray and he'd have fewer lines in his massive forehead if it were.

'Gwen was a simple person. She loved art and music and me,' Jared started to sob. When he'd collected himself, he said, 'She was ambitious and she would have had a wonderful gallery of her own someday. I was prepared to back her, but she said she wanted to do it herself. She'd saved quite a bit — I was amazed, in fact — and was sure she could find some silent partners, besides me. But for now, she felt she still had a lot to learn from Nick. Oh, Faith, it was all going to have been so perfect. I'm sorry. I have to hang up now.'

'We love you, Jared. Come when you're ready.' Faith heard him put the phone down and did so herself, feeling inexpressibly sad. Life would never be perfect for Jared, no matter what happened in the future. There would always be Gwen, always that body lying on the floor. The unperfect ending.

★   ★   ★

108

Suitably, Anson Scott lived at the end of a long, twisting road in the northern part of Aleford, bordering on Byford. The woods came up to the pavement and had been carefully cultivated to remain deep and impenetrable. Branches from towering oaks formed a canopy over the drive and filtered the sunlight. The mystery writer's house was large and sprawling, designed at the height of the Arts and Crafts movement. The slate roof appeared to have been draped over the brown-shingled outside walls. A long eyebrow window ran across the third story, duplicating the roofline. Faith walked up to the elaborately carved oak front door and rang the bell. The writer himself answered almost immediately.

'Mrs Fairchild, lovely to see you. Come in, come in. My humble abode.' He swept his arm out, an indication of both welcome and proud ownership.

Faith hadn't told him why she wanted to see him, afraid he might refuse. Now she thought it appropriate to say something right away, but she was dumbstruck at the home's interior. There was no entryway or foyer. She'd stepped directly into the living room. The walls were painted red — red with a great deal of gold. They shimmered above the dark wainscoting and were interrupted on two sides by a bank of leaded-glass windows. A stained-glass medallion with a single ruby poppy was centered at the top of each. The floors were covered with brilliant Orientals, azure, crimson, purple, deep orange. True to the period, the furniture consisted of Morris chairs, Stickley tables, and glass-fronted bookcases, in addition to extraordinary single pieces by master craftsmen Faith couldn't identify. A fireplace large enough to provide shelter for a family of four filled one end of the room. The opening was surrounded by tiles that, taken altogether, formed a forest frieze of green, blue, lavender, ocher, and brown. The tree trunks seemed to recede as she looked, while the cloudlike branches fell forward. She realized that the room forced an awareness of color, perhaps because it was dark, the beamed ceilings low, and the light from outside dimmed by the leaded window-panes.

'This is such a beautiful room,' Faith said, aware of the under-statement but at a loss for a way to express how exquisite it all was, except in the most clichéd phrases. 'These tiles . . . ' She gestured toward the fireplace.

'Gruebys. The company was in Boston. You've probably run across the tulip ones — a single blossom against a dark green background? I'm very fond of this period, both in Britain and in the United States. The notion that everyday items should have as much artistic integrity as paintings or sculptures is a credo of mine, too. Do sit down.'

Faith was tempted by one of several window seats, covered in Morris's Strawberry Thief pattern, but she chose the leather couch, nearer to hand. Scott nodded approvingly, murmured, 'Original upholstery,' and selected a remarkable-looking oak chair across from it. The chair's tall back started at the ground and was made up of thin verticals, the outside one on each side forming the legs. It loomed thronelike even over Scott's height.

Faith took a guess. 'Charles Rennie Mackintosh?'

'Close, close, but it's Frank Lloyd Wright, designed for the Robie House in Chicago around 1908. Well' — he rubbed his hands together — 'you've discovered my passion, one that I was fortunate enough to develop early. When all this was considered junk. Either your grandmother gave it to the Salvation Army or it was relegated to the children's or servants' rooms. Or even worse, tossed out. I found one Stickley chair by a curb in Cambridge on trash day.'

There was a massive sideboard against one

wall and it was covered with art pottery. 'That stuff' — he pointed to the vases and bowls — 'I mostly picked up in yard sales and flea markets. Now Sotheby's auctions it. But you didn't come here to chat about Rookwood versus Weller.'

'No, although I'd like to hear about it sometime.' She knew he was talking about the pottery, but the differences were hard to distinguish. The colors were similar, as well as the use of organic forms. Her mind was wandering. She brought it back.

'This may sound a bit odd, but I wondered if you'd give me your impressions about what happened on Saturday night. I mean, you invent this kind of thing and perhaps — '

'Perhaps I could take a busman's holiday and solve the crime? What a novel idea! A plot in and of itself! I am honored. Shall we unravel the threads over tea? Or sherry, if you prefer, although I think tea would better suit what I hope is in that package by your side. We'll have it in the library. I've a fire there, and it's also where I work. The muse pervades its air and may speed us along.'

A bellpull hung on the wall. It was embroidered with an intricate design of vines and roses. Anson got up and gave it a hearty yank. A woman who could have been anywhere from forty to sixty appeared. She was dressed in a dark sweater and skirt. Her starched white collar stood out. Nothing else about her did.

'Sir?'

'Tea, please, Margery, in the library, and my guest has brought provisions.' He took the bag from Faith and handed it to the housekeeper, who gave a small nod and disappeared.

'Come, let us cogitate,' he said. At this point, Faith didn't care whether he gave her any ideas or not. The whole experience was fascinating and getting curiouser and curiouser.

In the library, in front of the fire, he sat still, like a pointer by a fallen bird. Finally, he said, 'An interesting choice of venue. A murder mystery dinner. There might be something there. The plot was childishly simple. Who wrote the thing?'

In concentrating on the murder, Faith had overlooked the fact that the whole point of the evening was murder — or solving one. She had no idea who'd written the story. It was probably something Paula had bought. Faith had seen them for sale, along with those mystery jigsaw puzzles, in any number of stores. She realized that she didn't even know who the murderer was.

'I was paying more attention to the menu. I

assume Paula Pringle, who was in charge of the event, bought one of those mystery dinner party kits.'

'No doubt, no doubt, but it's a possible angle. Our killer reads it beforehand and tailors the crime to fit. Many murderers are quite conceited and love to play tricks like this. Evidence in front of your nose, that sort of thing. The basic fact of a premeditated murder is that he or she has total confidence in his or her ability to get away with it — fool the world. So, the game — which, by the way, was quite obvious and I was correct.' He smiled engagingly. 'I read ahead to the solution printed at the end of our booklets, as did several other naughty guests at the table. I spotted them. The old man was killed by his grandson, in part because the grandfather objected to the lad's taste in fiancées — although, the lass *was* totally unscrupulous and interested only in young Willoughby's healthy cash flow. But the main motive for the young sprig was righting an ancient wrong. He'd nursed this grievance for years. Seems his grandfather had been indirectly responsible for young Willoughby's mother's descent into alcoholism and early death. When she'd married into the family, Forbes senior had insisted that she cut herself off completely from her own family, humble but honest

114

yeomen, and even though she complied with his wishes, he continued to treat her as nothing more than a servant. Unlike our murder, it was murder committed in a fit of passion. The grandfather's objection to the fiancée was the match to the shavings.'

Nothing at all like Anson Scott's books, Faith thought. There was passion, but it was never straightforward, and certainly *much* bloodier than the country house crime enacted at the dinner. The grandfather would have been found in several parts, scattered about the estate. If they'd been following a Scott script, no one would have been able to eat.

'Gwendolyn Lord was playing the fiancée,' Anson continued. 'I was the butler and, let's see, wasn't your husband playing Willoughby Forbes the Third?'

Faith nodded. Yes, the good reverend. Tom. Tom, her husband. The murderer.

The housekeeper arrived with a loaded tray. The silver tea service gleamed. Sliced lemons, hot water, milk, sugar, Faith's muffins and scones, arranged with the housekeeper's addition of tea sandwiches and thin sugar cookies — it was all there.

'Thank you, Margery,' Anson said approvingly, and got up to stoke the fire. The housekeeper silently disappeared.

'Will you be mother?' he called over his shoulder to Faith.

'I am and I will,' she replied. It was getting to be more and more like an Oscar Wilde play. She expected Lady Bracknell at any moment.

'Milk or lemon?'

'Milk and three lumps of sugar, please. I'm terribly greedy.'

She put the cup down in front of him and poured one for herself. He was already eating one of her muffins with great relish. Looking behind him, she could see rows of bookshelves filled with leatherbound copies of his titles, as well as the translations into virtually every tongue on the planet. The walls were decorated with framed posters of the books that had been made into movies, as well as with a variety of scrolls and plaques, most of which were decorated with skulls, daggers, or gore of some nature.

'I've been trying to think of a motive. Gwen wasn't wealthy, so money is out.' Faith was feeling hopelessly outclassed.

'But there are so many, many more motives. More interesting ones — love, hate, fear, jealousy, pride — hubris, overweening pride, that is.' He was smiling broadly. The man obviously loved his work.

'What about the choice of poison? What

does that say about the mind of the killer?'

'The psychological approach, yes! Poison is often a coward's choice — one doesn't necessarily have to be present to kill. Murderers are frequently cowards, you know. Terribly, terribly fearful people. Presumably, the killer was in attendance in order to get at the dessert and saw the death throes of the victim, hence perhaps, although a poisoner, not such a coward after all. More tea, if you will be so kind.'

He put several sandwiches and a scone on his plate. 'I assume you will be visiting my fellow scribblers.' The look he gave Faith was definitely mischievous.

'I hope to — if they'll see me.'

'Take food, my dear. No one will refuse you. And come again to see me, even without your sumptuous victuals. I'd like to hear what they have to say. I'll be out of town, plugging my latest effort, for the next week, but I'll be back for a good while thereafter.'

The housekeeper appeared in the doorway. 'More tea, sir? Is the water still hot enough?'

'Everything's fine, thank you.'

She melted away. With that, it was time for Faith to return to her own family, accompanied by the famous man's ruminations. Ruminations — she was starting to sound like him. She laughed to herself.

* ★ *

The visit to Adder Chase, for such was the name of Scott's house — his first bestseller had been *The Adder's Smile* — had put Faith in a good mood. She was doing something. What that was was not exactly clear, but the mystery writer had given her a great deal to think about and had issued an invitation for her to return and 'cogitate' some more at 'a moment's notice.' If each author provided similar fodder, she should have the whole thing figured out in no time. She knew it was a brave thought.

Tom was home for dinner. Afterward, Faith bathed Amy, tucked her in, and went to clean up the kitchen while Tom read some *Harry Potter* to Ben. From the sounds she heard, it was hard to say who was enjoying it more. She'd poached some boneless, skinless chicken thighs and breasts, then covered them with a sour cream and caramelized onion sauce. There had also been herbed basmati rice and haricots vert, the thin French string beans steamed just to the point of tenderness, but still crisp. As she dried the last pot, the doorbell rang. Her heart sank. Damn this job. The cozy evening in front of the fire with her husband, the kind of evening they hadn't had for weeks, vanished with the sound. The bell rang again. She hastily dried her hands and went to answer it.

'Hello, Faith. I'm sorry to bother you at night, but I wondered if I could talk to Tom for a moment. You, too, actually.'

It was George Hammond, the principal of Aleford's Winthrop Elementary School. Ben's principal. What on earth could her kindergartner have done that required a home visit from the principal? And why hadn't she been called? There was a boy named Jerry, whom Ben kept talking about. Jerry was always getting into trouble. Each day, there was a new Jerry tale — broken crayons, shoving in line, and, worst of all, talking back to Mrs Black! Maybe there wasn't a Jerry. Maybe Jerry was Ben!

Her thoughts raced as she smiled graciously, offered coffee, which was refused, seated the principal and headed upstairs, two at a time, to get Tom. Ben was beginning to drowse, Faith gave him a quick kiss and turned off the light, pulling Tom into the hall.

'George Hammond is downstairs.'

'I thought I heard the bell.' Tom moved down the hall.

'What do you think's the matter? What could Ben have done?'

'Ben? I'm sure it has nothing to do with Ben. His teacher would have called,' Tom said sensibly. 'George probably wants to corral us into volunteering for something.'

Which could be worse.

But it was neither. George came straight to the point. 'I've gotten a couple of nasty phone calls, and the latest one has accused me of molesting the children at school. It will be all over town soon, and I haven't the slightest idea what to do about it except resign.'

5

Tom found his voice first. 'This is monstrous, George, and obviously the work of a very sick individual. I'll do everything I can to help you. Have you notified the police?'

The principal shook his head. 'Thank you, Tom, but I don't think you understand. I came to tell you what was happening before you heard it from someone else. There's really nothing you — or anyone else — can do about the situation.'

Faith felt the fury that had been welling up inside her boil over. 'That's crazy! I mean, the whole thing is crazy! People know you — some of them all their lives. You're one of the most trusted and loved men in town.' George was among a small handful of residents who'd twice received the Bronze Musket Award, presented every year on Patriots' Day to a resident who best typified the spirit of Aleford.

'I think I'll have that coffee after all. You're new to the school system and there's a lot you don't know,' George said ruefully.

They moved into the kitchen and soon Faith placed a steaming mug of coffee into his hands. She set a dish loaded with oatmeal lace cookies on the big round table and took a seat herself. What George had said was true. Since the beginning of school in September, she'd felt overwhelmed by her ignorance of school mores. Pix was a wonderful guide through the labyrinth, but Faith was sure that even Pix would be stunned by this curve.

George spoke calmly and evenly. It was his normal demeanor. 'Over the years, a climate of hysteria has taken hold, to the point where any and all accusations are accepted as fact, even when the individual is proved innocent. I've watched colleagues of mine in other parts of the state and country try to deal with this issue either for themselves or their staff. Their lives become a nightmare — and, in some cases, not worth living. There have been several suicides and any number of sudden 'car accidents.' The worst part of it is that we can't be the kind of teachers and administrators we want to be. The kind we used to be.'

He sipped some coffee. The cookies went untouched.

'It's been years since I've been able to comfort a crying child by giving him or her a hug. No more encouraging pats on the back. No outward signs of physical affection or support at all. We've had faculty meetings about it. I tell my teachers they have to make

122

their words palpable; their voices the equivalent of a nurturing hand. They understand. They're scared.'

Faith was remembering her elementary-school teachers — warm individuals; one in particular, who had a rocking chair and a large lap.

'What happened to trust?' she said bitterly. 'I don't want Ben and Amy to miss what I had growing up. Kids need pats on the back, hugs, and someone at school to dry their tears!'

George nodded, then continued to speak. 'Sexual abuse in childhood is just about the worst thing that can happen to a person, particularly if the abuser is a close authority figure like a teacher. I don't want to minimize that. But the incidence is minuscule. Familial abuse is far more common, and we are always on the alert for it. The public, however, thinks otherwise. We're with children all day. There's proximity and that gives an automatic credence to any accusations.'

'How many calls have you had?' Tom asked.

'This was the second. The first was three weeks ago. I'd kidded myself into thinking that it was an over-the-edge parent dissatisfied with teacher placement or something like that who was making a onetime obscene phone call. The person didn't come right out with the accusation, unlike the latest one, but rambled on about my character in general, until I hung up. Maybe I missed the point, because I didn't want to deal with it, but there was no missing the message tonight. The call convinced me it's not going to stop — not just the phone calls but also the rumors that will be spreading soon. I came here for solace — and to be sure you knew the truth, too, I suppose.'

'We would never believe anything like this about you!' Faith protested.

George Hammond smiled slightly. 'I hope not — and yes, I'm sure not. But you'd be amazed at what people will believe if they think their children are affected.'

'We can organize parents — and the rest of the town — in your defense. We can't let you be driven out by this kind of witch-hunt. It's McCarthyism all over again,' Tom said. 'The parish will support you.' He was already framing a sermon.

Again, George smiled. 'Any more coffee? I appreciate all this, Tom, but I'm not sure I have the energy to fight — and a fight it will be. A nasty, knock-down-drag-out fight. Headlines not just in the *Aleford Chronicle*, but the *Globe* and the *Herald*, as well. TV. This stuff is a gold mine for boosting circulation and ratings. Do I want every aspect of my life placed under this kind of microscope? And what about the town? The superintendent and the school committee are going to be put on the line. I'm not sure I want to know where they stand. You folks are still not getting it. This means the end of a career, no matter what the truth may be.'

'What will you do?' Faith whispered. Her eyes were filled with tears.

'Well, Polly and I had always planned to move to our cottage in Maine when I retired. After she died, I held on to it, even though I wasn't sure what I'd do. Now, it's beginning to look very attractive. My kids are scattered all over the place, and Maine is the one constant in all our lives. The problem is that if I resign, it will be tantamount to an admission of guilt. If I don't, it means I'll be smack in the middle of this ugliness. I'd like to see the year out, but I may not be able to. Let's just say I know I'm leaving; I don't know when or how.'

'It may be that we don't fully appreciate all the ramifications of the situation, but I'd like you to consider at least telling Chief MacIsaac and immediately getting caller ID — I assume you don't have it — so you can get a lead on who's making the calls. It could be someone who is such an obvious crackpot — and you know we have those in Aleford

— that no one will believe the charge,' Tom said forcefully.

George finished his coffee and rubbed his forehead. 'God knows, I don't want to leave my school. I'd hoped for at least three more years,' he said. 'I'll call the phone company in the morning — and go see Charley.'

'A man or a woman?' Faith asked. 'On the phone.'

'Impossible to tell. The voice was disguised. But during the second call, there was a TV on in the background. I could faintly hear the theme song from that children's show *Wishbone* when I first picked up the phone; then it sounded as if a door shut.'

'So, definitely a parent — or an adult with juvenile tastes — but much more likely a parent who's parked junior in front of the TV in the next room while making the call. And you're sure both calls were made by the same person?'

'Definitely. Same voice. I guess there's a silver lining here. At least I don't have two people after me.'

'What did you say back?'

'The first time I asked who it was a couple of times and then hung up. Tonight, I asked again, but when the person kept on talking, I lost it a little and said, 'Goddamn it, leave me alone,' and whoever it was hung up.'

But you didn't deny it, Faith thought with dismay — not that it would have made any difference to someone crazy enough to bring the accusation in the first place.

They talked some more and even managed to laugh together at Ben's utter devotion to Mrs Black. 'She still gets Christmas cards from the families of kids she had fifteen, twenty years ago,' George told them.

He stood up to leave. 'A school night, you know.' Both Faith and Tom hugged him. And he hugged them right back.

* * *

Faith had one arm around Tom's waist. They were lying in bed together, like spoons. She could tell he was wide-awake. After the principal left, they had talked of nothing else. It seemed to Faith that poison, real and figurative, was seeping from Aleford's every pore.

'You can do more about this than I can.' Tom rolled over and propped himself up on one elbow.

'What do you mean?'

'You're in the school a lot more than I am. Find out if any parents have particular grudges against George — or any teachers. We should have asked him that, and I will, but he may not be aware of everything that's going on, even if he is the principal. But mothers are — the mothers who are at Winthrop all the time.'

Faith was surprised that Tom had picked up on all this. It was true that mothers ran the nonacademic side of the school and father volunteers were few and far between, to the point where they were suspect.

'Here's a time when you can use your powers of investigation — and without any danger. You're good at this. We can't simply stand back and watch a man's whole life be destroyed.' Tom was extremely agitated. Faith had seldom seen him so worked up. 'There's an unhealthy tendency in this town, any town, to feed on rumors like this without questioning the source. A man's reputation is at stake here. It's the damn whispers, not the shouts, that bring people down,' he added bitterly.

She wanted to ask whom he was talking about now, but she said instead, 'I'll try to find out as much as I can. We'd better get some sleep.'

Tom rolled back over, and soon Faith heard his regular breathing. Heard it while lying wide-awake. Tom wanted her to find out who was launching this attack on George and why. She wanted to know, too. But she did not intend to stop her other investigation — the one Tom didn't know about. She'd moonlight.

Her plate was pretty full at the moment. Maybe the cancellations weren't such a bad thing after all. Sleep began to descend. Aleford. A sleepy little New England town. Give me the city that never sleeps, she thought as a sharp pang of homesickness struck. When this was all over, she'd take the kids to visit their New York grandparents. When this was all over — whatever 'this' was.

★ ★ ★

The obvious place to start investigating what Faith was calling 'the problem at Winthrop,' as opposed to 'the problem at Ballou,' was next door — at Pix's house — although there she could cover both. After getting everyone off for the morning, Faith went over, stuck her head in the back door, and called, 'Pix, are you home?' Just as she was about to leave, figuring that her friend was out walking the dogs, since the car was in the driveway, Pix called back, 'Pour yourself some coffee. I'll be right down.'

Faith poured herself a cup. Making good coffee was Pix's solitary culinary accomplishment. Everything else concocted in this kitchen was hit-or-miss. Gastronomically challenged, there was an unpredictability to her offerings that left her friends and family completely in the dark. It wasn't a question of feast or famine, but feast or what could this possibly be?

Coffee was the elixir of life in suburbia and coursed through innumerable everyday encounters — coffee to wake up, midmorning coffee with a friend, coffee at meetings, afternoon coffee, coffee as an offering, the container something to hold. It wasn't even really necessary to drink it. It had to be given — and taken. A rite.

'I promised myself that I would just shut the door and not get worked up about the mess in Danny's room, but I totally lost it this morning when I went in to wake him — he forgot to set his alarm again — and discovered that a wet towel he'd thrown on top of a pile of dirty clothes under his bed was producing an odor not unlike Limburger cheese. I've been cleaning, and from now on, it's going to be like camp — inspections from Mom. What's up? You're holding that mug with two hands in what looks from here like a vise grip, and you haven't drunk a drop.' Pix pushed back a strand of hair that had fallen across her cheek from the wrong side of her part, ended the outburst, and flopped into a chair across from her friend.

Faith put the mug down and told her what had happened the night before.

'I know you won't tell anyone, except Sam. And anyway, George seemed to think it would be all over town soon.'

Pix listened in silence, her face stricken. She'd sat up straight after the first sentence.

'Oh, it will be all over town all right. And all over every town in Massachusetts and other parts of New England. And why something like this has to happen to probably the best person ever to work in our school system is totally beyond me. A real test of faith. I know all about bad things happening to good people and I believe God is not a puppeteer, but wasn't it enough for George to lose Polly to ovarian cancer? He kept her home, and I can tell you, it was a hard death. Now this. I don't know whether to be relieved or sad that she's not here.'

'I'm sorry I never knew her. She died just before we were married. Tom has spoken of her often. She must have been wonderful.'

'She was,' Pix said emphatically. 'And a strong woman. She would hold her head high and get George through this. But it would also have been horrible for her to watch the town she loved and grew up in tear her husband to pieces, because that's what will happen. He's right. There will be defenders and supporters, but he'll always be remembered as the principal with the problem — no matter whose problem it turns out to be.'

'Tom wants me to try to find out who it is.' As Faith told this to Pix, she realized that she wasn't sure how to take Tom's words from the night before: 'You're good at this.' It was an affirmation. It was also a challenge. And a funny sort of challenge if you added 'You think' to the beginning of the sentence — words she had felt hanging in the air. It was a command performance. There had been an edge to his voice. It was that edge that had kept her awake.

Pix was nodding. 'I agree with Tom. I can't think of anyone in a better position. You can check things out at school and in the congregation. George is on the Anniversary Campaign committee and has been pretty vocal about using the money for the crypt.'

Faith was horrified. 'You can't possibly believe that one of the steeple lovers would do something like this!'

'I don't really, but you've often said yourself that you have to consider every angle.'

This was true — or, as Dorothy Sayers put it, 'Suspect everybody.'

'Okay, I'll keep steeple/crypt in the back of

my mind — or bottom and top — but I think it's more likely that it's a parent,' Faith said. 'And a current parent, someone with an elementary-school-aged child, given what was on television. Plus, *Wishbone* is a PBS show, so a parent with high standards.'

'That narrows things down,' Pix said sarcastically, which was an indication of how upset she was. Pix was never sarcastic.

'Okay, so it applies to virtually every parent in the school, every parent in town. Now how should I go about this? Have you heard anything negative about George as a principal?'

'Not for a long time. When Winthrop jumped on the Whole Language bandwagon and started using invented spelling, everybody in town became an immediate authority on education, as opposed to the principal. The school system ended up keeping the good parts of the program and ditching the rest, as usually happens. At the moment, there's all the MCAS business, but nobody blames the schools for that — especially since our scores are very respectable.'

The MCAS was recently mandated state-wide proficiency testing, and it either wasted most of the spring for fourth, eighth, and tenth graders or provided an opportunity to assess how well they were being taught, depending on your point of view. The idea of an MCAS-crazed parent was appealing to Faith, who weighed in on the side that believed it was a waste of time. Say little Johnny or Janie had been one of the few kids to do poorly and, thinking this might prevent early admission to one of the Ivies, the parent decides to make a statement by getting rid of the principal.

'But have you heard any direct complaints about George's ability as a principal, decisions he made on his own? He's had the job for a long time. All these hard-driving boomer parents. Some of them must think he's old hat.'

'If they do, he'd be able to come right back at them. He's always taking courses at the Harvard Ed School, and invited to speak at the Principals' Center there. But remember, I haven't been around Winthrop in over two years. Not since Danny was there.'

'Come on, Pix, I know for a fact you were still running the book fair last year.'

Pix Miller was the person Aleford called for any and all volunteer activities. Her husband, Sam, teased her by saying she was the epitome of 'I'm Just a Girl Who Can't Say No,' but without having any fun.

'I'm not doing it this year. Janice Mulholland is. You know her. She was at my table at Ballou House' — Pix gave a slight shudder at all the memories those words conjured up — 'and she's a member of First Parish.'

'The one with Rosemary's Baby for a kid, right?'

Pix laughed. It cleared the air for a moment.

'I wouldn't go that far, but Missy *is* a little difficult. It can't be easy for Janice. Apparently, shortly after they moved to Aleford, her husband ran off with his twenty-one-year-old secretary.'

'Men can be so unimaginative,' Faith commented, but it didn't alter her view of Missy Mulholland. The child was a little demon.

Pix continued. 'She's particularly bitter, because it's the old story — Janice dropped out of med school to put him through; then when she finally went back years later, she was only there a short while before she discovered she was pregnant. She dropped out again after Missy was born. I think she's given up at this point.'

'So Missy became her calling,' Faith said. 'I guess Janice would be a good place to start. I can volunteer for the fair and infiltrate the school that way.'

'The fair is in the spring. School book fairs

are always in the fall and spring. Winthrop's is in April, because we sell wrapping paper in the fall. This metamorphoses into magazine subscriptions when the kids hit middle school, so that grandparents and other relatives are able to dig out from under the thousands of rolls of the stuff accumulated during the elementary years.'

The prospect was daunting. Faith hated to sell things, except comestibles of her own making, and she had the feeling she was going to be forced to impose on any number of her near and dear for years to come. Unfamiliar as she was with school, it was still clear who made the actual sales, drove those totals up. She hoped the paper was nice. Her mother was very particular.

'So I'll volunteer for wrapping paper. How hard can it be?'

'Not hard at all, but volunteering to help out in the school library will put you on the spot and you'll hear more. Just make sure to get on a shift with a chatty mom, which shouldn't be hard. Most mothers who aren't working outside the home are very happy to talk to anybody other than the cat.'

Pix never failed to impress Faith with her knowledge.

'I'll call the librarian right away. No, better, I'll go over there.'

Having a plan always made Faith energetic. But before she left, she wanted to talk to Pix about Gwendolyn Lord. The visit to Millicent had stayed with Faith like yesterday's garlic — no matter how often one's teeth were brushed, there remained a hint of it in the back of one's mouth. Faith wanted to know if Pix had any ideas about the murder, but she didn't feel much like talking about it with Pix. Pix, her best friend. Pix, who could see through her.

It was Pix who introduced the subject. 'Mother thinks whoever killed Gwen Lord is someone with no connections to Aleford. Someone Gwen knew from somewhere else — from her work, perhaps.'

This was good news. There was enough going on in Aleford at the moment. And Ursula Rowe was seldom wrong in her hunches. Years of living in Aleford and on a small island off the coast of Maine had provided invaluable training in assessing human nature.

'I suppose you're looking into it,' Pix continued with studied nonchalance.

'You mean am I trying to solve the case because she died after eating my food and dancing with my husband?' It was out. 'Yes, I'm looking into it,' Faith said, and felt good to have it all on the table.

Pix grinned and stood up, opening the back door for Faith to leave. 'You know where I am. Anytime — day or night.' The smile faded. 'But please, please, do be careful, Faith.'

★ ★ ★

Faith drove to Winthrop Elementary a little too fast, downshifting at corners to transform her sensible Honda into a Miata. Patsy wanted to meet later in the afternoon. She said she'd leave work early and come to the house, despite Faith's objections. She didn't want Patsy to try to fit another thing in. She knew the volume of Patsy's work, and at the moment, it was enough to know that she was around and could jump in whenever Faith needed. Besides, Patsy hadn't been able to find out any more than what Faith knew from Dunne and Charley. She could, Patsy had explained, if she presented herself as Faith's legal representative, but neither of them thought that was a good idea. 'No sense running up a flag,' Patsy had said. She hadn't repeated 'Don't worry,' and Faith was thankful for that — thankful also in the end that Patsy was coming. Legal counsel was very reassuring, even if one hadn't broken any laws. The catering cancellations had infuriated Patsy as much as they had Niki. The thought hovered over the wires between them — if Have Faith's reputation wasn't definitively cleared, the only food-related job in Faith's future would be making fries at McDonald's — possibly.

Faith parked the car by the playground and went in the back door of the school, making her way into the well-stocked library. Countless book fairs and other PTA fund-raising had supplemented the diminishing contribution from the town budget. There were several computer terminals, comfortable reading areas, and books, books, books. Susan Glidden, the librarian, was processing some new ones with obvious pleasure.

'Mrs Fairchild, how nice to see you. Ben is just tearing through books. And he's already quite proficient on the computer.'

While this was well and good for a mother to hear, it wasn't what Faith was there for, and she plunged in, offering her services during what she referred to as a 'downtime' at work.

'Fantastic! We can use all the help we can get. When can you start?'

'How about now? I have about an hour.'

'It's tedious, but would you mind shelving books and helping if anyone comes in to check books out? It's very simple. I'll show you, then I'm due to read to the third grade.'

Sue left, with *Charlotte's Web* tucked under her arm, and Faith got to work. It was pleasant to have such a mindless task and she felt a bit like Charlotte herself, waiting for a fly to walk in. When one did, she hadn't expected it to be such a catch. It was Mrs Black, patron saint of the Fairchild household but also a veteran teacher, who would be more apt than most others to know what was going on in the school. She'd served as principal herself the year George took off — Polly Hammond's last year of life.

'The children have gym now,' she explained to Faith. 'I thought I'd pull some books on birds. We're making feeders and starting a life list for each child.'

This was a very New England thing, Faith had learned. Pix kept a little red leather notebook, embossed on the front with a robin, in her purse. Her mother had given it to her as soon as she was able to toddle in Ursula's footsteps and tote her own binoculars. Pix was always saying things like 'I see the yellow-tamped warblers haven't left yet' in a ruminative tone, suggesting that their suitcases should be at the door. At night, when it was too dark for most birds, she'd say fondly, 'Oh, look, good old Pegasus's great square is directly above us.' Faith had discovered that many of the people she'd met were on similar speaking terms with nature. She herself was not. Apparently, her children would be.

How to begin?

'I have a bit of spare time at the moment and thought I'd help out in the library.' Establish her presence and score a few points for later when she refused to make blue jay costumes or whatever.

'Sue can always use extra hands. She really needs an assistant now that the library functions as a computer center, too.'

Faith wasn't about to volunteer for that, but it gave her an opening.

'Perhaps the PTA could raise the money for one. I've been thinking I should get more involved in fund-raising, since I have some business experience. Who are the movers and shakers in that department?'

Mrs Black stopped selecting books and scrutinized Faith, who felt distinctly uncomfortable under the teacher's gaze. No one, child or adult, was going to put anything over on this lady.

'You should come to the next meeting and speak to one of the officers. They move and shake about equally.'

Faith flushed. She was going about this all wrong. And she wasn't getting anywhere. She made a sudden decision. After all, if she couldn't trust her son's kindergarten teacher, whom could she trust?

'I do want to get more involved in the school, but I also want to get to know people for another reason. I wonder if you've heard anything negative about the principal recently? My husband and I have become aware of something and want to find the source. We care about George very much.'

'We all care about Mr Hammond,' the teacher said sharply. 'I don't know exactly what you've heard, but if it's what I think it is, the best thing you can do is stay as far away from it as possible and keep your own mouths closed.' She was clearly angry.

Faith took a deep breath. Not only was winning Mrs Black over crucial to her investigation but vital to Ben's well-being. The way things looked at the moment, he could kiss Giant of the Week goodbye and count himself lucky with Dwarf of the Day.

'I agree with you — in theory. But the problem with rumors of this sort is that they don't go away. If those of us who know George and want to defend him keep quiet, the playing field is wide open for those vicious enough to start and spread the lies. If I know and you know, then we can assume the whole Winthrop community has some inkling, and we have to trace it back to the source. How did you hear? From someone on the faculty or from a parent?' 'Playing field' — Faith couldn't recall ever having used this particular phrase before. It must be the sight of all these low tables and small chairs, plus inspirational posters that urged children to make lemonade when given lemons and reach for the stars.

Mrs Black paused a moment before answering. Faith sensed the teacher knew that the mother in front of her hadn't been an eraser monitor in her day, but she hoped her words would convince Mrs Black to help. The pause ended and Faith was reassured. 'You're right,' Mrs Black said in a resigned but determined tone. 'And I apologize for overreacting, but George has made this a place where teachers love to teach and students love to learn. It's his achievement, his leadership. I can't bear the thought that he might have to leave — and what will precede it. I've seen it happen in other school districts, and someday I hope we'll look back at this particular era and see it for the Salem it is. I heard the rumor from another teacher and promptly asked the same question. She'd heard it from a parent, who had requested anonymity. The parent didn't want to get involved in anything. She just wanted to know whether it was true or not and was satisfied when the teacher told her that there had never been even the slightest indication of that kind of behavior — or any other accusations before. Of course we've been talking about it among ourselves, but we can't figure out why George is being targeted — or by whom.'

'For a start, we have to find out who that parent was. Anonymity doesn't count in a case like this.'

'I agree and I'll work on it.' She reflected for a moment. 'George has never had enemies. Oh, the occasional fuss over a student's placement — you'd be amazed at how passionate parents can get about the need for their child to have a specific teacher — but he's remarkably adept at smoothing ruffled feathers. And placement decisions are made with the teacher the child is leaving. There's nothing arbitrary about it. We spend an endless amount of time on it each year. We try to accommodate parents — educating a child is a collaborative effort between home and school — but often they'll fix on one teacher and refuse to accept our reasons for why another might be a better match.'

Faith nodded. Pix had mentioned the parent grapevine — that certain teachers were preferred, often for no discernible reason, but simply because the gossip mill deemed them the best. Thinking about what lay ahead seemed almost as complicated as what lay before her at present.

'How about the faculty?' she asked. 'Any problems there?'

She smiled. 'We're a fairly good-natured bunch, and most of us have taught together for a long time. George did have a problem a couple of years ago with a prima donna teacher. He was convinced that his way was the best and only way, that he was the only innovative teacher here. He had his kids plowing up the playground and planting crops to teach them about the struggles of the early settlers. He even built a sod house with money they raised by selling the vegetables. It's the type of curriculum that looks wonderful from the outside and the media loved it. He also had quite a bit of parent support. George was concerned that the students weren't learning enough of the fundamentals in math and reading that they'd need to move on to the next grade. He also saw that the kids who were benefiting the most were the ones who were highly self-motivated. They formed a kind of club with the teacher within the class, excluding other kids, particularly those with less self-confidence and ones with special needs.

The teacher resigned at the end of the year and sent a bitter letter to the newspapers denouncing the school, and George in particular.'

Faith felt a surge of hope. 'Where is this teacher now?'

'The West Coast — software development, of course. Making a fortune. Any vegetables he's involved with at present are designer vegetables.' Mrs Black definitely had a sense of humor.

Faith was crushed. She'd worked out the whole thing in her mind. Now it was apparent there was nothing the ex-teacher could gain, unless he had been smoldering with spite these last years, but success tends to blunt this kind of reaction.

'I've got to go pick up my daughter at day care. Will you call me when you find out who the parent who mentioned the rumor is? And I *will* go to the next PTA meeting. There might be something in the air.'

'Oh, there will definitely be something in the air. Don't worry.'

Mrs Black lugged her stack of books over to the counter and started to check them out. Faith pulled her coat on. She was almost out the door when the teacher called, 'I'll wait until you figure this all out before making Ben one of our Giants. It's not that it takes much time, despite what you hear, but you should be able to have some leisure to enjoy his week with him.'

Faith smiled gratefully at this vote of confidence, as well as at the postponement of the project, thinking at the same time, *And that would be when?*

* * *

Patsy Avery arrived shortly after Faith had put Amy down for her nap. Ben was staying for extended day, and Faith now blessed her son's desire for independence. The last thing she needed to think about was occupying a five-year-old. Leave it to the pros.

'Let's sit a minute and see where we are,' Patsy said, refusing coffee and accepting a tall glass of milk and some of Faith's oatmeal cookies instead. 'The police can't think you're involved; otherwise, they wouldn't have let you reopen. Have you heard from either Chief MacIsaac or the state police detective in charge of the case? What's his name again — Dunne?'

'Yes, John Dunne, as in 'Ask not for whom the bell tolls,' except with a *u*, not an *o*.'

'Very enlightening. Now, I'll tell you what I know — although it's not much — and then it's your turn.' There was a slight but unmistakable emphasis on the word *your*.

Patsy opened up a small notebook. 'It was, as you know, cyanide — in the dessert, and only her dessert. Gwendolyn Lord, age twenty-five, born in Framingham, Massachusetts. No siblings. Father worked for UPS and mother sold cosmetics at Jordan Marsh until she died of breast cancer when Gwen was eighteen. Her father died of lung cancer two years ago. Gwen was number one in her high school class and on full scholarship at Harvard. Reputation for keeping to herself and working night and day.' She looked up. 'Someone in our office was in her class and remembered her.' She returned to her notes. 'Let's see. Ms Lord interned at various museums during the summers and seemed headed for curating. She had started her graduate work when she took the job at Nick Gabriel's Undique Gallery. *Undique* is the Latin word for 'from everywhere,' by the way. The gallery specializes in twentieth-century prints — lots of Chagalls, Dalís, Mirós, and Picassos — but Gwen mounted several exhibits showcasing new young artists in a variety of other media: painting, sculpture, photography, as well as print-making. At the time of her death, she had a very nice portfolio herself — stocks, that is — and left an estate of close to a million dollars.'

'What! Where would she have gotten money like that?' Faith was stunned. 'Did she have a will?'

'Yep — and Jared is the beneficiary, after some minor bequests to a few charities like Rosie's Place and AIDS Action. As to the amount, if she'd been shrewd enough to buy and sell some of her discoveries, she could have accumulated that much in a relatively short period of time.'

'I had no idea the Boston art market was this hot.'

'Regional prejudices showing? The Big Apple is not the only place in the country with big money — or big talent. Bostonians stopped painting still lifes with teacups and fruit a long time ago. You need to broaden your horizons — have a look at Aaron Fink, Jon Imber, Jill Hoy, Jody Klein, Henry Horenstein, Walter Crump — I could go on.'

Faith pressed on. 'Anything else about her personal life? Men in the past; men in the present?'

Patsy shook her head. 'That's not the stuff I can dig up without hiring someone, which we can do if it comes to that, but that's your job. Assuming it is your job?'

Faith didn't have to answer. It was written all over her face. It was her job all right.

Small whimpering noises from upstairs indicated that Amy was awake and unhappy at having to stay in bed — even her new, big-girl bed. Faith sprinted up the stairs before the whimpers became wails. Patsy followed. Faith hadn't told her what she'd been up to and obviously Patsy didn't intend to leave until she knew what her client had been doing.

Faith dumped a container of blocks on the floor and a box of small wooden animals sent by Faith's own aunt Chat. The two women sat on the window seat while Amy played, delighted by the audience.

After hearing about Faith's visits to Millicent McKinley and Anson L. Scott, Patsy remarked, 'I sometimes think there aren't any places, just place names. Every town and city has the same people, the same situations. We had our Millicent, only she was called Miss Belinda — knew things about you before you did yourself. And Scott could be Mr McBride, who wrote long novels filled with family secrets — his and everybody else's. Wore a white suit with a gardenia in the lapel — year-round, of course — looked like Truman Capote and talked like Orson Welles.'

'I know what you mean. Every city is a village and vice versa. Human nature, or, in this case, inhuman.' She paused. 'There's something else going on, but I don't know if I have the energy to go into it.'

'Oh yes you do. You don't put pie on the table without a knife and fork. Now, what's up?' Patsy asked. From the very beginning, she'd sensed that Faith was keeping something back. Now here it was at last.

But it wasn't what she had expected — something involving Faith directly, involving Faith personally. Patsy listened gravely as Faith told her about George Hammond, and she made all the right responses. She continued to listen as Faith described her visit to Winthrop Elementary. Outside, the sun was dipping down toward the horizon. Its rays caught the silk bursting from the milkweed pods in the field beyond the next house. Amy was putting an animal on top of each block. The elephant kept falling off. Patsy murmured a comment or two and kept listening some more as Faith feverishly outlined a jam-packed schedule filled with interviewing the other three mystery writers who had been guests at Ballou the night of the murder, making a trip into town to the Undique Gallery, hanging out at the school library, attending the next PTA meeting, and calling Paula Pringle to find out more about the murder game setup. It was an ambitious plan of action, especially considering the fact that hearth, home, and work had to be squeezed in. Faith would be so busy, she would scarcely have time to think.

No time to think — exactly the whole idea.

6

The Tiller Club's annual autumn game dinner was one of its most popular events — next to the annual summer lobster feast — and thirty of its thirty-seven members would be attending with a guest on Saturday night. The Tillies, as they affectionately referred to themselves, had started as a group of sixteen sailing buddies who'd known one another 'forever' up on the North Shore. They regularly left Pride's Crossing, Hamilton, and Manchester-by-the-Sea for prep school and college, but they always managed to get home for the summer and spend every free moment on the water. At age sixteen, the sixteen of them had decided to formalize the bonds of friendship with a club and immediately agreed to limit the membership — adding only one carefully selected new Tillie as they aged a year. When Niki Constantine had heard this, she'd exploded with laughter.

'I can never get enough of these quaint WASP customs! Now, obviously the person, the man, of course, has to be the same age as the rest of them to keep the whole age/number thing the same, so when they're all ninety-nine, which without a doubt they assume they will be, they'll be beating the bushes with their canes for a suitable candidate. Someone no one would blackball. Someone named Somerset or Chandler and still breathing.'

It was Friday morning, early, and the following evening's game dinner was very much on both Faith's and Niki's minds.

'Savenor's is delivering the meat this morning. Everything except the quail and the rattlesnake will need marinating,' Niki said.

Savenor's Market on Charles Street had the best meat in Boston, maybe in the country, and was a favorite of Julia Child. They stocked a wide variety of game — everything from lion to moose. The Tillies had given Faith a free hand with the menu, their sole demand being chocolate cake for dessert. Boys will be boys. She'd done the event last year, as well, and she'd promised some new dishes to supplement the venison they considered de rigueur.

'Real men don't eat quiche, so I told the chairman the first course would be rattle-snake tartlets. As soon as Savenor's comes, put everything else away, but start parboiling the snake to get the meat off the bones so we can get these done today. There's plenty of pâté brisée for the pastry shells in the freezer.'

'Can do. Can do the whole thing, in fact. Why don't you get out of here and get on with *your* work.' Niki gave her boss a playful shove.

Faith was not averse to the idea. The dinner was under control. Besides the rattlesnake, they were serving roast venison with juniper berries; quail stuffed with wild rice, pecans, and spices in a sweet Madeira wine sauce; and a bear ragout — the stew tenderized the meat and produced succulent gravy. Roasted root vegetables in a garlicky vinaigrette, mashed Yukon Gold potatoes with plenty of cream and butter, plus a bread basket with buckwheat/walnut and sourdough rolls, Parmesan bread sticks, and rosemary focaccia filled out the menu. The Tillies were providing their own wines. They fancied themselves connoisseurs, and last year, in fact, Faith had been impressed with the selections. Nary a jug in sight. Or a keg, as in their youth, but then, these guys might well have been the ones with the Mouton Rothschild at their tailgate picnics.

'And the cakes?'

'I'll do them in the morning. Don't worry!'

The dinner itself was at one of the yacht clubs in Marblehead and the club was providing the waitstaff and equipment, but it didn't prepare meals off-season. All Faith had to do was appear with Niki and the food. It was indeed a piece of cake.

She'd been half-expecting a phone call to cancel, but either they hadn't heard or didn't care. A steady hand on the tiller. The Tillies wouldn't be driven off course by something as trivial as a little cyanide. Now, a tsunami . . .

Faith had spent the many moments before sleep the night before planning every minute of today. She'd left for work the moment her family was out the door, having arranged earlier for Amy to go to her friend Jeremy's house for the afternoon — a treat that had caused Amy to be dressed and ready before the rest of the family was awake. In honor of the occasion, she was wearing a bathing suit, tutu, and Easter bonnet. It had been a struggle to get her to change and Faith had given in on the tutu, but she'd replaced the one-piece bathing suit with a turtleneck and warm pants. Amy's relatively recent mastery of toilet skills would have been severely challenged. The bathing suit had had to go. Also the hat. It was cold out, and only by reminding her daughter that Jeremy had a terrific swing set and she'd need something warm on her head to go outside had Faith finally managed to carry the day. It was exhausting. Ben had been jumping up and down, almost at the point of tears, since his snack wasn't ready.

'Mom, the bus will be here any second!'

He was staying for extended day again and Faith had added a second bag for the afternoon, feeling enormously and inexplicably guilty. Ben loved going. He was ready for all-day school. She wasn't doing anything bad. But it must be, a little voice inside had said. It's convenient and makes your life easier, so something has to be wrong with this picture.

As she drove down Route 2 toward Cambridge and Boston, Faith thought some more about this conundrum that haunted her life, and the lives of most other women she knew. If it's for me — whether the 'it' be time, material goods, or situations — there was supposed to be a thorn, a sharp reminder of priorities. She'd suggest to Tom that the four of them do something together Sunday afternoon. Go to Family Place at the Museum of Fine Arts or to the Children's Museum. Then she remembered it was Halloween and they'd be going trick-or-treating. Ben wanted to be a robot. She'd promised to help him with his costume. The box, aluminum foil and other components, was in a corner of his room — exactly where it had been all week. Tonight, she'd get to it. Tonight. Amy was going to be a ballerina and help her mother give out the candy. No problem there.

She flicked off the radio in order to concentrate on where she was going.

Veronica Brookside, the mystery writer, lived in Jamaica Plain. Faith had spoken with her earlier in the week and set up the appointment. Veronica hadn't been as warm as Anson L. Scott had been and she had told Faith not to bother when she'd offered to bring some raspberry/peach scones. Maybe she was behind on her deadline. Maybe she was on a diet. Maybe she didn't want to get poisoned.

Jamaica Plain was an interesting place, Faith noted. She hadn't been in this part of Boston before. Veronica had been quick to claim she lived in Jamaica Plain, not Boston, and Faith had the feeling that many of its residents shared the same sense of identification. She drove down Centre Street, noticing several interesting ethnic restaurants that might bear future investigation, as well as equally diverse shops, galleries, and bookstores. She almost missed her turn.

Veronica's house was a well-maintained Victorian with plenty of gingerbread. Remnants of what must have been a glorious flower garden last summer occupied the front yard. She saw the curtain twitch, and the writer answered the door before Faith had time to ring. Clearly, minutes were going to count.

She stepped into the hall and was stunned by what she saw. Veronica herself was dressed in a long black Lycra skirt and a soft gray cowl-necked sweater. Very minimalist. Very nineties. 1990s. Everything else within sight was also nineties, but 1890s — frilly, madcap, Gay Nineties. The woman who wrote one of the most hard-boiled series going favored antimacassars and knick-knacks. Every surface was covered with one or the other. A lot of angels. A lot of cats and kittens. She motioned Faith into the parlor and indicated a seat — a velvet-covered slipper chair with several needlepoint pillows. Faith sat down.

'I don't believe in amateur sleuths.' Veronica's voice was as impressive as Faith had remembered, but not as sultry. She wasn't upping the wattage for her current audience. 'Dempsey Lansky has a PI license.'

Faith hadn't read any of Veronica's books, but she knew that this was her character — a character who was obviously very real to her creator.

'They get in the way and mess things up for the professionals. I simply don't believe in them.'

159

Or Santa or fairies or the efficacy of vitamin E. But Faith knew exactly what Veronica was talking about. She'd heard it before.

'Until the police or someone else finds out exactly how Gwendolyn Lord died, my business will be virtually nonexistent. Almost all of the jobs I had have been canceled.'

Veronica didn't look particularly sympathetic. She lit a cigarette and didn't offer one to Faith. Faith wouldn't have accepted, but she would have liked to have been asked.

'I see, but exactly what do you want to know from me?'

'I wondered if as a professional, you might have given any thought to the case. If it were your plot, where would you go with it?'

'You're talking to each of us?'

'Hoping to, yes.'

'Whom have you seen so far.'

'Only Anson Scott. I haven't been able to reach Bill Brown or Tanya O'Malley.'

'She'll be back this weekend. We're on a panel Sunday night. Bill is hard to get. When he's working, he doesn't answer the phone or even check his messages. The mystery-writing world is a small one. We tend to know what's going on with one another.'

Suddenly, she was being helpful, and Faith wondered about the abrupt change. Veronica hadn't asked what Anson's take had been, and this also was a surprise. She hadn't acknowledged his name at all.

'What would Dempsey make of it?' Veronica mused. She blew a smoke ring and got away with it. She really was very beautiful. 'Why that particular place and time? So public. Someone wanted to make a statement. It's terribly easy to kill people, of course. Perhaps the killer wanted a challenge. Cyanide. Not a pleasant death, nor an exotic method. But the setting — that would pose some difficulties. It's very important. Place can be another character, you know.'

Faith didn't know, although certainly Ballou House had character to spare. She nodded. Anson had mentioned the choice of Ballou as the murder scene also, but he hadn't put the emphasis on it that Veronica was.

'What about the mystery game? Was that merely a coincidence? Would Gwen have been killed if the fund-raiser had been, oh, I don't know, a bingo night or a plain old dance?'

'Rather too much of a coincidence, don't you think? I suspect our killer has a sense of humor. So many of them do. Twisted, but funny.'

Faith thought she'd stop at the bookstore she'd seen on the way, Jamaicaway Books &

Gifts, and buy one of Veronica's books. Dempsey Lansky might have something to say to her.

Veronica put her cigarette out in a cut-glass ashtray. The interview was fast coming to an end. She stood up.

'What about motive?' Faith asked hastily, rising from her chair. 'Gwen did have some money, but it was all left to her fiancé, and aside from my knowing him very well, he'd have to be an extraordinary actor to fake the grief he's displayed.'

There was no mistaking the patronizing smile on Veronica Brookside's face.

'But — what was your name again, Fairfield? — but, Mrs Fairfield, murder *is* an extraordinary act. And each murderer plays his or her part to perfection.'

The front door closed on her last word and Faith walked down the path and through the curlicued iron gate, feeling like a complete fool.

She bought her book and sat in the car. Her plan had been to drive straight to Newbury Street and visit the Undique Gallery, where Gwen had worked, but she realized she was not far from Brookline, where Bill Brown lived. Her interview with Veronica had left Faith wanting more, much more. If he didn't answer his phone when he was working, she reasoned, he wouldn't answer his door, either, so she wouldn't be disturbing him. Brown lived on Tappan Street. She found it easily in the atlas a realtor friend had given her. She pulled out of her parking space, and as she drove down Centre Street, she muttered, 'I don't believe in amateur sleuths' in a mocking approximation of Veronica's voice. Who did the woman think she was? Amateurs indeed! Faith had always believed it was much more likely that people would tell all to someone without a badge or license — a point she had made repeatedly to Detective Lieutenant John Dunne in the past and one she now saw the possible need for repeating in the not-so-distant future.

Bill Brown's apartment complex was an older one and had been elegant in its time. The brick building surrounded a pretty courtyard, still well kept up. An elderly woman was sitting in the sunshine, seemingly oblivious to the cold. Her coat was open at the neck and she wore no hat. She greeted Faith cheerfully. 'Isn't it a beautiful day! So restorative!'

Faith agreed, 'Yes, lovely. We need all the sunshine we can get at this time of year.'

'Oh, yes. Daylight saving ends this weekend. Always such a shock to the system.

163

I don't know why they don't simply keep the same time all year long. My husband, God rest his soul, used to try to explain it to me, but I never cared much for logic.'

She patted a spot on the seat next to her and Faith accepted the invitation, sitting down for a moment. It really wasn't all that cold, and the woman was a kindred spirit. There were many times Faith didn't care much for logic, either.

'I haven't seen you before. Are you looking at the Meyersons' apartment? Very clean people, and they put in a new kitchen two years ago.'

Faith was filled with a sudden, almost overwhelming desire to rent the Meyersons' apartment and walk into another life. Just for a little while.

She sighed. 'No, I'm not. I'm looking for Bill Brown.'

'He went out for breakfast — he doesn't cook — but he's been back for several hours. He's in three B, on that side.' She gestured to the left. 'Nice man. He came and opened a jar for me once. He's a writer, you know. Mysteries. I don't read his books. Too violent. But people say they're very good. I do crosswords. Can't get into trouble with them.'

Faith stood up. 'I ought to go and see whether he has time to talk to me.' She smiled down at the woman. 'It was very nice meeting you.'

'Very nice meeting you, too, sweetie. My name is Muriel and I'm usually here. Come again.' She was still waving when Faith went into the building.

Brown's voice crackled over the security system after a short interval. 'Yes?'

'I hope I'm not disturbing you, but my name is Faith Fairchild and I wondered if I might talk to you about last Saturday night, the event at Ballou House? I was — '

'The caterer. Come on up, Faith. Don't know what I can do for you, but I'm pretty curious to know what you think I can.' There was that voice again. Which southern state produced it? Faith wondered. Virginia? It made everything he said sound like good news.

He buzzed her in and was waiting when the elevator doors opened on the third floor.

Aside from exchanging a tuxedo for worn corduroys and a blue oxford-cloth button-down shirt with fraying cuffs — both neatly pressed — Bill Brown looked the same. Very neat, very clean. The apartment reflected his appearance. After her experience with Veronica, Faith had wondered whether Brown would be wallowing in psychedelic clutter — he appeared to be the right age for long hair in the sixties — but the room she'd stepped into from the hall was Spartan. A linen-covered couch, a pole lamp, a coffee table — bare — and one beige easy chair. There was nothing hanging on the walls. The windows were uncovered and the spines of the books in the shelves that ran from floor to ceiling on one wall provided the only color in the place.

If Bill Brown was annoyed with the interruption, he didn't show it. He was looking at her with warm humor. 'I never met the woman, so you can cross me off your list. You are trying to solve the crime, right? Otherwise, your business is toast.'

Got it in one. She *definitely* had to read his books. She recalled Spenser's Mystery Books was not far from the gallery on Newbury Street. If the day produced nothing else, at least she'd be going home with a lot of new books.

'Apparently, most of my customers have begun to have doubts about my ingredients — against all logic.' She smiled to herself, remembering her encounter in the courtyard, and added, 'But then, there are those who don't care much for logic.'

'You've met Muriel,' Bill said. 'My favorite little old lady. Complete unto herself. Doesn't even need a pet.'

Faith looked again at the furniture. It was so drab, she knew she'd be completely unable

166

to describe a single piece once she'd left the stark space. There wasn't even a rug on the hardwood floor.

'May I sit down? And to satisfy your curiosity, what I want is your take, as a mystery writer, on the whole thing. Isn't fiction just reality written down?'

'If you made that up yourself, it's not too bad. Very quotable. Yeah, let's sit. But I've got to warn you, it takes me months to work out a plot.'

'I've talked to Anson Scott and Veronica Brookside. So far, I've learned murderers like to fool the whole world, are filled with overweening pride, think they're too clever to be caught, have twisted senses of humor, are fearful cowards, and are consummate actors. Would you agree?'

With a bow tie, he'd look a little like Gary Moore, she thought as he took his time answering.

'Again not bad, and eminently quotable. Profiling is a big deal nowadays and every killer is unique, but yes, I'd agree with that list, especially the part about thinking they'll get away with it. But I'd add something — something pretty obvious and only implied by Anson and Veronica. Murderers are crazy. Insane. Not cuckoo. Not quirky. But very, very, terrifyingly nuts.'

He leaned back in the chair.

Faith was startled. It was a given, yet she hadn't thought about the killer this way. It had been a premeditated crime. The product of intelligence, not sudden rage. Not madness in that sense.

'Not everyone would agree with me, but the older I get, the more I believe it. Murder is an act of total insanity. Including crimes of passion, maybe especially crimes of passion. You leave the world of reason, even if only for a short time. The beast leaps, strikes, and you come to with your wife and her lover dead in front of you. What made sense in the universe of insanity becomes inexplicable back at home base. You've taken a life, maybe more.'

Faith nodded. She wanted him to continue.

'When I was a kid, I didn't read mysteries. I read about real cases. Like Leopold and Loeb. They wanted to know what it felt like to kill somebody. Smart boys. Very smart boys. Clarence Darrow got them life imprisonment on the basis of 'mental instability.' Legally, they were sane, according to the experts, so he had to argue that their instability was abnormal. Great lines — 'Why did they kill little Bobby Franks? They killed him as they might kill a spider or a fly, for the experience. They killed him because they were made that way.' Mental instability, hell. They were crazy.

Maybe they should have been following what was going on in Germany — a war would have done it for them. They would have had plenty of chances to experience the thrill. They were tried in twenty-four and we didn't enter the war until forty-two. Even if they had known, they couldn't have waited that long. Something else for your list. Most murderers are not into deferred gratification.' Bill Brown liked to talk. His face was animated as he described the case.

It was an interesting train of thought — all of it. Faith thought about the two young men and killing for the thrill of it. War might have been different. She gave words to her thoughts. 'War. That would have been random. And most of the time you're not face-to-face with your enemy, your victim. Maybe they had to kill someone they knew. They did know him, right?'

'Yeah, they knew him. He was a cousin of Loeb's. It's true, though. Much harder to kill someone face-to-face. After the war, when army officers talked to GIs about how they felt in combat, it was found that three out of four couldn't pull the trigger when they could see the person they were about to shoot, which is pretty amazing. And it brings us back to Ballou House. The killer was there, because I'm assuming — unlike your asshole customers, pardon me — that you didn't put cyanide in the young lady's dessert. Unless, of course, your husband was fooling around with her, which again strikes me as unlikely, not because he wears his collar backward, but because you live in a very small town and by the time one of them had kicked a shoe off, people would have been talking about it at the grocery store.'

Faith had felt a hot flash of anxiety at his first words regarding a possible motive for herself, then immediate reassurance. It would have been all over town. And no one had been giving her any of those pitying, knowing looks Aleford inhabitants perfected at an early age. Millicent had dropped her land-mine hints, but again, the look hadn't been there. If anything, Millicent had seemed sorry for Tom, but that was normal.

Brown continued. 'So the killer was there and able to watch. Kind of like a snuff movie come to life.'

Faith shuddered.

'I keep wondering, Why Gwen? And I can't imagine that her fiancé, Jared, had anything to do with it. He was the only one who stood to gain by her death, and he has enough money himself.'

'There's no such thing as enough money for some people, probably most people.'

Faith looked around the room. Whatever he was making, Bill Brown seemed to have enough for his needs, a notch above the needs of a Carthusian monk.

He followed her glance. 'I don't like to accumulate anything except books. My bedroom looks like this, too, except for a table with my computer, a chair, and the bed. I don't like extra stuff in my life. And no, I'm not married.' He laughed. 'Never was. But you should see my girlfriend's house. And her storage containers. I come back here to breathe. And work. But enough about me.'

Faith was getting tired of trying to think like Hercule Poirot. She wanted to stop in at the gallery and the time on her Mom-o-meter was running out.

She posed one more question, a catch-all. 'Anything else that occurs to you about all this?'

He half-closed his eyes. It didn't seem affected. She felt comfortable with him — more so than with the other two writers. Maybe it was knowing how he helped Muriel with her jar. It seemed he didn't want to add any more. She started to get up.

'Well,' Bill Brown said in his slow, deep voice, stretching the word out around a bend, 'you've probably thought of this yourself and I'm sure the cops have, but are you positive Gwendolyn Lord was the intended victim?'

Veronica Brookside had made Faith feel inadequate, while providing very little insight herself. In contrast, Bill Brown had pointed out a crucial piece of the puzzle lying on the floor, but instead of berating herself for the oversight, Faith felt invigorated and ready to move to the middle from the outside edges. Reaching Newbury Street, she found a parking space right in front of the Armani Emporio. The sun was shining. She hadn't felt this good in weeks.

The Undique Gallery was close enough to the Public Garden end of Newbury to be desirable, yet far enough away for a merely outrageous, not catastrophic, rent. The current show was titled 'Millennial Moods.' Faith went in, nodded to a young man sitting behind a desk, whose bright red hair seemed only slightly unnatural, and slowly walked past the drawings and prints. It really should have been called 'Millennial Nudes,' she thought, and several were quite striking. She took the price list from a pedestal next to the door. It was striking, too. The Chagalls and the Dalís were probably good investments even now, but buyers today would never make the killings earlier ones had. Of course, you had to have had the money back then to buy art, instead of, say, food. It was always the way. Think of all those wealthy Americans snapping up Impressionists for a song, lyrics that went on to reap royalties for the next and the next generation. You had to have money to make money in the normal course of things. Why was she thinking about all this? It was the street, certainly. Looking past the artwork and out through the large plate-glass window to the sidewalk beyond, she could see a parade of ladies who lunch — at the Ritz — in Chanel suits, mink coats, platinum from the rings on their fingers to the streaks in their Sassoon coifs; men in well-cut cashmere topcoats, cell phones to the ear, slim Bottega Veneta briefcases clutched in one hand. And the street youth, impossibly slender and European, even when born and bred in Ohio, they came to Boston for an education — what to order at L'Espalier, where to max out a credit card, and how to say 'I'm sorry, this isn't working for me' in six different languages. Gwen had been part of this scene. She'd protested to Faith that she didn't have the time or money to patronize the local shops, but the moment she stepped out the door, it was all around her. Faith remembered how much fun it had been living as a single woman in New York, out of college and starting her catering business. Boston was very decidedly the Little Apple, but she imagined the sensation that the world held limitless possibilities must have been the same for Gwen. Gwen had loved her work, was excited about uncovering new talent, and, being bright, beautiful, had fit right in. Fit right in until someone killed her. Faith turned from the window and went over to the desk. The young man looked up and smiled. 'Anything catch your eye?'

It was disarming. Not hard sell, not soft, and the implication was that she had an eye. In some New York galleries, she'd been made to feel that she had to sell herself as a legitimate buyer with taste before they would even let her look — let alone sell anything to her.

'Quite a few things. It's a lovely show, but I'm actually here to talk about Gwen Lord. I was there last Saturday night when she died. I was catering the event.'

He stood up and pulled another chair up to the desk.

'Omigod! You must have felt terrible! To put it mildly. I mean, it was your food! Jesus!'

I get it. I get it, Faith said to herself, then murmured aloud, 'Yes, it *was* horrible. And now, I'm sure you can understand, my business stands to be affected.'

'Stands to be? I would have thought it

already was. I know this sounds insensitive, but when you're looking for a caterer, you don't want the Grim Reaper.'

It was insensitive, but Faith had to laugh.

'I'm Faith Fairchild, by the way.'

'I'm Alexander Hoffmann. Sandy for short.'

'Did you know Gwen well?'

'Yes and no. I started working here last June and we saw each other most workdays. I liked her, liked her a lot, yet I can't say that I ever felt I really knew her. She was engaged, so there was no question of getting involved that way. I mean I'd tell her she looked sensational — she usually did — and she'd flirt a little, but she was crazy about Jared.'

'How about friends? Did they ever come by the gallery?'

'She'd have lunch with someone she'd known in college every once in a while, female. I think they'd been roommates. But any extra time she had — and it wasn't much — she'd spend with her honey. I can't imagine what the guy is going through. I mean, if she'd been hit by a car that would have been awful, but to have your girlfriend murdered!'

'So, there were no other men in her life as far as you know.'

He shook his head. 'None. She wasn't having any last flings, and there were no exs creeping around.'

So much for that theory, Faith thought.

'How did she get along with Nick? Her boss?'

'Oh, Nick's great.' Sandy's voice became slightly guarded. Faith realized Nick Gabriel might be in the back, where he probably had his office.

'Is he around? I'd like to talk to him, too.'

'No, he's not, but he's due back any minute, if you can wait.' So that explained the tone in his voice. Nick could walk through the door at any moment.

She looked at her watch. She didn't have any time. She had to pick Ben up and then tear Amy away from Jeremy, literally. Both kids tended to howl, as if they would never see each other again. Jeremy's mother said he wasn't good at transitions, whatever that meant. Faith thought it had more to do with being a relatively powerless two-year-old in a grown-up world. You stood your ground wherever you found it.

'I do have to leave soon.' She looked at Sandy. Her earlier elation was ebbing. 'Can you think of anything at all that might help identify Gwen's killer? Any visitors to the gallery whom she reacted to in an odd way? Anything?'

His face flushed and his eyes shifted from her face. 'I wouldn't want to make too big a deal out of it, but — '

'Faith. Lovely to see you. What brings you all the way into town? I thought you Alefordians didn't know how to get to Boston.' Nick Gabriel was coming through the front door.

Faith forced a laugh. 'It's not quite that bad. I was in town and thought I'd drop by. I've been thinking of getting Tom a print or a drawing for Christmas and it's not too early to be looking.' It hadn't occurred to her, but as she said it, she decided it was true. They must have something in her price range.

'No, indeed, it will be here before we know it. You're wise not to put your shopping off. This way, you'll get exactly what you want — and isn't that why you came?' Nick asked pointedly. 'I hope Sandy here has been taking care of you.'

'Absolutely,' she replied, slightly uncomfortable at his tone. What was he suggesting? 'Unfortunately, I have to leave now, but I'll be back.'

'Great. See you tomorrow.' He gave Faith an air kiss — she hadn't realized they were so close — and went through a door at the rear of the gallery. Sandy walked her to the door.

'What were you going to say?' she asked.

'I can't talk now.' He gestured with his

head toward the office. 'I'll see you tomorrow, too.'

It wasn't until Faith was putting her key in the door of her car that she made the connection. Of course they would see one another tomorrow. It was Gwen Lord's memorial service. She'd completely forgotten about it. And there hadn't been a single note of sadness in Nick Gabriel's voice.

★ ★ ★

The phone was ringing as she stumbled into the house carrying a bag of groceries, with Amy clutching at the hem of her skirt. She grabbed it just before the machine picked up.

'Hello?'

'Hello, Mrs Fairchild. It's Julie Black. Is this a bad time?'

'No, not at all,' Faith lied. Tossing a raisin bagel to each child, she pointed toward the small den, where the TV was. Ben practically sprinted out the door, dragging Amy. His TV time was very limited and no doubt he hoped the phone call would be a long one.

'I won't keep you, but I thought you'd like to know as soon as possible. I found out the source of the rumor about George Hammond. The mother heard it from Janice Mulholland. I told George, and he was as surprised as I am. Mrs Mulholland is a little high-strung and things have been difficult for her since the divorce, but I can't imagine why she'd attack George this way, unless she, too, heard it from someone else. Please don't say anything to anyone else except your husband. We're trying to think of the best way to handle the situation. We certainly don't want it to blow up in our faces, and that could happen if she thinks we're accusing her unjustly.'

'I understand and won't say a word. Please do let me know what you're doing, though.'

'Of course.'

'Let's just hope that whatever you decide will put an end to the whole matter.'

Julie Black gave such a heavy sigh over the phone that Faith could almost feel the coolness on her ear. 'I wish I felt more optimistic. Several more teachers and two parents have mentioned it to me since we spoke. We have to act quickly. I told George that, but I can't do anything until he does.'

'Please tell him to get in touch with us. I'm sure Tom has time to talk to him about what's best. We'll be home all evening.'

'I will. Oh, if you're still interested in the PTA, the meeting's Tuesday night. Ben should have a notice in his backpack.'

'I'll be there,' Faith promised. Janice

Mulholland was the secretary of the PTA. She'd be there, too.

'Ben handled his disappointment today nicely. Don't feel bad. Mothers forget all the time. That's why I keep extras.'

Faith thanked her profusely for she knew not what, hung up, and went into the den. She was so tired, she felt as if she were swimming in Jell-O.

'Ben, sweetheart. Was there something special going on in school today? Something you were supposed to bring things in for?'

He turned away from the screen.

'Only my Halloween costume,' he said, and turned his attention back to Big Bird. Big Bird never let anybody down.

'Oh, Ben! I am so sorry.' The adult note of bitterness in his voice was deeply upsetting. She switched off the TV. Amy said, 'Bye, Big Bird.' Faith gathered both kids on her lap.

'Things have been too busy around here. But that is no excuse. You brought the note home last week and we should have made the costume right away. We'll make it now and you'll be all set for Sunday.'

'And can we carve our pumpkins?'

Advantage, Ben. 'Yes, we can carve the pumpkins,' Faith said. 'The only thing I have to do is put the groceries away, and with my good helpers, that will be done in a minute.'

One of Faith's good helpers managed to drop a carton of eggs, much to her brother's disgust, but only one broke. The costume was so much easier to make than Faith had envisioned that she felt even more guilty, if that was possible. Ben had told her Mrs Black had given him a pirate costume, complete with eye patch, to wear in the school's Halloween parade. 'So this year, I have two costumes. I bet no other kid in Aleford, maybe the world, has two costumes. Right, Mom?'

'Right, Ben.'

They had dug all the seeds from the pumpkins, putting them aside to toast, when the phone rang again.

It was Tom.

'Honey, I'm with Jared. We're working on the service and it's going to take awhile.'

'Why don't you bring him over here for some supper when you're through?'

'I think we'll go over to the Willow Tree for chili and a beer. Jared suggested it when he came in.'

'I have chili in the freezer and plenty of beer in the fridge . . . '

'Another time, Faith. I won't be late.'

'Give him my love.'

'I will.'

And love to you, too, Faith thought,

181

putting the phone down.

'Okay, guys, let's carve some jack-o'-lanterns.'

Soon Amy was covered in seeds and chanting 'Jack-elanman' over and over to herself softly. Ben was drawing a huge toothy grin. Faith carved Amy's, adding stars and crescent moons on the sides and back of the smiling face. Then she helped Ben with his. They took them out to the front walk and lighted the candles inside, then stepped back to admire their work.

'These are the best ever!' Ben exclaimed. 'Look at the pattern your stars are making!'

They did look beautiful. Faith usually thought of this squash as a container or ingredient. Tonight, she went back to her own childhood and remembered the mingled fear and excitement Halloween always brought. She and her sister, Hope, had trick-or-treated at a few apartments in their building, then, accompanied by their father, they had first gone to their grandparents', then to Aunt Chat's, enjoying the novelty of traveling through the city in disguise. Sunday, Tom would take Ben to some houses in the neighborhood.

'Come on, it's getting very late and we still have to eat. Plus, you have got to take baths. You could be pumpkins yourselves, there's so much on you!'

They raced back into the warm house, giggling. She loved her children so much, it hurt.

Faith fed the kids toasted cheese sandwiches and split pea soup, then left Ben to put the finishing touches on his costume while she bathed Amy. 'I may need some help on this,' Ben said. 'Why can't you stay? Where's Dad?' His lower lip trembled.

'He's still working, and you know I can't leave Amy in the tub alone.'

'Don't let her play with my boats.' He picked up a Magic Marker to add to the dials he'd drawn.

Faith kissed him. 'I won't let her touch any of your things. I promise.'

Soon, Amy was asleep and Faith was reading *Harry Potter* to a clean and drowsy Ben. 'I'd be pretty good at Quidditch, don't you think, Mom?'

'I think you'd be great at it. Now go to sleep. Danny is going to watch you and Amy tomorrow morning. If it's a nice day, you can all go to the playground.'

'That'll be good,' Ben said, his eyes closed. 'But I don't want Amy using my shovel in the sandbox. She broke my last one. Tell Danny. Okay, Mom?'

'I'll tell Danny. I promise,' Faith said.

Promises, promises. To love, honor, and

respect. Until death do us part. Faith longed for Tom to come home. She moved throughout the house, tidying, picking up a book to read, setting it down. Ben's backpack lay on the kitchen floor, where he had dropped it after school. She opened it and took out a picture that had been carefully rolled up. It proved to be Ben's rendition of a Muggle, accompanied by a caption he'd dictated to his teacher. There was the notice about the PTA meeting and a booklet with order forms for the gift wrap. There were five forms. She calculated quickly. Two sets of grandparents, Aunt Chat, themselves, and maybe the Millers, although Pix probably had enough paper to stock Santa's workshop. Faith put everything on the counter.

Even though she hadn't eaten with the kids, she still wasn't hungry. She poured herself a glass of wine and lighted the fire, then sat in the wing chair, watching the way the flames made cities of conflagration out of the embers. Promises. All those promises and they'd said, 'I do.' Yet for the moment, death had parted them. Not their deaths, but a death. She wanted to talk to Tom. She had to talk to Tom — to Tom, her husband.

He came home at nine o'clock, looking exhausted. She went and put her arms around him. He held her close.

'Come sit by the fire. Unless you'd rather go to bed,' she whispered in his ear. He pulled away. 'I'm too tired to sleep. Let's sit for a little while.'

She hadn't been thinking about sleep.

'Kids okay?' he asked.

'Fine. Typical scene getting Amy to leave Jeremy's house, but fortunately, he's just as bad. Ben missed you. I read to him, but he said it wasn't the same. He's so passionate about everything. Not letting Amy touch any of his things. Having you catch up so you know what happened to Harry. I should have read something else.' She didn't mention the forgotten costume.

'That might have been a good idea. It's kind of our thing.'

His words stung her. She was sure he didn't mean them the way they sounded. It had never occurred to her that there would be things each child shared with them separately, but of course there would.

'Are you hungry? Thirsty?'

They were sitting on the couch, her head leaning against his shoulder. He smelled like the Willow Tree — grease, beer, and cigarette smoke.

'No thanks.'

They sat in silence for a while. Now that it

was autumn and they had fires, she should move the couch back. It was silly to sit away from it, staring out the window at the darkness. But then she'd have to put up with all the smug 'I told you so' looks as the parishioners marched through. She'd leave it where it was.

'Tom, we need to talk.'

That wasn't what she had meant to say. Men were genetically disposed to abhor those four particular words, and women were similarly programmed to say them.

'I mean, it's just that I've been feeling so distant from you lately. We never have any time together.' Faith flailed about for words. 'Last Saturday night was terrible. And then all this business with George Hammond. Our life is filled with these things, and I need you to be with me.'

'I can't.'

There it was. And she sat listening desperately for more.

'There is a lot going on in both our lives right now. But it can't be helped, Faith. I love you and I'm doing the best I can. You'll have to accept that.'

'But, Tom — '

'Look, what we need more than anything, or what I need, is sleep. I've got the service tomorrow and a full day after that. You've got that dinner tomorrow night. I don't want to talk anymore. I simply want to go to bed. Okay?'

'Okay,' she said. But it wasn't. It wasn't okay at all.

7

It was done so neatly. The head had been severed with a single sharp stroke and placed carefully next to the body. There was very little blood and what there was had hardened into glistening clots. Faith ignored the paper she'd come outside for, stumbled on the doorstep as she ran back into the house, and threw up in the downstairs toilet. Then she went to find Tom. The yard was filled with bushy-tailed gray squirrels, chattering in the trees, stealing all the bird seed from the feeders. This morning, there was one squirrel less.

'It's Halloween weekend, Faith, and celebrants, particularly adolescent boys, have varying interpretations of what constitutes a 'trick.' The definition of *treat* is universal, and I hope you got plenty of candy. We ran out last year, remember?' Tom wasn't taking the appearance of a mutilated corpse on the front steps seriously at all. 'Let Charley know, by all means, but I'm sure he'll agree with me.' He gave her a kiss on the cheek. 'Don't worry, I'll clean it up.' It had never occurred to Faith that she would have to dispose of the remains. Women are extremely good at dealing with large amounts of blood, levelheaded, applying pressure, bandages as needed — and extremely bad at handling small amounts, mice in traps, paper cuts.

After Tom's words, it took Faith an hour to decide to call the police. She felt foolish, but surprisingly the police chief wasn't as quick as her husband to chalk up the headless squirrel to a prank.

'Anything else? A note?' he asked.

'Perhaps there wasn't time and he'd only a few nuts to leave. No, no note.' She'd been trying to sound light-hearted throughout the conversation, as if to suggest that discovering dismembered animals with her newspaper were mildly annoying everyday occurrences.

'Funny, very funny, but I'm sure you weren't laughing when you found it.'

'No, I wasn't.' Faith sobered up immediately, grateful for the implied sympathy and glad to be taken seriously. 'Do you think this has anything to do with Gwen Lord's death — or the business with George Hammond?' George had met with Charley and Charley had called Tom afterward. 'The whole town seems to be going crazy.'

'Possibly, and the town usually is going crazy about something or other most of the time, but I can't really see how this relates

— I'm just going to keep it in the back of my mind. Remember, there are smashed pumpkins and trees decked in toilet paper all over. Lord knows what the next two nights will bring. I hate Halloween. Given that there was nothing besides the squirrel, I'd say it's kids — somewhat sick kids.'

'What do you think a note would have said?' Faith had been puzzled by Charley's question.

'Something like 'Mind your own business' — you *are* sticking your nose into all this, I've heard. Been out to Scott's place and talking to people.'

Faith was impressed once more by the efficacy of the Aleford grapevine.

'No chance a dog did it — killed the squirrel, that is?' Charley asked.

Faith thought of the neat decapitation. Maybe Lassie with a carving knife and fork could have managed it, but not your average canine.

'No, I'm sure it was something on two legs.'

'Then mind your own business.' Charley hung up almost immediately after the warning. Faith went about the morning's chores, feeling distinctly out of sorts.

Gwen Lord's service was scheduled for one o'clock and Danny Miller came to baby-sit at

12.30. Tom was already at the church with Jared. Pix was at the door with her son.

'Let's walk over together. I hope the press and other ghoulish onlookers won't try to crash.'

'Tom has Rhoda Dawson posted with the ushers, and if she can't tell who belongs and who doesn't, nobody can.' Ms Dawson was the formidable parish administrator, Tom's assistant, who transformed herself into 'Madame Rhoda, Psychic Reader' on her days off.

Pix laughed. 'Let's go.' She kissed her son. 'It's not public, just the parsonage, so don't 'Oh Mom' me. The service should be over in an hour, and if Faith still needs to be there, I'll change places with you so that you can get to your game.' Danny was on the Middle School soccer team.

Danny squirmed away from her kiss with the deftness of practice and told Ben and Amy to get their jackets and then they'd go to the playground. Their squeals of delight reminded Faith that she hadn't had time to take them herself in quite a while. *It was my suggestion, though,* she thought, consoling herself.

As they walked to the church, Faith told Pix, 'The service is mostly music, with some brief readings. Jared is playing part of one of his new compositions as the eulogy. He said it was inspired by his love for Gwen and it's what she would have wanted.'

Pix looped her arm through Faith's. 'It's too sad and horrible, but you didn't do anything. Okay?'

'Okay,' Faith said shakily. 'Okay.'

The church was packed, but as far as Faith could tell, everyone looked as if they belonged. Many were young — friends of Jared's and Gwen's, dressed in somber, grown-up clothes, with somber, grown-up expressions on their faces. The weather had turned cold and rain was predicted. Coats were kept on, buttoned up.

Tears began to well up in Faith's eyes from the moment musician friends of Jared's from Boston joined him in a heartbreaking rendition of Ravel's 'Pavane for a Dead Princess.' Tears coursed down her cheeks throughout Tom's readings, and by the time Jared played his own composition, 'Love Never Lost,' she was choking back sobs.

The conventional arrangements of funeral flowers were missing. No gladioli or white lilies. Nothing on the top of the closed coffin. Instead, there was a large burnished copper container in front of the pulpit, filled with hydrangea — white tinged with pink and blue, huge, lush blossoms. More of the flowers had been placed inside the entrance to the church.

Jared had selected only two readings. Parts of Keats's *Endymion*, including 'A thing of beauty is a joy forever,' which was no surprise and certainly apt. The psalm was also appropriate, but for different reasons. Psalm 55 — not a lyrical psalm, nor a psalm of consolation — a psalm of raw grief, of revenge and the recognition of betrayal. Faith could hardly bear to listen to the pain in Tom's voice,

> 'Fearfulness and trembling are come upon
>   me,
> and horror hath overwhelmed me.
> And I said, 'Oh that I had wings like a
>   dove!
> I would fly away, and be at rest.''

Jared had chosen an indictment, a gauntlet thrown down.

> 'The words of his mouth were smoother
>   than butter,
> but war was in his heart . . . '

Murder had been in someone's heart. Did Jared suspect someone? Someone close to Gwen?

By the end of the reading, Tom was almost

shouting from the pulpit, like an avenging prophet of old.

'But thou, O God, shalt bring them down into the pit of destruction;
bloody and deceitful men
shall not live out half their days.
But I will trust in thee.'

The last line was uttered so bitterly that a number of heads jerked up in surprise. Pix reached for Faith's hand and gave it a hard squeeze. They stood to sing 'I Cannot Think of Them As Dead,' and Faith was shivering under her thick coat. But not from the cold. Tom had been so passionate. So ... so involved. His face was flushed.

It wasn't an ordinary funeral.

There was a brief, almost hurried prayer. Then Jared came down from the choir loft and placed one perfect white rose on the coffin. It was over.

'You have to go to the reception,' Pix said.

'I know.' It wasn't what Faith wanted to do at all. She wanted to go home, crawl under the covers, and try to sort out all the conflicting emotions she was feeling. Sorrow and fear predominated. It was unutterably sad. And horrible. And frightening. And threatening. Tom and Jared had left the sanctuary immediately. Tom and Jared, the chief mourners?

'I'll take care of the kids. Go.' Pix gave her a gentle shove in the direction of the Parish Hall, where, Faith knew, a caterer — obviously not Have Faith, under the circumstances — had laid the New England equivalent of funeral baked meats: small white-bread sandwiches with anchovy paste, a millimeter of chicken or egg salad, and perhaps cucumber; trays of orange cheddar cheese cubes, Triscuits, and grapes; some butter cookies. And coffee, lots of coffee. She stopped at the ladies' room to postpone the inevitable.

Even under the best conditions — the deceased age ninety-something, hale and hearty to a mercifully swift end — Faith hated funerals. And she'd had to attend an enormous number of them over the years. It went with the territory. Making her peace with death was something she planned to do in old age, and until then, she preferred not to think about it. Of course she knew she was going to die. It would be unnatural not to, and when she did, she wanted Ben, Amy, their spouses, her grandchildren, whoever was around, to display noisy, no-holding-back, proper grief. But the notion of this ultimate change from all she had been accustomed to was one she kept securely locked up, along with other dismal inevitables like cellulite and gray hair.

She sighed and made ready to leave the security of the toilet cubicle, which had been growing more and more attractive. She was about to open the door when she heard two women come in. They were talking. She recognized one as a cashier at the market; the other was someone Faith couldn't identify.

'What a service! I don't think I could have stood much more.'

'I know. Poor Jared. What will he do? His music will be a comfort to him — and his friends, but his life will never be the same. I suppose he'll find someone else. But what a problem she'll face. How could you ever measure up to someone's fiancée who was murdered just before the wedding?'

'Maybe he won't marry. Just keep her memory forever fresh. It's like a movie.'

'I've never heard Reverend Fairchild read the Bible that way before. I expected to see a flaming sword appear in his hand.'

The other woman laughed.

'It really isn't funny, but I just got this picture in my head. You're right, though. He was pretty worked up and certainly seemed to be taking it personally.'

'Well, from what I've heard that's not so surprising.'

'You don't mean to say — '

One of them turned the water taps on and the rest of the sentence was drowned out. Faith had been standing still, far back in the stall. Unless one of them tried the handle, they wouldn't know there was anyone else in the bathroom.

The water stopped.

' . . . hadn't realized it was *that* well.'

'So they say. Let me finish putting my face on. I have to go back to work.'

'I'll walk with you.'

The door swung shut and they were gone. Faith slumped against the wall. So, the whole town did know.

Know what?

She entered the Parish Hall and from force of habit searched the crowd for Tom's familiar face. He was talking to Ursula Rowe, Pix's mother. Away from the sanctuary, the mourners had become more cheerful. The bulk were parishioners who had attended the service because of Jared, their music director. They hadn't known Gwen. Paula Pringle was at the center of a group of women, most of whom Faith recognized as having worked on the Ballou House event. Faith recalled that she wanted to ask Paula how she'd obtained the script for the game, but now was not the time.

John Dunne had told Faith once that a surprising number of murderers showed up at their victims' funerals. They'd talked about the various reasons one might have for returning not to the scene of the crime but to the aftermath. A subconscious wish to be caught? Thumbing one's nose at the inept police? Remorse? It was possible, therefore, that the murderer had been in church and was here now. The room smelled of coffee and wet wool — the Parish Hall's habitual winter aroma. It also smelled of fear. Or perhaps that's my imagination, Faith told herself. Yet, once planted, the notion bloomed and she was sure she could detect the undercurrent beneath the clinking of the cups and saucers, the banal pleasantries and chitchat. A week before, a young woman had been killed at the First Parish 250th Anniversary Campaign Kickoff. It was inexplicable — and frightening.

'So, what do you think?' a familiar voice asked. Faith turned in relief and gave Patsy a hug. She wasn't sure exactly why she was so glad to see her friend — her lawyer — but she was.

'I didn't know you were coming to the service.'

'We came to the concert last spring and Jared is a friend of a friend, so we wanted to come. Besides, I thought I'd better keep up with things.'

Faith was tempted to blurt out what she'd heard in the ladies' room, so she could get Patsy's reassurances — and Patsy would reassure her, wouldn't she?

Patsy looked at her hard. 'One of these days, you'll have to come clean and tell me what's bothering you, besides what's bothering you, just so I know. Not that I'm pressuring you, but it is written all over your face.' She'd slowed down and emphasized each of the last words.

'Maybe tomorrow,' Faith said, trying to turn the corners of her mouth up. 'Tomorrow's another day. Not now. I'm doing a dinner up on the North Shore.'

'Anytime, Miss Scarlett. Now I have to get Will home before he gets so hungry that he succumbs to one of these white folks' sandwiches. I shudder to think what my mother would say about a spread like this. Talk about respect for the dead — you should have seen the food at my father's funeral. The entire city of New Orleans could have eaten for a week, and eaten like kings.'

Faith laughed and started to walk across the room with Patsy to find Tom, but halfway there, the crowd separated them. Faith was about to push through politely, when the young man with the red hair who worked at the Undique Gallery grabbed her by the arm.

'I've been looking for you. I need to talk to you, but not here.'

Faith thought quickly. 'It's Saturday, so there won't be anyone in the child-care center downstairs. We can go there.'

'Tell me where it is and I'll meet you. I'd rather we not be seen leaving together.'

Faith gave him instructions. She didn't think anyone had ever said those particular words to her, even in her footloose single days, but in this instance, the connotation was not the usual. It wasn't that he didn't want them to be seen *leaving* together. It was that he didn't want someone to know he was telling her something. Telling her what? She drank a cup of lukewarm coffee, then went downstairs.

Sandy Hoffmann was sitting in the teacher's rocking chair, moving slowly back and forth and looking pensively out the window. He jumped to his feet as Faith entered the room.

'I've never been to the funeral of someone I knew. I mean, I did go to my grandparents', but they were — '

'Old,' Faith said, finishing for him.

He nodded. His pale, drawn face seemed even paler because of his shock of red hair. His freckles looked like jimmies on a vanilla ice-cream cone. 'I kept thinking of how she looked the last time I saw her; then I'd see the coffin in front of me and think about what was in there.'

He took a deep breath. 'Anyway, ever since yesterday when we talked at the gallery, I've been trying to decide what to do. I mean, it could be nothing — or it could be everything.'

Faith waited for him to get to the point. She was nervous. The throng upstairs would start to thin out soon and their absences might be noted — if someone was keeping watch, and obviously Sandy thought someone was.

'Why don't you just tell me about it and we can go on from there.'

He nodded and went back to the rocker. Faith took one of the children's chairs and sat in front of him. Clearly, it was storytime.

'Okay. Right after I was hired, I returned to the gallery unexpectedly. It was a Monday, when we're closed, but we almost always have work to do for part of the day, so we're in and out. That Monday, I was supposed to deliver a painting to one of our clients, take her some flowers, chat her up. She buys a lot from us and likes the personal attention. When I called her that morning to confirm the time, she told me it would have to be another day, so, eager beaver that I was, and wanting to make a good impression, I went in to work.

'The door was locked, of course, but I had a key and went to my desk to do some paperwork for a show that was coming up. The door to Nick's office in the back was open, and as soon as I walked in, I heard the two of them screaming at each other. I couldn't believe it. Both Gwen and Nick are like the ultimate cool types. Nick kept saying over and over, 'You fucking bitch! Nobody does this to me!' and she said, 'You did it to yourself, asshole!' Then he said, 'I made you! If I hadn't hired you, because of your boyfriend, you'd be checking catalog copy for some two-bit museum!' Then he started again with the bitch stuff. She kept quiet for a while. I was afraid if I tried to leave, they might hear me, but I was getting even more afraid that if I stayed, one or both might come out. He stopped raving and she said, 'It was a game and you lost. You know what I want. It's all up to you.' He told her to 'get the fuck out' and I ducked behind the desk — a lot of good that would have done — and she said, 'Fine, if that's what you want, I'm only too happy to leave.' Then he got mad again and said, 'No way,' and slammed the door — at least I figure he must have been the one — and I got the hell out of there. The next day when I went in to work, you would never have known there had been a cross word between them. But I remembered what they'd said to each other. I guess because it was so out of character. So not like Gwen. So not like Nick.'

Nick Gabriel. He'd been at Ballou House. He'd been right there at the table. Jared's money from his grandfather's trust would go to second cousin Nick, unless Jared married and had kids. Faith realized she should have thought of Nick before. But she hadn't thought this murder was about money. Was it?

'Has the gallery been having financial problems? The rent must be pretty high.'

'*Au contraire*. This has been a fantastic year. People are buying art as an investment — and occasionally because they like it,' he added wryly. 'Undique is very much in the black. Nick not only has a great eye, he's a good businessman, and that's a rare combination. I've worked in two other galleries. One went under because of poor management. The other, bad taste.'

'Was this the only time you ever heard them quarrel?' Faith asked.

Sandy shook his head. 'That's my problem. If it was just what I overheard last spring, I wouldn't give it a second thought. A lost sale, a client pissed off, something like that. But, they had another knock-down-drag-out fight the afternoon before Gwen was killed. I got back early from lunch, unlocked the front door, and went to Nick's office because I heard voices. I thought I should let him and whoever else was there know I was opening up. 'You can't get blood from a stone,' Nick was saying. They were both really ripping. You could tell. But they shut up as soon as they saw me.'

''Blood from a stone' — again, it may have been about a client. Trying to get somebody to settle an account,' Faith offered the possibility. She wanted to hear Sandy knock it down.

'I don't think so. This was different. Personal. They were glaring at each other and Gwen said she had an appointment and left right away.'

'Why was the gallery closed? I'd think that a Friday lunch hour would be a time when people might drop in.'

'Normally, we would have been open, but when I went to lunch, Gwen said she might close. She had to be someplace and she said if Nick didn't come in on time, she'd lock up. It would just be for a little while. I offered to come back early, but she told me it didn't matter. That most of the lunch-hour crowd were 'Thinkaboutits,' meaning they say they'll think about it and come back, which they never do.'

'So you were surprised that they were there.'

'Yeah. I guess I was. Not Nick, but Gwen.'

'How did they act when she came back?'

'I never saw her again.'

The words stood in bleak contrast to the bright primary colors surrounding them. Then Sandy said, 'I have to go. I came with some other people who knew Gwen through the gallery and they're probably ready to go. It was just a fight about a show or something else minor, right? I don't have to tell the police, do I?' His eyes were begging her to tell him he was right, even though they both knew he was wrong.

Faith wanted some time to think about what this all meant — to think about Nick Gabriel and what Gwen might have had on him. That much was clear. It explained why she'd been able to amass such a substantial nest egg. It wasn't merely a question of wise art investments and thrift. It was, Faith had a strong feeling, blackmail. But over what?

Sandy left first, and after five minutes, Faith followed.

Upstairs in the Parish Hall, the mourners were indeed dispersing and the tables looked suitably bereft. Only a few forlorn sandwiches remained and the cookies had disappeared. There were, however, several virtually un-touched sizable mounds of orange cheese cubes. She looked around. Tom and Jared

— and Nick — were gone. She knew where Tom and Jared were. Gwen was being buried beside her parents in Framingham and the graveside service was limited to Jared and the Reverend Thomas Fairchild. Perhaps Jared had asked his cousin to accompany them at the last minute.

There were still people by the coffee urn, though, and Faith saw Janice Mulholland. All thoughts of Gwen and what Sandy had revealed were suddenly edged out of the way by Janice's appearance. Here was a situation she could do something about, and Faith felt a surge of adrenaline. Janice was going to have to go public and clear things up about George Hammond. The woman had probably been miffed about her little darling's role in the school play, a tree, instead of the fairy princess or whatever. Julie Black had said not to do anything until George gave the word, but that didn't mean Faith couldn't employ some very strong innuendoes. As she got closer to Janice, she noticed that Mrs Mulholland seemed to have lost ten pounds over the course of the week and gained at least twenty facial wrinkles. She was frowning over her coffee now. Janice wasn't a small woman, yet what had been lean now appeared gaunt and she seemed to have shrunk. She wasn't bad-looking — in an aging cheerleader sort of way — but the streaks in her hair had been gold a week ago. They were a dull bronze now. It gave Faith pause. What was eating Janice? Witnessing Gwen Lord's death, or Janice's own personal smear campaign? Or a combination of both?

'Hello, Janice. How are you?' Faith asked. It was the best opening she could come up with at short notice.

'Fine, and you?'

'Fine, thanks.' Now what? She couldn't ask the question straight out. She'd have to approach the subject sideways.

'I've started volunteering in the school library and I plan to be at the PTA meeting on Tuesday night. Parents really need to get involved with their children's schools, so they can keep an eye on things, don't you think?' This should do the trick.

And it did. 'I couldn't agree with you more. I'm sorry to say this, but even with a school system as well respected as Aleford's, you have to monitor what's happening with your child every minute. They just don't seem to get it that nobody knows better than a parent what's best for an individual student.' Color rushed into Janice's face like a riptide and she was off, swept away by the current of her convictions. 'You'd better get used to the fact right away that a parent's relationship with a school is often adversarial. I strongly advise you to take the opportunity to visit both first-grade classes and even the second-grade ones, if you have time during visiting day next month.'

Faith was bewildered. 'But I thought this was the time when parents were supposed to visit the classes their kids are in.'

Janice gave a sigh of pity. Clearly, this was one mom who had a lot to learn. 'No one spends more than a few minutes in a son's or daughter's class. It's shopping time. How else are you going to know which teacher to pick? The day is called Class Visitation Day, and this means that any parent can go to any class.'

Her voice carried the ring of truth, and Faith knew that when she checked with Pix, she'd find that parents did indeed use the time to scope out next year's prospects — and even further down the line. Janice would probably spend the afternoon at the Middle School. At the moment, though, Janice was right where Faith wanted her.

'Surely we can trust the teachers, and particularly the principal, to do class placement.'

Janice's cup hit the saucer violently and she snorted. 'Trust! I wouldn't trust George Hammond as far as I could throw him!'

'Goodness.' Faith opened her eyes wide. 'Don't tell me the rumors I've been hearing are true!'

'True and then some, from what *I* hear. It makes me sick to think that a — well, let's not mince words here — a pedophile has gotten away with being the principal of our elementary school all these years.'

Faith thought she might lose it. How could this woman in her demure deep purple Maggy London Jersey dress stand there accusing George of unspeakable acts for which she had no proof? Could she actually believe it? Faith had thought all along that the person who made the calls had an ax to grind. And since apparently Janice was the one who had started the rumor in the first place, she must have been the caller. But now she was talking as if she'd gotten her information from someone else.

'Janice, this is a very serious accusation. I dismissed what I heard until now. Where did you get your information? Was a specific incident mentioned?'

'I can't tell you any more. Not here. It's very upsetting, but believe me, it's true.' Her eyes were the eyes of a fanatic. Faith took a step backward. She'd been feeling sorry for Janice. An abandoned wife with a difficult child. Now she began to think that Missy and her father might be the ones deserving sympathy.

'So hard to believe that only a week ago that young woman was alive,' Janice said, firmly changing the subject.

Faith nodded. But to her, the night of the campaign kickoff at Ballou House seemed several years ago.

'Did you know Gwen?' Faith asked. It wasn't an entirely idle question.

'No, I'd never spoken to her before last Saturday.' Janice paused, then spoke rapidly. 'I don't want to think about what happened. It's all a blank. I can scarcely remember anything about the evening. The police kept asking me questions, but I couldn't remember a thing, except Mr Scott, the mystery writer. He was so kind. I don't know what I would have done if he hadn't been there to talk to. He made sure I got home safely. He knew how upset I was, so he followed my car. But that's all I remember.'

And all you want to remember, Faith said to herself. Amnesia for Janice. She wasn't the type, yet the shock — or something else — had wiped the slate clean.

'I'd seen Gwen Lord in church once.' Janice's voice switched rpms and almost sounded normal. 'And she was at the concert last spring.'

'It will be so hard for Jared to do this year's. I suppose Missy is already rehearsing.' Missy Mulholland was in the youth choir, and Jared started working with them in the early fall to get ready for the annual concert, assigning music and generally getting the basic program down.

'Missy is the star of the choir, as you may recall from their performances — she has perfect pitch, a gift she was born with — although apparently Jared has been persuaded otherwise. I don't want to name names, but there are some parents in the church who have more influence than others, and Missy does not have a solo. Yes, she's rehearsing — Missy is nothing if not a team player. However, I don't think she's getting much enjoyment from it. I know *I'm* not.'

The woman gave new meaning to the word *paranoia*. Everyone was out to get her kid — and, by extension, herself. It was truly scary.

Faith glanced at her watch and panicked when she saw the time. She should have left for Marblehead and the Tiller Club dinner by now. Tom wouldn't be back from Framingham yet, but the sitter she'd hired, since Danny had a game, must be at the house by now. If not, she'd have to impose on Pix yet again.

'I'm sorry I have to leave. I didn't know how late it was. I'm catering a dinner on the North Shore tonight.'

'Did you say you were catering it or attending it?' Janice had heard what Faith had said, but obviously she couldn't believe her ears.

'I'm *catering* it,' Faith said firmly, aware that she was clenching her fist. She planned to clock the woman — parishioner, PTA honcho or no — if she impugned one more thing.

'Well, I guess you'd better run, then. See you Tuesday night — and remember, be a squeaky wheel. It's the only way to get what's best for your child.'

When she stepped outside, Faith took a deep breath. The fresh air felt wonderful and she stood in the church driveway for a moment, letting the oxygen clear her head. Then she dashed across to the parsonage and into the kitchen. Pix was still there, and Faith's heart started to sink.

'Don't worry. The sitter's here. I just wanted to see how you were. Do you want me to come along tonight? Sam's out of town and Danny has a friend coming over to watch *Star Trek* tapes — not my idea of fun.'

Pix worked part-time for Have Faith, keeping the books and bringing her considerable organizational skills to ordering supplies and scheduling events. She had agreed to take the job, provided she would not be required to have anything to do with actual food preparation, not so much as turning on an

212

oven or stirring a pot.

'It's a long drive. Stay home. Read a book. Niki will be there. But thank you. I'm all right. Really.'

'Patsy called. She said to remind you that you're to call her tomorrow.'

Faith was sure her two friends had been talking about her. She was surprised Patsy wasn't waiting in her kitchen, as well.

'She and Will are going to see Bill T. Jones dance tonight in town. I told her you'd be late anyway. But don't forget to call her.'

'Yes, mother.' Faith grinned, then stopped. *Mother*. The word reminded her of Janice Mulholland.

'Am I wrong or is Janice Mulholland a very, very crazy parent?'

'Not noticeably more nutso than a lot I know. Why?'

'I'll talk to you about it tomorrow. I've got to change and go. But quickly, do most parents really use Visitation Day to pick out a teacher for the next year and even the year after that?'

'Some years, I was the only current parent in my kid's class. All the rest were on spec.'

'Maybe Janice isn't as crazy as I thought. No, she is. It's not just Winthrop Elementary but the choir, too. Nobody appreciates Missy enough.'

'Replace choir with Little League, piano, or soccer and you've got a bunch more just like her.'

'Thank God I had totally disinterested parents.'

Pix raised her eyebrows.

'They loved us, made sure we were healthy, relatively happy, but I doubt if they had more to do with our schools than knowing the teacher's name and showing up if we were performing, which, in my case, wasn't often.'

'And you never had a teacher who put you down or a situation at school with another kid that upset you? But then, you turned out okay — that *is* what you were going to say, right?'

Faith tried to laugh, but the thought of a certain sixth-grade teacher's ridicule all year and a group of girls who teased her for being a PK — she didn't even know it stood for preacher's kid until years later — made her laughter a bit strained. 'Point taken. A happy medium. I get it. Now I'd better change and head north to the land of port, starboard, and the Tillies.'

★　★　★

Niki was already at the yacht club and had unloaded the van. For the next few hours, they worked hard. The first task was getting the hors d'oeuvres out. The Tillies were gathering for aperitifs at 6:30. Someday, Faith told herself, I'll get used to New England's totally uncivilized social hours — or not. And it wasn't that they wanted to be home in time for Leno or Letterman. They wanted to be home in time for bed.

The yacht club itself was a wonderful late Victorian wood-shingled structure that meandered imposingly along and above the shoreline. A porch stretched across the back, facing the water. It was still light enough to imagine what it would be like to sit on it and watch the races in the summer, sipping iced tea or something stronger. The porch was bare now. Faith was sure it was crowded with comfortably cushioned wicker in season. The long-ago ghosts of women in shirtwaists and men in straw boaters or commodore's caps lingered throughout the year. The sea beyond was beautiful, and after a gray day of rain, the sky had cleared up enough to suggest there would be at least one last glorious sunset before the clocks would have to be turned back. A sunset to ease the prospect of the short, dark days ahead. Inside, the club was luxuriously appointed — deep-pile carpeting, with good Orientals spread on top, massive easy chairs, sofas, and, in the main room, a large fieldstone fireplace under the club's insignia, which was carved on an elaborate gilded wooden plaque. The walls were hung with ancient knot boards, crossed oars, pennants, awards, plus photographs and paintings of all sorts of boats with all sorts of sailors — sailors in groups, sailors alone. Glass trophy cases displayed glittering testimonies to the members' prowess. It was the kind of place mentioned in an offhand kind of way as 'the club' by those who belonged, and completely unknown, or off-limits, to those who didn't. You could only see the building from the water, and the dock, needless to say, was private.

Maybe the newest Tillie would be someone who would introduce a note of diversity. Last year, all the faces had been white — flushed, but white. Black, Asian, Latino? Faith wasn't counting on it, and a survey of the crowd from the pass-through in the butler's pantry confirmed it.

'A cheerful crowd, wouldn't you say, boss?' Niki commented, peeking over Faith's shoulder.

'Absolutely. What do you think the invitations said? 'Brooks navy blazers only'? 'Women in pants stay home'?'

Niki laughed. ' 'And be sure to polish your buttons.' They're a pretty well-preserved bunch, too. I'm looking at a lot of time at the gym here and more than walking Bowser for the ladies. Plus, they've still got their summer tans.'

'I think they sail pretty much year-round. Tom told me real sailors never stop, just change locales, or outerwear, and go 'frost-biting.' Anyway, thirty-seven is not that old. 'Well-preserved' will describe them when they're in their seventies, at least.' Having crossed the great divide to her thirties, Faith was a little touchy on the subject of age.

It was time to serve the first course, then the main courses. With the club settled and the wait staff in attendance, Faith sat down at the counter next to Niki, who was digging into a plate filled with mashed potatoes, the roasted root vegetables, and venison. 'Yum, yum. I didn't have time for lunch and I'm starving. I'll bet you didn't, either. Grab a plate,' Niki said.

Faith hadn't eaten, but she wasn't hungry. Thinking about what Tom had said about sailing had started her thinking about — Tom.

'All I have is a quarter,' Niki said, digging into her pocket and tossing the coin on the counter. 'No pennies, so I should get a lot for my money. Thoughts, that is. The Tillies are going to be busy scarfing down the food for at least another half hour. Remember how much they ate last year? And the cake is all ready to go. So, spill your guts, Faith. This has gone on long enough.'

She was serious. So was Faith. She picked up a piece of focaccia and began to pull it apart.

'There's the murder — and the business with George, although I'm pretty sure I've figured that all out and now it's a question of what to do — but mostly it's Tom.'

'Okay. Go on. What's happening with Tom?'

'Nothing. I try to get him to talk, but he's totally uncommunicative. It's stupid to think there was anything between him and Gwen, but he's taking her death so hard. Even complete strangers have noticed.' She told Niki about the conversation she'd overheard in the bathroom after Gwen's service.

'I don't know what there is about the sight of gleaming white porcelain that causes mouths to flap. You can't imagine some of the conversations I've had in bathrooms. People will tell you anything — I suppose because they think they'll never see you again. Not to mention what I've overheard. It's just gossip, Faith, idle gossip.'

'I know that deep down, but why can't I get Tom to talk to me about all this? I tried last night but got nowhere.' Her hands were covered with crumbs and little pieces of rosemary. She wiped them on her apron.

'Faith, Faith, Faith. And all along, I thought *you* were the one who knew everything. It's a guy thing.' Niki continued to eat, secure in the knowledge that she had solved the problem. She reached for more potatoes. Thin and wiry, she possessed an enviable metabolism, the kind that immediately burned up whatever calories entered her system, converting them to instant, observable energy. She had short dark hair, tightly curled, like a pot scrubber. At times like these, it seemed to spark.

'When did you ever think I knew everything, and what do you mean 'guy thing'?' Faith asked.

'Men don't talk. *They don't know how.* They are not communicators. You are asking for behavior that is not in Tom's repertoire. Yes, even perfect Tom. If you really want to talk to someone, talk to me — or Pix, or Patsy. We're good at it. Men can give speeches, flirt, make jokes, and on occasion bring forth appropriate remarks — but talk, no. When you see them with their cell phones, they're checking a point spread or making an appointment.'

Faith did know this and had, in fact, given a similar speech to her sister, Hope, once after yet another possible Mr Right turned out to have much in common with Marcel Marceau. As she recalled, she'd told Hope that women should really marry other women if all they wanted was open, frequent, emotional conversations. Something like that.

Niki was continuing, mimicking. 'I can't get him to open up. Well, duh, of course not. Once in a blue moon, maybe. Or if he's Greek. Greek guys talk, except it isn't always what you want to hear.'

The waiters returned with the Tillies' clean plates. Some of them appeared to have been licked. 'They're roasting the chairman during dessert. And we're to serve the sauterne immediately,' one of the staff said. 'I just hope we don't have another incident like last year.' An exuberant member had leaped up on to one of the tables, which promptly crashed beneath his weight.

Niki looked at Faith. 'This is how they communicate.' She sounded as if she were referring to a newly discovered tribe of aborigines. 'They can't come out and say, 'Fitzwilliam, you're a wonderful friend and I love you,' so instead, they run him down, and the worse it is, the more they care. Go figure. A woman would be destroyed — in tears. A man is in his element.'

The cake and wine dispatched, Faith and

Niki went to the pantry to watch the festivities. 'I feel like I'm nine years old, spying on one of my parents' parties when I was supposed to be in bed,' Faith said.

'We'd better count the lamp shades when they leave,' Niki advised.

The Tillies and their guests were roaring with laughter. At the height of the frenzy, most of them stood up and threw their napkins, tied into knots, at the speaker and the honoree, who immediately threw them back, starting a jolly melee that ended only when the waiters circulated with seconds of cake. No one wanted coffee. Cigars were lighted, cognac produced, and Faith began to get sleepy. They'd packed up everything they could. Now they had to wait until the Tillies wound down.

'Why don't you go home?' Niki suggested. 'To put it mildly, you've had quite a day.'

'No. I'm not tired at all. We'll finish this together.'

'This is the beginning of the evening for me. I'm supposed to meet a date at Axis at one. I'll tell you what. You take the food in your car — there isn't any cake left — and leave it at work. I'll take the van. I can change here. My stuff is in my bag. Sometime tomorrow, I'll bring the van out and get my car. There isn't much to do for Monday's dinner, but we can be sure we have everything.'

It was a good plan, especially since Faith had lied. She was tired, and the idea of slipping into bed in an hour was irresistible.

'Okay. But if the Tillies get out of hand, don't hesitate to call the authorities.'

'Mater and Pater? A stern talking-to will do it, and I'm up to it, but I think they're running out of steam. The napkin snowball fight did some of them in. One woman lost her headband.'

'Okay, I'll go. But you're sure?'

'I'm sure.'

Driving down Route 128, Faith thought longingly of home — and Tom. Niki was right. Tom had said as much himself: He couldn't handle talking about all this now. She felt guilty. He'd had to deal with Jared's grief and planning the memorial service, plus everything else that was going on in the parish. People were ill, troubled, and then there was George. She knew the principal's situation was preying on Tom's mind. They'd talked about it again last night and he was so angry, he couldn't sit still. At least she could tell Tom about Janice Mulholland and what was going on there. She'd accomplished something. She sped up past the Burlington Mall, its parking lots unaccustomedly barren.

It wouldn't take her long to put the food in the refrigerators at Have Faith's kitchen; then she'd be home in ten minutes. Tom would be asleep, but she was sure she could make it worth his while to wake up.

There were no streetlights on the back roads leading to Aleford. This had come as a surprise after the Great White Way she'd grown up with, and she remained unsure whether the lack of illumination was due to parsimony or the belief that if one was out after dark, then one could take one's chances. She pulled up to the small building that housed the catering firm and let herself in. She turned on all the lights, inside and out, then rapidly transferred the food from her car to the refrigerators, saving only the generous platter she'd prepared in case Tom was in need of sustenance.

It didn't take long. She shut off the lights and locked up. Turning left on to the back way to the parsonage — slightly faster than through the center of town — Faith became aware of a car following her.

'You should be home asleep,' she told the headlights reflecting in her rearview mirror. As if in answer, they switched to high beams. Suddenly, she felt uneasy. The car was moving closer. She sped up. So did the other car. She was annoyed that she hadn't gone straight through the center of town, with its reassuring orange halogen lights — still controversial after several years — and the small but adequate police station. She'd be home soon. She was perfectly safe. She hit the lock button, although she'd done it when she'd gotten into the car. *Click.* Nothing could happen. I'm perfectly safe, she told herself again. This is Aleford. An animal darted across the road. She swerved and missed — and increased her speed. To begin the day with a dead animal and end with one would be too much. She tried to get the image of this morning's maimed squirrel out of her head, yet it pushed its way in, accompanied, inevitably, by the memory of Gwen's dead body, bright blood bubbling from her mouth. A week ago. Only a week ago. She put her hand up to signal the car to lower its beams. Nothing happened. She tried to see what kind it was or who was driving, but the road was narrow and full of sharp curves. She didn't dare turn around.

Then suddenly, it was gone, disappearing as fast as it had come. She stopped and, shaking, watched the taillights disappear down a side road.

Faith was alone now — alone with her thoughts.

8

Tom was sitting in the wing chair, staring at the ashes in the fireplace, when Faith pushed open the kitchen door, intending to creep upstairs and slip into bed next to his warm body. He looked up and his face frightened her more than the unnerving encounter she'd just had. It wasn't the expression. In fact, that was what was so terrible. There wasn't any expression.

'Tom, are you all right?' she asked anxiously.

'Yes. Well, actually, no. Today was pretty rough,' he answered, then added, 'You must be tired. How did it go?'

'It was fine and I'm not tired.' Suddenly, she wasn't. 'Let me get you something to eat.'

'Thanks, honey, but I think I'll turn in.'

Faith became even more alarmed. When Tom was awake, he was always hungry — at thirty-two still your typical rangy, big, hungry boy. By the time Ben was a teenager, they'd have to keep a herd of dairy cows to keep the family in milk.

'Are you sure? I saved you some of the game we served, plus mashed potatoes.' Tom

225

loved mashed potatoes. 'Or you could have some chocolate cake' She'd hidden one piece from the Tillies. Tom loved chocolate cake.

He shook his head and stood up. 'Let's just go to bed. It's late and I have to perform tomorrow.'

Faith had never heard him refer to his ministry as a performance. What was going on?

He put an arm around her shoulder and drew her close, moving her toward the stairs. Her cheek rubbed against the soft wool of the sweater he was wearing and she breathed in his reassuring smell — his shampoo, a faint whiff of the Penhaligon aftershave she bought for him, and something else, something that belonged only to him.

'Kids okay?' she asked as they entered their bedroom.

'More than okay — sound asleep,' he answered.

★ ★ ★

It was a first for them — and Faith knew she sounded scripted. 'This happens to everyone. Don't worry. You're exhausted, physically and emotionally. It's late. Come on, darling, let's get some sleep.'

Tom started to say something, then turned

over after kissing her quickly on the cheek. Within seconds, it seemed, he was asleep.

Don't worry. All right for you to say, Faith told herself. Even when they were quarreling, they could always make love — maybe because they were quarreling. But the point was that Tom's mind was elsewhere. She had to hope his heart wasn't, too.

★ ★ ★

November 1, All Saints', was the next day and they were singing 'I Sing a Song of the Saints of God,' as was traditional at First Parish. I seem to be spending an inordinate amount of my life in one church or another, Faith thought as she tried to muster some enthusiasm for the hymn. By the time they got to the end — 'For the saints of God are just folks like me/And I mean to be one too' — she'd put some vigor, if not belief, into her voice. It was one of the more singable hymns, but the likelihood of being a saint herself . . .

As if to make up for last night's disappointing performance, Tom had given his all to the sermon, but — as sometimes happened — Faith could not keep her mind focused on the subject, though it was certainly food for thought, 'New Wine into Old Bottles or New Wine into New Bottles?':

The Transformation of the Self.' Instead, she had been distracted by the back of George Hammond's head several rows in front of her. She planned to grab him after church and invite him back to the parsonage for lunch. Up early, she'd gone over to work and hastily assembled a game pie from last night's left-overs. It was ready to pop into the oven, and this along with a salad and fruit cobbler for dessert should entice George should he show any signs of hesitation. They weren't having anyone else, and she always fed the children separately, so they would have a chance to talk. She'd mentioned the plan, as well as her conversation with Janice, to Tom before he left for church and he'd agreed enthusiastically. She'd felt better than she had for days. Maybe she should simply let the police solve Gwen Lord's murder and trust that the catering firm's reputation would draw people back little by little. Even as she considered the option, she acknowledged how hopeless it was. The case could remain unsolved and she'd always be known as 'the caterer of the corpse.'

As soon as Tom gave the benediction, Faith stood up and made a beeline for George. One thing at a time.

' . . . and we'd love to have you come.'

George Hammond looked Faith straight in

the eye. She was glad she hadn't any spitballs on her conscience. 'Tom's had a hard week and I'm sure he'd rather put his feet up and watch the game than have company, but you've got something to say — and it's always a pleasure to eat at your house, so thank you very much.'

'Good. I'm leaving now, so come whenever you want.' She was going to skip the coffee hour to get ready.

He nodded. 'See you soon.'

Less than an hour later, Tom and George came into the house together.

'Dinner in ten minutes,' Faith greeted them. 'Why don't you have a glass of sherry?' This was a staid ecclesiastical custom, akin to the absence of any frivolity on earlier Sabbaths. Both men would probably have preferred a beer. Faith made sure the cellar always had a good dry sherry, and Tom poured a glass for each of them.

Ben stood shyly in the doorway. Amy was napping. Faith had told her son he could stay with the grown-ups until dinner was served, but then he had to go upstairs to his room for a rest.

'Come and sit down, Ben,' the principal said. 'I hear you're enjoying your bookmaking.' Each child was writing a story and illustrating it, which parent volunteers typed up, then helped the student bind into a 'real' book.

'Mine is about a magic boy who can turn people into anything he wants by looking at them cross-eyed.'

'A handy trick,' the principal observed.

'He doesn't leave them that way,' Ben hastily assured him, then segued into the subject uppermost in his mind, saying in his best adult imitation, 'On the subject of rests . . . '

'Time to eat. Ben, we'll see you later. I'll let you know when to get up, and please don't wake your sister?'

Ben scowled. Faith looked at him and sighed. The fact that life was monumentally unfair was written all over his face. There was no doubt in Faith's mind that at the moment, the little boy in front of her was wishing he could turn his mother into a bat. He'd regaled them at breakfast with a multitude of facts about bats that Mrs Black the all-knowing had imparted.

'Come on, then.' Faith gave him a gentle push toward the door and tucked two big chocolate-chip cookies into his hand. Bats couldn't make cookies, she reflected. Maybe she was safe.

As soon as the food was served, George turned to Faith and said, 'I can tell you what's been happening in the last few days, and I'm sure you have things to share with me, too.' Apparently, there wasn't going to be any small talk, no discussion of the weather, or the proposed change in paint color for the shutters of the library.

'It's not completely clear, but one possible source for the rumor — and possible caller — is Janice Mulholland, whom, I believe, you know from the parish. She's the secretary of the PTA and we've had some disagreements over her daughter's teacher placement, as well as a few other issues that have come up about Missy, but frankly, I was surprised. Janice has been so involved at Winthrop, and I never suspected she would do something like this.'

'She probably wouldn't under normal circumstances, but I think she's really gone off the deep end when it comes to her daughter. I spoke to her yesterday about the school in general and she mentioned the necessity for being a 'squeaky wheel' and that parents were often in an adversarial relationship with their child's teachers and the principal. I'm afraid she also repeated the rumor with the utmost conviction, but she wouldn't give me any specifics. She seems convinced it's true.'

George Hammond nodded. He didn't appear upset, simply resigned.

'Obviously, the police have got to talk to

her and straighten this out,' Tom said firmly. 'They should be able to determine if she's been making the calls. She came to me a few times for counseling after her husband left, and although she was extremely emotional — not uncalled for, given the situation — she seemed honest.'

'I'm sure she is. And she honestly believes I'm a child molester. And now, so do other people.'

'What are you talking about?' Faith asked.

'The superintendent and I met Friday afternoon. He'd had a call from a school committee member who'd had calls from two Winthrop parents. Both the school committee member and the superintendent affirmed their belief in my integrity, but it's been suggested that I take a leave of absence while this gets sorted out.'

'You can't!' Faith realized she had raised her voice. The last thing she wanted was for Ben to come running in. She lowered it. 'We'll call the superintendent right now.'

'It's no use, Faith. I told you this would happen, and it's happening. Pretty soon people are going to be 'remembering' all sorts of things. 'Didn't he seem overly fond of little so-and-so?' 'Didn't someone bring this up when he was a Scout leader?' That's the way these things go.'

'At least let me talk to Janice Mulholland. You have nothing to lose from that.'

'Talk to anyone you like. I'm meeting with my teachers tomorrow after school and I plan to leave at the end of the week. Mrs Black will take over, as she did when I was gone before, and a new kindergarten teacher will be hired for the rest of the year.'

It was all Faith could do to keep from wailing out loud. It would be bad enough for Ben to lose his beloved principal, but Mrs Black! The psychological scars would keep him on the couch for the rest of his life.

'Don't do anything hasty,' Tom advised. 'What does Charley say about all this? Obviously, there have been no charges of any kind.'

'I haven't had a chance to talk to him, but I'll stop by the station on my way home.'

'It just seems to me that everyone is jumping the gun here. Two phone calls to a school committee member — and do we know who they were from? One could have been Janice — and you're out the door. It's gotten way too serious way too fast.'

'It's always serious when your boss tells you that you'd better get a lawyer, Faith. Now, could I have another spoonful of whatever this delicious meat thing is we're eating?'

As she cleaned up the kitchen after lunch, Faith wondered how she was going to squeeze everything in. She wanted to call Janice and go see her immediately, but she'd made an appointment to see the fourth mystery writer, Tanya O'Malley, and she didn't want to cancel. The woman had sounded reluctant enough, saying something about her animals. She lived in Wayland, which wasn't far, but Faith couldn't see both women and be home in time for the early trick-or-treaters, the little kids. Tom would be taking Ben around, and in any case, she hadn't told him about her interviews with last Saturday night's honored guests. Hadn't told him that she was investigating Gwen's death at all. It appears neither one of us is communicating well, she thought ruefully. Although not telling Tom she was getting herself involved in yet another murder was an established pattern of behavior, born of necessity. He worried too much.

Once more using her atlas of the Boston area, Faith had located the address Ms O'Malley had given her. She turned off Route 126 and found herself passing a series of open fields, occasionally coming upon old, extremely well-maintained farmhouses and barns. One resembled Monticello, and it was startling to see it tucked at the end of a drive with a prominent, oversized rural-route mailbox in front. It was unusually warm, so Faith hadn't bothered to put on the suede jacket she'd pulled from the closet. A few trees still blazed with color and she thought that October was definitely something about New England she would keep. Boiled dinners, blackflies, February, and ancestor worship could disappear without a trace and she wouldn't care, but October could stay.

The house numbers were on the mailboxes and Tanya O'Malley had helpfully added her name, as well. Her house was one of the farms — one of the most beautiful ones. Horses were grazing in sloping fields surrounded by venerable stone walls. There was a large gray-shingled barn, but the house itself, although traditional architecturally, was the color of Campbell's cream of tomato soup. The shutters were shiny black and the trim glossy white. Somehow, it worked. Faith was looking forward to meeting a woman who would dare to stray from Farmhouse White so dramatically. She hadn't seen her at Ballou House, or if she had, she hadn't known who the woman was. Paula hadn't asked her to play a prominent role. She hadn't asked Anson Scott, either. Maybe she'd known what their answers would have been. Something like 'I'll come, eat, and smile, but that's it.' Maybe not even the smile part. Tanya had sounded extremely brusque on the phone.

She rang the doorbell, then after a while rang it again. Of course it opened immediately, as it always does when you ring twice, which makes you feel both rude and overly anxious.

Tanya O'Malley did not look like an author. She looked like a farmer. She was wearing overalls over a sweatshirt, and rubber boots. Her gray hair was cut short and further kept from getting in the way of her face by a kerchief tied peasant-style at the nape of her neck. The kerchief struck the only incongruous note — Faith recognized it immediately as a Liberty of London silk scarf.

'You'll have to talk to me in the barn. I have a sick ewe.'

Given the context, Faith realized Tanya was talking about a sheep, and she followed her through the house. As she went, she took a quick inventory of the house's furnishings. Like the exterior, the interior was filled with color. Either Tanya had exquisite taste or her decorator did. The rooms opened off the long hallway, two parlors in the front, one of which was obviously a study; it was lined with bookshelves and sported an iMac on a beautiful Sheraton desk. The walls were covered with dark green damask striped wallpaper. Buttercup yellow silk drapes hung at the windows; they were tied back with green-and-gold tassels and puddled at the floor. She quickly shot a glance to the other side. A Scandinavian blue-and-white porcelain stove stood at one end and French doors led to a terrace. The walls here were Prussian blue, the drapes unabashedly red. Couches and chairs had been selected for comfort, and books were stacked on low tables, in large baskets, and on more shelves. She glimpsed a portrait of a mother and child either by or in the style of Lilian Hale, the American Impressionist. Two doors were closed. A bathroom? A closet? Another door into the large living room? Then they were in the kitchen, which occupied the entire back of the house and included a dining area. A round table surrounded by Shaker-style chairs was set in front of an enormous arched window, commanding a view of the fields. The rest of the kitchen was almost as well equipped as Faith's own — a Viking range, Sub-Zero refrigerator, and all sorts of other essentials.

'Grab a mug,' Ms O'Malley directed, pointing to the counter. Faith did and then they exited through the mudroom. Crossing the yard to the barn, Faith felt jealous. She'd be an old lady before she had a house of her own. The Fairchilds had built a small cottage near the Millers', on Sanpere Island in Maine, but it was a summer place, not a real house. They might change parishes, but she'd always be in a parsonage, and you didn't paint those red, even cream of tomato red.

Tanya O'Malley, unlike the other authors, wrote nonfiction — true crime — and Faith had been particularly eager to speak with her. The woman was more well known than any of the others, except Anson Scott, and had made the *New York Times* bestseller list several times. She'd written about the Pamela Smart case — the New Hampshire high school teacher who'd used sex to persuade one of her students to kill her husband. Then there had also been one about the Stuart case. Charles Stuart had murdered his pregnant wife, then spun a tale about being attacked by a black man. His story was immediately believed by the Boston police, who promptly found a suspect before some glaring discrepancies and Stuart's sudden suicide revealed the real killer, as in 'It's *always* the husband.' O'Malley's latest book was about the mother who hired a hit man to bump off the mother of a rival cheerleader when her own daughter didn't make the squad. Faith thought of Janice Mulholland. Mothers did get very, very crazy. How crazy was Janice? She wasn't happy with Jared, given his lack of appreciation of Missy's talent. That was clear. But unhappy enough to kill his fiancée? A gigantic 'So there'?

'Just look at her eyes. She's been off her feed, but she ate a little while ago. I want to watch and make sure it stays down.'

The ewe was gazing up at Tanya plaintively. Faith had taken the kids to Drumlin Farm in Lincoln, run by the Audubon Society, and this sheep didn't appear to look any different from Drumlin's, but there were obviously subtleties here that would forever escape Faith.

'You must be having a hell of a time getting anybody to hire you after last Saturday,' Tanya observed as she sat down on a low stool and motioned Faith toward another. The barn looked like an illustration from Swedish illustrator Carl Larsson's *The Farm*. It was immaculate and smelled pleasantly of hay, with just a whiff of barnyard. That could change if the ewe has digestive problems, Faith thought as she joined Tanya in keeping watch. It was definitely one of the most unusual circumstances in which she'd ever questioned someone. She took a sip from her mug. She'd almost forgotten she was holding it, she'd been so fascinated by the surroundings. Mulled cider, not too sweet, delicious.

'I'm afraid you're right. I catered an event on the North Shore last night and I have a booking tomorrow night, but that's it.'

'People are such sissies,' Tanya observed. 'Besides, you didn't kill her.'

'Thank you, but why are you so sure?' Faith was beginning to hope that today would be the start of a long and beautiful friendship with this unusual woman. She liked what Ms O'Malley had to say — and she wanted to see the rest of her house.

'Too obvious even to be a plan. Unless you intended to get out of the business, you'd never jeopardize your livelihood that way. You'd come up with something else.'

Why hadn't she thought of this? And proclaimed it loudly and clearly. You didn't shoot yourself in the foot, or, in this case, fall on your own boning knife. Faith turned to the business at hand with a sense of encouragement that had been missing for days.

'As I said on the phone, I've been asking each of the authors who were present for any thoughts. If they were writing it, who would they suspect, or, in your case, does it remind you of any other case? Who do *you* think killed Gwen Lord?'

Tanya O'Malley sat still, then reached over to pat the ewe, burying her fingertips in the animal's coat.

'I've thought a lot about that night on and off this week. A murder game turned lethal. The victim a strikingly beautiful young woman. I'd watched her dance — my table was directly adjacent to the dance floor — and there had been an almost determinedly reckless quality to it. Others were having fun, whooping it up, yet she seemed to be acting a part, the part of someone having a good time. Every once in a while, the smile would leave her face, and I thought she looked tragic, almost desperate. Her partner, a handsome young man, seemed worried about her, solicitous even. He obviously cared about her deeply.'

This was the time to say that the handsome young man had been her husband, but somehow the words stuck in Faith's throat, gagging her.

'Something was on her mind. I fancy myself an animal behaviorist and a pretty good observer. She wasn't a happy person.'

Faith drank some cider. It had never occurred to her that Gwen might not have been happy. She'd been engaged to someone who adored her and whom she showed every indication of adoring back; she had a job she loved, no money worries. It was sad that she had lost her parents the way she did and had no siblings — although Faith knew some people for whom that would have been a blessing. Fortunately, she was not one of them. But what on earth could Gwen have been distressed about that night? The argument with Nick? Trouble at work? It had to be that.

'What exactly are you suggesting?' Faith asked, although she had a good guess what the answer would be.

'I think she killed herself.'

'Except why there and why that way? It was horrible and she must have been in terrible pain.'

'True, but not for long, and of course she wouldn't have known that ahead of time, would she? If no one ever killed him- or herself because of the imagined pain involved, we'd have virtually no suicides. And as to the place, perhaps she'd been carrying around the cyanide — it was cyanide, wasn't it? I saw the body — ' Faith nodded and Tanya continued. 'Carrying it around until she felt brave, or desperate, enough. It could have been the sight of all those merry-makers that pushed her over the edge.'

'Wouldn't the police have found the container? They're treating this as a homicide.'

'Easy enough to empty it on to her dessert, then go to the bathroom and flush it down the toilet. It would have been glass. All she'd have had to do was wrap it in a tissue and grind it up with her heel or walk out on to the terrace and do the same. It rained this week, but there still might be some particles of glass.'

Faith assumed the police had checked the grounds, but she'd tell Dunne Tanya's theory. It made sense, except, unfortunately, it wouldn't help Have Faith. The one person who could confirm the story and clear the firm's reputation was dead.

'She didn't leave any kind of a note. The police have searched her apartment.'

'Contrary to popular belief, most suicides don't. But you don't want to hear all this. It doesn't help you. You need a killer and you need to catch him — or rather, the police do. I can't imagine your efforts extend to actual apprehensions.' She smiled benevolently.

Well, they have in the past, Faith was tempted to say, but it sounded like boasting.

'According to all the other writers put together, murderers are filled with overweening pride, cowards, great actors with senses of humor, and insane. What would you add to the list?'

Tanya answered immediately. 'I'm surprised no one mentioned sex. So many murderers experience a sexual thrill in the act

— and while thinking about it both before and after. They get off on death.'

Faith thought about Leopold and Loeb and what Bill Brown had said. He'd been suggesting the same thing.

'And in this case, the target was a very sexually attractive woman,' Tanya added.

I know this; we can move on to something else. The words echoed in Faith's head.

'What a good girl,' Tanya was murmuring softly to the sheep, stroking her fleece. 'That's my little Jean Louise.' She looked up. 'Scout's real name in *To Kill a Mockingbird*. This is actually Jean Louise the Third. I've been keeping sheep for many years. The book is my favorite and I always like to have a Jean Louise around the place.'

'It's my favorite book, too. I read it or *Pride and Prejudice* whenever I'm diseased in body or mind.' Tanya O'Malley seemed to elicit this sort of expression.

The woman nodded. 'I've fitted up a nice place in the loft to read out here. I like the company.' They sat in companionable silence for a while, drinking their cider.

'The Druids had it all wrong,' Tanya observed.

'Oh?' said Faith, wondering how they had strayed from Maycomb, Georgia, and Jane Austen's Hampshire so much further back in time and place.

'Halloween. Of course, they didn't call it that — that came later, All Hallows' Eve, the vigil of Hallowmas, All Saint's Day, November first. The Druids had some other name. But it was a great autumn festival. Huge bonfires. It was to celebrate the sun deity and give thanks for the harvest, but I think they really just liked to make enormous piles and torch them. The Druids thought big. But they believed that Saman, the Lord of Death, called all the wicked souls that had been condemned to inhabit the bodies of animals for the past year together to wander the countryside in a terrifying pack. Later, it was simplified to ghosts and witches. It should have been the *good* souls who got to inhabit the bodies of animals. Look at Jean Louise. She'd be a treat for some newly departed and could never for an instant permit wickedness to share her inner space.'

Faith looked at the sheep. There was a simple goodness in her placid face and it was hard to imagine a devil within. Tanya O'Malley was very, very much in tune with her flock.

'I agree,' Faith said. 'Jean Louise is the soul of goodness.' Especially since she's kept her food down, Faith added to herself. A regurgitating sheep would have killed the mood.

245

All Tanya's talk about Halloween reminded Faith that she had two little trick-or-treaters at home, by this time growing anxious for her arrival. But Tanya had one more piece of Halloween lore to dispense. 'They still light bonfires in the British Isles, and in some places, everyone who is there places a stone in the dying embers. If yours has moved when you come back to check the next day, you're sure to die within the year. I've always thought it would make a good plot. The murderer deliberately moves the victim's stone and then over the course of the year insidiously uses the power of suggestion, and some near misses, until the person kills himself or simply dies of fright.'

Faith shuddered. She planned to stay away from any bonfires.

'It's all superstition. Even a sheep knows better.' Tanya stood up with Faith and put her hand on Faith's shoulder. Faith felt the flood of friendship return. Throughout the visit, she'd had an uncanny feeling that Tanya knew everything she was feeling. It was odd the way this happened every once in a great while. You met someone at a party or somewhere else, began to talk and soon felt as if you had known each other forever. And you stayed friends, although you might not see each other often. You always picked up where you left off. Women. She realized with a jolt. It was always with women. Niki's words from the night before came back to her. Well, it must be a girl thing, or make that woman thing.

'Good luck tonight,' Faith said as they walked together around the house to the drive where Faith had parked her car. 'I'm sorry I can't come to the panel, but I'll be handing out unhealthy food.' She knew from experience that no kid likes to get an apple or box of raisins on Halloween, and so she stuck resolutely to chocolate.

'I like being on a panel with Veronica. She carries the ball and everyone is happy simply to listen to her read in that wonderful voice of hers. I don't know the third author. Writes some sort of mysteries with recipes in them. Recipes for what? Arsenic pie? I'm not sure I get the concept. Oh, sorry.' She laughed. 'You'll be back in business soon enough, Faith. Don't worry.'

And Faith found that she wasn't. She was feeling positively light-hearted. 'Anson Scott has a marvelous voice, too. I suppose he's too busy to do a library panel.'

Tanya's face darkened. 'Or too something else. Don't get me started on him. The Druids would have put him in an animal for sure, but I wouldn't do that even to a — well, a coyote. They go after my chickens,' she added, apologizing for the maligning of a four-footed furry creature.

Faith could understand how a fellow writer might find Anson's habit of sucking all the air out of a room a bit annoying. He did tend to occupy center stage — and stage left and stage right.

'Come to see me again. Bring your children to visit the animals.'

'I will,' Faith promised, then drove off. Tanya had described herself as an 'animal behaviorist.' Faith wanted to ask her whether that was why her genre was true crime. It seemed such a contrast — the picture-book farm filled with living things, the joy of nature, and a livelihood that depended on nature gone awry — but then it was *human* nature.

* * *

'If I wear my jacket, I won't look like a robot,' Ben explained patiently. 'Robots don't have red arms.'

At dusk, it was still warm. Indian summer come at last for a tantalizingly brief moment before the cold of winter. So far, only a few of the youngest children had come to the door, dressed as tiny pirates, witches, fairy princesses, and one unicorn. Ben was old enough to go out in the dark — with his Dad — and also apparently considered himself old enough to make his own clothing choices. Tom, flashlight in hand, was ready to go, but Ben had balked at Faith's demand for outerwear. She was secretly pleased that he was already showing sartorial taste. The red Rugged Bear jacket did ruin the effect.

'Okay. How about your gray sweatshirt? Robots can have gray arms.' Faith was halfway up the stairs to get it before Ben could object, but he didn't.

'Robots do have gray arms,' he told her when she returned with the article of clothing in hand. She helped him put it on, then lowered the robot box over his head and kissed him. He was out the door, with Tom streaking behind him, trying to catch up after having settled on the couch for what had promised to be a long wrangle. Faith smiled as she heard him say, 'Wait, Ben! Now remember, Daddy likes Kit Kats,' before they went to the Millers', next door, their first stop.

Amy had been watching the goings-on, alternately jumping up and down in a toddleresque Margot Fonteyn imitation and sitting squarely on the floor, her chubby little legs stretched straight out in front of her, admiring her pink ballet slippers.

For the next several hours, the doorbell

never stopped ringing. The parsonage was directly across from the Aleford green and its central location made it a prime target. Faith was beginning to panic that she might run out of candy again, when the flood turned to a trickle, and it had all but stopped by the time Ben and Tom returned.

Amy was asleep on the couch. Faith hadn't had time to put her to bed and greet Harry Potter numbers fifty to ninety-six, complete with brooms and the occasional owl puppet.

'I'll take care of her, honey,' Tom offered.

Ben had struggled out of his costume and was waving his Unicef box and bagful of treats wildly. 'Wow, Mom, come on and see what I got!'

'How about we do it in the kitchen? I want to make something for your father to eat, and maybe you'd like a cup of soup or a bowl of cereal before you go to bed?'

'I'm not hungry and I don't have to go to bed yet!'

'Not yet. First things first, but tomorrow is a school day.' The moment she said that, Faith wondered whether this was some sort of response programmed into a mother's brain the moment she acquired a child. She'd hated it when her mother said it to her, but here was the same phrase popping out of her mouth like the toads in the fairy tale.

'Any more of that pasta?' Tom asked as he entered the kitchen after reading to Ben, who was now hopefully fast asleep.

Faith had whipped together a sauce by boiling down some leftover squash soup, adding Parmesan and some grilled vegetables. She'd mixed it with orecchiette, and there was still plenty. She placed a steaming plate in front of her husband. 'Beer, or some of that nice Australian Rosemount cabernet? Kit Kat and milk?' She felt like a stewardess and was tempted to add, Or me? Very tempted to add it.

'Let's have a glass of wine.' While Faith poured two glasses, Tom picked up an orange plastic pumpkin lying on the table. Amy had been insistently dragging it around all weekend. 'All Hallows' Eve. I remember my dad taking us out on Halloween, standing with the other dads, who were all carrying their flashlights and waiting at the end of the sidewalk while we ran up to ring the doorbells. Mom always made our costumes. I usually went as a cowboy; then one year, I wanted to be Elvis and came up with my own outfit — early Elvis, you understand, so not too hard, only I didn't know the marker I'd used for my sideburns wouldn't come off. I borrowed my brother's guitar. Very cool. That was the last year I trick-or-treated. Now I'm the dad on the sidewalk.'

'You sound sad.' Faith wasn't sure what Tom was mourning and hoped it was simply lost youth.

'I guess I am a little. You don't get that same feeling of anticipation in adulthood. You know, standing in front of someone's door, maybe someone you know, maybe a stranger, and when it opens, they'll say your costume is great and who could it possibly be? Plus, you walk away with candy.' He smiled and lifted his glass. 'But I have Ben — and Amy can go with us next year.'

And me, you have me, Faith thought.

'It was pretty much the same in the city, except hallways mostly instead of sidewalks. My father took us, too. Moms handing out candy apparently crosses state lines.'

Tom looked skeptical. He knew his wife and her sister had been born and raised in New York City, but the concept was so alien to him as to be the stuff of myth.

'My mother bought our costumes at F.A.O. Schwarz. I know she must have had a sewing kit, but the only needle I remember seeing is one she used to take splinters out of our fingers. The costumes were great, though, and we didn't mind recycling them with a few new additions. I was usually a gypsy, but one year, Hope gave up Cinderella and demanded to be an astronaut. They'd just started including women in the space program. There were a lot of jokes about having 'the right stuff,' as I recall. The last year I went out, a friend and I went as our grandmothers, so we could wear their minks. Fur and bright red lipstick. My grandmother wouldn't be caught dead in either now.' Faith realized Tom wasn't listening. She also realized she was babbling. She reached for his hand. She had an idea where his mind might be.

'It was a beautiful service yesterday. We've been so busy, we haven't really talked about it.'

'I don't know if I could have done what Jared did without breaking down. He's an amazing man. It was all his doing — all his planning, even the flowers. They were from their friend Priscilla's garden.'

'How did things go at the interment?'

'Oh, I read all the things you're supposed to read, but again, it was Jared who made the whole thing a real tribute, a real good-bye. He sang 'Amazing Grace' to her, softly, then put another white rose on the coffin before we left. Nick was with us, and he was crying like a baby.'

Faith could hear Jared's fine tenor voice. She had tears in her eyes, too.

'Oh, Tom, I wish it had all never happened!

I wish we could fall so far back that someone could grab the spoon out of Gwen's hand before she took a bite! And now I wish we knew who killed her, so it can all be laid to rest.'

'I do, too, honey. I do, too.' Tom squeezed her hand hard.

Faith remembered what Tanya O'Malley had suggested.

'Do you think there's any possibility that Gwen may have taken her own life? That she was depressed?'

He dropped her fingers as if they were covered with thorns. 'Where on earth would you get an idea like that?' He sounded angry. 'Is this the result of all your nosing around? I know you are — you can't help it. But please keep this thought to yourself, especially don't mention a word to Jared.'

'Of course I would never say anything to Jared.' Faith was deeply wounded. How could Tom think that she might be so insensitive? 'And I'm only raising the possibility because it all seems so inexplicable.'

Tom put his face in his hands for a moment, and when he took them away, he wasn't angry anymore. His face sagged as if punctured. 'I'm sorry. You're right. It is totally and completely inexplicable. It forces us to question all kinds of things. Maybe she did kill herself. But if I thought that, I'm not sure how I could live with myself.'

'What do you mean, Tom?' Faith was frightened.

'I'm just talking crazy. Let's go to bed.' He stood up, put their dishes in the sink, and walked to the doorway. She followed, turning off the light. The sharp click the old switch made sounded harsh in the silence.

'Could you please blow the pumpkins out?' Faith called downstairs. Tom had gone into his study for a book. She heard his mumbled reply and soon they were in bed. Tom was reading, but Faith's light was out and she was praying for sleep and oblivion.

★　★　★

She looked at the clock: 3:00 A.M., really 4:00 A.M., according to her body, which was wide awake and thirsty. Not that she was an early riser, but she knew that for the next few days, she'd be at odds with time. Water satisfies parched children, but adults are not so easily pleased. She wanted juice — orange juice. And that meant getting out of bed and going downstairs. It was warm and cozy under the duvet. Tom's steady breathing was so familiar, she could almost believe everything was all right. Sighing, she slipped

255

silently from under the covers and tiptoed across the room — her precautions completely unnecessary, as only a sonic boom or a cough from Ben or Amy would wake her husband.

She stood in front of the fridge and poured juice into a large tumbler, drinking some greedily, then pouring more. The cool liquid traveling down her grateful throat across her chest felt like a biology text's diagram come to life. She put the pitcher back and, holding the glass, returned to the living room. As she started up the stairs, she noticed a faint flicker of light at the front window. The pumpkins. Tom had forgotten to extinguish them. They would probably be fine until morning. She'd used tea lights, encased in aluminum, so there was no danger of a candle tipping over. But a dry leaf, or several, could blow in and ignite. A spark would find its way to the parsonage and the whole thing would go up like a house of straw. After her parents' first visit, Faith's mother had insisted they put in supplemental smoke alarms. A real estate attorney's worst nightmare was fire, and this coupled with genuine maternal concern had provoked several comments of the 'quaint New England death trap' variety from Mrs Sibley. Faith knew she had to put out the candles. If she burned the place down, she would never hear the end of it — and she could forget about lunch — in this town again.

It looked cold and she was barefoot, but Faith opened the door and dashed out to the pumpkins. She could see from the streetlights along the green that someone had flung a stuffed dummy on her lawn. It was one of those that — with corn husks, fake spider-webs, and strings of Caspers — had graced many houses since mid-October, to the children's delight and Faith's ongoing bemusement. Aleford took the holidays, even one with satanic overtones, seriously.

She blew out each flame and put the tops back on the pumpkins. There was a pleasant smell of smoke and squash. She looked at the lifeless figure again. And again. The cold flagstone sent a chill straight up her legs into her spine. She wrapped her arms around herself and forced her feet to move forward; each step was an effort. It took a long time for her to get near enough to see that the figure was indeed lifeless.

And that the figure was Jared Gabriel.

9

The Druids had been right. Saman, the Lord of Death, had been abroad, accompanied by the souls of the wicked. Jared was lying on his back in the moonlight, his eyes wide open, staring toward heaven. He looked startled. His mouth hung slack. For a moment, Faith couldn't move. She was trying desperately to take it in. Then she bent down to check for a pulse, placing her fingers on his neck — patiently waiting, going through the motion, a motion she knew was pointless. Jared was dead. She wanted to close his eyes, pull shut the unbuttoned coat that had fallen to either side. Every instinct called for respect, but this was murder, and murder kills all respect. She couldn't touch him. Not even stroke his smooth cheek, brush back the hair that fell across his forehead. She couldn't disturb the evidence.

There wasn't much blood. Just a small stain above his heart, the blood having seeped in a circle on his white shirt. The seconds stretched into minutes and still she didn't move away from the body. Every detail came into sharp focus. He'd been carrying his briefcase. The contents were strewn next to him — a pitch pipe, some music, copies of yesterday's order of service, a train schedule, and a yellow order-form receipt. Faith felt as if she were in a dream, a play, a film. She was watching herself act out a script, a script that wasn't, couldn't, be real. She stood up and then crouched down again, closer to the briefcase. The train schedule was for the MBTA Boston/Fitchburg line. It stopped in Aleford at peak hours. Jared often took the train. But it was the order form that had drawn her eye. She'd seen the same kind before. She knew what it was. Jared had bought some wrapping paper. Wrapping paper to benefit the Winthrop Elementary School PTA. She scanned the sheet for the seller's name and found it at the bottom, written in expert D'nealian script, Winthrop's preferred method: Missy Mulholland. It was so unexpected, and yet expected, that Faith thought she would faint. Her heart raced and she struggled to stay conscious. The film was very real now. She put her hand on the walk to steady herself and stood up. Again she felt herself begin to fall down, descending into a long black tunnel.

Faith looked at Jared once more, then ran into the house and called the police. When they arrived, she was on the couch, soundlessly screaming into a pillow. She hadn't been able to move — even to get Tom.

★ ★ ★

By the time the children woke up, the front yard was festooned with yellow crime-scene ribbons and there was a state police cruiser parked at the end of the walk to deter sightseers or macabre souvenir hunters. Jared's body had been removed. That all of this might escape Ben's notice was as likely as his overlooking a *Tyrannosaurus rex* that had wandered by. Faith and Tom had agonized over what to say to their son. When Ben was born, Jared had given him a music box in the shape of a little French sailor. It played 'Somewhere Beyond the Sea' and had been one of his favorite toys, an instant antidote to fussiness. It still stood on his chest of drawers. Jared was one of the adult guests every year at Ben's birthday, along with Pix Miller and Tom's parents. He always brought his guitar to lead some singing, and like the giant soap bubbles the children blew, Jared's songs were one of the things that didn't change, even though Ben did — moving from Winnie-the-Pooh parties to Inspector Gadget. Next year, when he was in first grade, Ben would be old enough for the junior choir, and he had talked about it earnestly with Jared, who assured him he would do fine, that he had a lovely voice. As soon as they heard Ben stirring, Tom and Faith went into his room. It was early. He was still on the old time, too.

'Ben,' Tom said. 'I'm afraid we have some bad news for you. There was an accident in front of our house last night and you'll see a police car there, besides some other things the police need to have on our lawn just for now.'

Ben sat up in bed, alert. For once, he wasn't asking questions. Faith had her arm around him and she could feel his little body tense.

'Our friend Jared was in the accident and he's dead.'

A look of horror swept over Ben's face; he blinked, then screamed, 'Noooooooooooo!' and began to cry, still repeating 'No' in between sobs and gulps for air. The noise woke his sister, who came padding into the room in her sleeper. The scene that greeted her eyes was a puzzling one. Tom picked her up. 'Ben get a boo-boo?' Faith was trying desperately not to cry herself, and this was almost too much. It was frightening for children to see their parents out of control. She reached over Ben, who was burrowed in her arms, to take Amy's hand. 'Yes, Ben's sad.' Amy looked from parent to parent. 'Mommy, Daddy, make it better?' she asked anxiously.

'Yes, honey.' Faith's voice acquired a note of resolve. 'We'll make it all better.'

It seemed like hours before the kids were off to school and day care, and it *was* longer than the usual amount of time, since they were up so early — an amount of time normally filled with the frantic attempt to get everyone dressed, fed, and out the door. Tom took Amy across to the church while Faith waited for the school bus with Ben farther down the street, away from the parsonage. Tom had called George Hammond with the news and Mrs Black had called almost immediately to say she'd take good care of Ben, keeping a close eye on him.

'Will there be a new choirmaster?' Ben asked, not only allowing Faith to hold his hand while they waited but holding hers tightly.

'Yes, but not right away. And you know we'll never forget Jared. He will always be with us.'

'I'll have to practice. He wanted me to be in the choir. I have to do it, Mom.'

'Of course you do, and he'll be listening.'

Ben got on the bus, waved a tremulous good-bye, and Faith returned home, feeling emotionally exhausted. As she entered the back door, the phone was ringing. It was Tom.

'Nick has been with the police and, as you might imagine, he's pretty strung out. He's on his way here. He needs to talk. Do you think Ben is going to be all right at school?'

Faith recounted their curbside conversation, which reassured Tom. Ben had never lost anyone significant — especially not someone so young. It would take awhile, but he would be okay. She hoped he would always miss Jared. For herself the notion of not talking to him, laughing over some parish foolishness, or taking a walk was incomprehensible. There was a hole in her universe where Jared had been, and it would always be there.

It all left her with a heightened sense of purpose. Bill Brown had been right. Gwen wasn't the intended victim; Jared was. The dessert was supposed to have been his. Perhaps Gwen had switched, thinking her portion larger. Women did that. Women watching their weight. Beautiful women. Faith had a lot to do, but there was one thing she had to do right away. Should have done the day before. And if she had, would Jared Gabriel still be alive?

Janice Mulholland was dressed in sweats and a T-shirt. She'd obviously just come in from a run and had been headed for the shower when she'd stopped to answer the door. She was in her stocking feet.

'Mrs Fairchild, Faith, hello,' she said with obvious surprise. 'Please come in. I'm sorry I'm such a mess, and I don't have any coffee on, either. I never eat before I run, but I can start some, if you like.' No proper Aleford hostess ever forgot to offer coffee.

'No, thank you, I've had more than is good for me,' Faith said, which was true. Janice did not look like someone who had been grilled by the police during the wee hours of the morning. She did not look like a killer, either. She looked like a healthy suburban housewife approaching forty well armed.

The house was an oversized Cape and the living room looked as if it had been transported intact from an Ethan Allen showroom, right down to the silk tulips in a tole coal scuttle.

'Tell me, what can I do for you? Is it something about school or First Parish?'

So she hadn't heard. Faith had beaten the police, which she'd figured was a long shot, but it gave her a sudden advantage. Still, it didn't make sense. Why hadn't they been here?

It was as if she'd spoken aloud. 'I'm a morning person. I start my run at six, after getting Missy up and going, then loop back to make sure she's eaten what I've left out. You'd be amazed how picky children can be, even Missy, who is such an adventurous eater. Imagine, she asked for caviar last week! Then we go to the bus stop and I finish from there. It gives me the whole day.'

To do what? Faith wondered. But she didn't have time for speculation about that or Missy's 'Let them eat cake' food demands. Janice was going to hear about Jared's death sooner or later, and it might as well be from Faith. She couldn't question her about the wrapping paper or she'd be in big trouble with the police. She could ask questions around it, though, and she could certainly find out more about Janice's campaign to get rid of the principal. She took a deep breath.

'Jared Gabriel is dead. He was killed sometime last night or early this morning.'

'My God!' Janice clutched her throat. 'Gwen and now Jared! It's the work of a madman. A serial killer! What are the police doing? Why didn't they cancel school? Are they sure it's safe for anyone, especially children, to be walking about town?' The color had drained from her glowing face. Actors. Veronica Brookside had said that murderers were consummate actors. If so, then there was a golden statuette in Janice's future.

'It's been a terrible shock, but I don't think we have to worry about the safety of our children, just their reactions to the loss. The police are investigating, of course,' Faith said, thinking, Now, it's your turn to say, Why, Missy just sold him some wrapping paper. But Janice Mulholland was shakily opening a drawer in the coffee table and taking out a crumpled pack of cigarettes.

'I never smoke in front of Missy, but would you mind terribly?'

'Go ahead.' Faith waited until Janice took a long drag, and then she said, 'What we were talking about on Saturday — this business with George Hammond. You know him from church. He's been at Winthrop for years and is one of the most respected people in Aleford. You've *got* to tell me what evidence you have to back up your accusation, because it's you, isn't it? Nobody else told you about George. This started with you.'

Janice continued to smoke, taking another long drag before she spoke. 'You have children yourself. You ought to understand how important they are. How you have to watch them — and everyone who comes in contact with them. Anything can happen at any time. Whenever Missy walks out that door, I don't know what will happen to her.'

'But, Janice, you can't live like this. It's bound to affect Missy, too. Parents transfer their fears. We live in a safe town with a wonderful school system — '

Janice interrupted her, raising her voice. 'A safe town! Two murders in a little over a week!'

'They have nothing to do with our kids, with George. I want you to tell Charley MacIsaac what you did. That you made the calls. Maybe you believed what you said at the time. Maybe you thought you had good reason, that George was somehow doing something that you saw as harmful to Missy, a teacher you didn't want for her, or some other issue. But please, just tell him — or talk to my husband. Tell Tom.' Faith was prepared to go on. She saw something like the possibility of relief cross Janice's face, a letting down of her guard.

Then the doorbell rang.

Detective Lieutenant John Dunne, Charley MacIsaac, and another plainclothes police officer, whom Faith recognized as Detective Ted Sullivan, 'Sully,' Dunne's right-hand man, more than filled the door frame.

'Mrs Mulholland,' Charley said, 'we'd like to speak with you for a moment.' It wasn't a question, and Janice stepped back to let them in. Dunne saw Faith and scowled. 'Paying parish calls, Mrs Fairchild?' He would have been happier to see her anywhere else, an alternate solar system, for example.

'I was just leaving.' Faith stood up.

'No,' Janice said firmly, putting her cigarette out. 'I would like Mrs Fairchild to stay. I'd also like to know if you think I should call my lawyer.'

Dunne lowered himself on to the couch and motioned everyone else to sit. 'Do *you* think you should call your lawyer, Mrs Mulholland?'

'I believe it's my right, and if you're going to start making accusations about me regarding George Hammond, I want a lawyer here and, until then, Mrs Fairchild as a witness.'

'Hammond? George Hammond?' Dunne turned to Charley. 'Who the hell is that?'

'The principal of our elementary school. He's been getting some unpleasant phone calls.'

'Well, most principals do, but how is Jared Gabriel involved?'

'He's not.'

Dunne sighed. These Aleford cases took a

268

lot out of him. He'd much rather have a straightforward hit in Revere or somewhere like that.

'Okay, let's start again. Hello, Mrs Mulholland. I'm Detective Lieutenant John Dunne of the Massachusetts State Police, Chief MacIsaac you know, and this is Detective Sullivan. I'd like him to take notes for me, which you may read and accept or not accept. You may call your lawyer, but we are not interested in your elementary school principal. We are investigating the murder of Jared Gabriel, which, I assume from Mrs Fairchild's presence, is a fact not unknown to you.'

Janice relaxed visibly and nodded. 'Poor Jared. We didn't always see eye-to-eye, but he was a fine musician and I don't know what the church will do without him.'

'Just to get it out of the way, could you tell us where you were last night?'

'Why, I was here, of course. I seldom leave my daughter, Missy. She's in third grade. And when I do, I have an excellent woman who baby-sits. I wouldn't use a teenager. Drugs, you know.'

Dunne nodded and waited.

'I especially wouldn't have left Missy on Halloween. Her pumpkin was smashed last year. Very little is done to control the youth of

269

this town, I'm afraid.' She shot an accusatory look at Charley, who winced.

'So, you didn't leave the house.'

'Only to take Missy and a friend trick-or-treating. We were home by seven. It was a school night. You can check with the Montegnas. I left their daughter at their house shortly before then.' She was answering all the questions crisply and dispassionately, in her best PTA manner.

Dunne reached down to his briefcase. Like his apparel, his accessories were top of the line, and the thin leather envelope with the discreet Longchamps logo seemed more suited to an executive than a cop. He took a sealed evidence bag from it and leaned over, holding it in front of Janice's face.

'Do you recognize this piece of paper?'

Faith did, and for a moment the room whirled around as she recalled where she'd last seen the sheet, but she forced it to stop so she wouldn't miss Janice's reaction — or her answer.

'Why yes, it's a receipt for an order of the wrapping paper we're selling at Winthrop to raise money for the school.' She studied it in detail.

'It's made out to Jared — and that's Missy's name at the bottom.'

Faith knew she was going to piss Dunne

off, but she couldn't help it. 'Janice, maybe you should call your lawyer before talking much more.'

But it was Janice herself who appeared annoyed. 'I don't have anything to hide. What is. this all about? What does the wrapping paper have to do with anything?'

'The receipt was found next to the victim's body, apparently having spilled out from the briefcase he was carrying. Did Missy sell him some wrapping paper? That would explain it,' Charley said kindly. John Dunne and Sully exchanged looks. It was a little more information than they would have given. Actually, a lot more. Small-town cops. You gotta love 'em.

'Not directly, but he must have picked up the form at the church, which was very good of him, although naturally it's invalid now.' Like Paula Pringle's comment about the silent auction after Gwen's death, Janice's revealed a similar mind-set. It must be something about fund-raising that, in the midst of tragedy, still kept those columns of figures firmly in place. Faith vowed to stick to volunteering in the library.

Janice looked about the room with obvious relief. It was all clear now. 'I had Missy sign a bunch of order blanks and we made a little display on the table under the notice board at church. We left the sample book and the forms with a poster she made urging people to support the school.'

Faith remembered seeing it — and thinking how Missy had gotten the jump on all the other First Parish kids who attended Winthrop. It had annoyed her at the time, but apparently it hadn't offended Jared — or he'd needed wrapping paper.

'The table is still there. You can go see for yourself. You've seen it, haven't you, Faith?'

'Yes,' she replied. 'It's to the left of the church office.'

'So anyone coming into the church would be aware of it?' Dunne queried.

'Yes,' Faith said again, thinking of the number of people at Saturday's and Sunday's services who would have walked past on their way to and from the parking lot.

Janice summed it all up nicely. 'So, I really don't see what this has to do with me at all, and I have a very busy morning.'

Faith jumped up — she'd taken the chair nearest the door — and said, 'I'm afraid I have to be getting along, as well.' She nodded to the group in general and her good-bye was lost as she raced to the door and shut it behind her. She had no intention of leaving with the rest of them, letting herself in for, at the very least, a stern reprimand from

Dunne, Charley, or probably both.

She'd walked over to Janice's. It wasn't far, and now she was so intent on what the woman had and hadn't revealed that she almost collided with Patsy, who was coming from the direction of the parsonage. Anyone who thought Aleford wasn't a busy place had only to track her for a few days, Faith reflected.

'You're not home,' Patsy said.

'I know. Let's not go there, though.' The thought of facing the yellow ribbons was suddenly too much. 'How about the Minuteman?'

'Too public. Come to my house.'

Faith agreed. Besides, Charley took his coffee breaks at the Minuteman Café. Even the presence of the state police wouldn't keep him from his blueberry muffins.

'I was planning to call you,' Faith said, feeling slightly guilty. After all, Patsy was her lawyer, and another body had turned up on Faith's watch. This time in her front yard.

'But something came up.' Patsy was smiling broadly as they walked toward her house. She'd been very worried when she'd heard about Jared's death — and the location of the corpse — but she could see that Faith was more like her old self. She unlocked the door and they headed for the kitchen.

'You didn't have breakfast, did you?' It was more like a statement.

Faith shook her head. She'd been too busy trying to get everyone out of the house to do more than drink coffee. Then she'd raced over to Janice's.

Patsy was rummaging around her refrigerator, emerging with eggs, cream, and butter. She reached back in for some cranberry juice and poured Faith a large glass.

'Thank you,' Faith said gratefully. She'd had enough caffeine.

'What we need is some of my grandmother's *pain perdu*. Very stimulating for the brain,' Patsy said as she whisked two eggs and a cup of light cream together with a spoonful of sugar. A lump of butter was melting in a huge cast-iron skillet. Patsy soaked several slices of thick white bread she cut from a loaf on the counter and put them in to brown.

'It smells heavenly and I'm starving,' Faith said.

Patsy flipped the bread and sprinkled the cooked side with cinnamon sugar. *Pain perdu* — lost bread — a New Orleans way to turn old bread into a banquet of French toast.

Faith cut into her portion hungrily. 'You should be the caterer, not me. Or open a restaurant using your family's recipes.'

'I don't want to work that hard. I'd never see Will. Okay, enough small talk. What have you been up to? I told you on Saturday that we had to talk, and we do.'

Faith nodded. 'Of course I didn't kill Jared.'

'It never crossed my mind, but you did find the body, right? That's what everyone's saying.'

'Yes. I found him.' Faith gulped some juice and told Patsy about Halloween and also about her conversation with Sandy Hoffmann at Gwen's funeral. And about the conversations with the mystery writers. And about Janice. Patsy made another round of *pain perdu* while Faith talked and talked.

'So Jared was the target all along and Gwen got the wrong dessert. It's the only thing that makes sense,' Faith concluded.

Patsy used the last bite to mop up the sugar on her plate. 'My, my, we've been a very busy girl, haven't we?' Faith still hadn't told her what was goading her to all this activity — it wasn't simply concern about the business — yet after watching Tom at the memorial service, Patsy now had an idea.

'Tom helping you? Talking to people, too?' she asked in a neutral tone of voice.

Faith answered quickly. 'No — and I don't want him to know I'm doing any of this.' She tried to smile and attempted a lighter tone. 'You know how he is — a big worrywart.' It didn't work. 'He does want me to find out who's behind the rumors about George, though.'

'And you think it's Janice?'

'I'm positive it's Janice, and I would have gotten her to admit it — and agree to tell Tom or Charley — if the police hadn't come barging in the way they did.'

'Never a cop when you want one, always one when you don't,' Patsy said, glad that Faith wasn't being charged with obstruction of justice, tampering with a possible suspect, or any number of other things she'd risked by knowingly going to Mrs Mulholland's before the police had a chance to question the woman.

'Exactly,' Faith said firmly.

'So what's the deal?' Patsy reached for the yellow legal pad never far from her hand. 'If it was Jared, then why? If it was both of them, why?'

'Who? That's the question. Who?'

They talked for another hour, going over every possible suspect and motive. Everyone at the table the night of the fund-raiser and everyone they knew who was in any way connected to the victims.

'We need to find out more about the guy

276

who works at the gallery, Sandy Hoffmann. He could have been blackmailing Gwen about something and she threatened to tell Jared. The story about hearing her fighting with her boss makes a good smoke screen,' Patsy offered.

'I agree, but Gwen had money coming into her account, not going out.'

'Then he was blackmailing Jared.'

Round and round they talked, but it all kept coming back to one person: Nick Gabriel. Who benefits? With his cousin out of the way before his marriage to Gwen Lord, Nick would have stood to be a very wealthy man.

'I'll find out just how solvent Undique is — maybe Sandy Hoffmann is right, maybe not — and you use your not-insubstantial talents to figure out what Gwen might have had on Nick Gabriel. Cheating on his wife?' Patsy suggested.

'He's not married.'

'Okay, then on a jealous lover — and maybe a lover who's got money in the business. And what about the business itself? You know the gallery scene better than I do. What could Nick have been involved in?'

'I know the gallery scene in New York, but I suppose it's not that different here. There's bound to be all sorts of things. A cover for some other activity. Money laundering, for example.' The term always conjured up a clothesline of greenbacks secured with wooden pins, flapping gently in the breeze.

'Certainly a possibility.'

'I have an old friend I can call who knows all about this — been involved in the art world forever, and not just in the city.'

'Good enough. In the meantime, try not to find any more bodies, okay?'

★ ★ ★

There were a bunch of messages on the machine. Most of them from Niki about that night's dinner, urging Faith to stay home. Niki said that she could handle it, with the help of Scott and Tricia Phelan, who often filled in at Have Faith affairs. There was one from Tom, saying he was still tied up, but none from the school, so Ben was fine. She decided to get Amy and pick up Ben, too. This wasn't a time for extended day. She wanted her son home. She checked the messages at work. More from Niki, but happily — and surprisingly — none canceling the job that night. Faith intended to go. She had to. It was the proverbial getting back on the horse. And she had to keep busy. Very busy.

★　★　★

Late in the summer, Jim Morton had called Faith about a surprise birthday party for his wife, Daisy. Ursula Rowe had once told Faith that women with flower names were born either before 1940 or during the sixties, and, as with most of Ursula's pronouncements, Faith had found this to be true. Daisy Morton was turning sixty. Jim was an engineer, MIT '59, and had worked everything out precisely. Daisy and some of her lady friends (Jim's term) would be having lunch and going to the Museum of Fine Arts to see the 'Pharaohs of the Sun' exhibit, getting back to the house at about six. 'It depends on how long they stay at the show — the museum closes at four-forty-five, but we'll all be in position from five-thirty on.' Faith imagined not a few sore backs after all that crouching behind furniture, but it was Jim's plan, down to knowing that the museum closed at 4:45, not 5:00, not 4:30. 'After she comes in, we'll yell, 'Surprise,' and then you can come in with the champagne and some kind of canapés. I leave it to you.' Which was a good thing, because Faith had a strong hunch that, to Jim, canapés meant pimento cream cheese on Ritz crackers. 'Counting us, there'll be fourteen.'

279

Faith had prepared a menu and made some suggestions about flowers. Jim had dropped by the kitchen, approved it all, given her a deposit, and said he'd see her on November 1.

'Why am I so nervous?' Niki complained as the two women drove to the Mortons' house late in the afternoon. Tom had returned home to watch the kids and it was one of those ships-passing-in-the-night things again. 'I left you a note,' Faith had said, brushing his cheek with a kiss and hugging Amy and Ben. After Faith had picked them up, they'd spent a quiet afternoon. Ben took his rest in his parents' big bed, dozing while his mother read 'The Owl and the Pussy-Cat' and other deliberately nonsensical rhymes.

'Because Jim Morton didn't call and we didn't call him. I thought about it, but I couldn't think of a way to put it. 'Are you still sure you want us to cater your wife's birthday dinner? I mean, I have been involved in two murders very recently, one of which was a poisoning.' Something like that.'

'The guy has got to have heard.'

'Not necessarily. The Mortons aren't members of First Parish and they weren't at the Ballou House event. I'm sure Daisy and her friends have been talking of nothing else all day, but even if Jim did hear something about it, he wouldn't connect it to Have Faith. I imagine he's like my dad. They're the same vintage. Even when you tell him a juicy piece of gossip straight to his face, it doesn't register. Jim may have heard something, but his mind is on other matters — like whether Daisy will like the pearl circle pin from Shreve's he got her.'

'You're making that up!' Niki squealed.

'Yes, the circle pin part, not the rest. More likely, he got her something in the shape of the flower. Trust me. I know the man. He's a sweetie.'

They pulled into the driveway, drove to the rear of the house, got out, and rang the bell at the back door. Jim answered right away, rubbing his hands together. 'You're here. Good, good, good. Daisy's going to be so surprised!'

He left them to their work, and by 5:30, they were ready. The table was set — Faith had placed a large centerpiece of Michaelmas daisies mixed with deep purple sedum and soft mauve dahlias on the sideboard, opting for several small vases tightly filled with Mon Cheri roses on the table itself. The Mortons lived in a large brick house on several acres, built by Daisy's family in the early twenties. They'd raised three children here and the long table must have seen many family gatherings. Jim had told Faith proudly that there were three more leaves.

Since she'd worked with Daisy Morton before, Faith knew her taste. Good food, plenty of it, and nothing too fussy. Accordingly, she'd prepared two warm hors d'oeuvres — mushrooms stuffed with toasted walnuts and assorted miniquiches — plus two cold ones — snow peas filled with a lightly smoked salmon cheese spread and caramelized onion with fresh tomato bruschetta. Jim wanted oysters for a first course, and Faith had convinced him to try oysters Rockefeller — that rich combination of spinach, Pernod, and bivalve — instead of raw with cocktail sauce. They briefly went back and forth on the main course, from duck to beef, then duck it was, which Jim knew in his heart his wife would prefer, although he said he'd really liked the filet Faith had made for an earlier dinner with 'those big mushrooms.' As a variation from duck à l'orange, Faith had glazed tonight's *canard* with cassis. She was also serving asparagus, wedges of sautéed polenta, and plenty of rolls to fill in the cracks. After salad, there would be birthday cake, of course, for dessert. Niki had made an old-fashioned layer cake — devil's food with butter cream frosting covered with crystalized sugar daisies. 'Perfect,' Jim said when Niki reverently took the cake from the box.

'Absolutely perfect. Hey, you gals might like to see this.' He reached in his pocket and took out a small velvet-covered box, opening it to reveal a diamond-petaled daisy with a sapphire center. Faith was touched. There was no 'He loves me, he loves me not' going on here. Daisy had told her that the Mortons had been married for forty years, and it looked like they were good for forty more.

The guests who were not part of the luncheon/museum plot had all arrived, and it wasn't long before a car pulled up to the front of the house. Poised in the dining room with the trays of champagne and hors d'oeuvres, Faith could hear Daisy say, 'Good-bye, girls. What a fun day. I'll have to turn sixty more often. Maybe every year from now on!' It had been thoughtful of her husband to plan an outing that meant she'd be suitably dressed for a party and not in her bathrobe, ready for a tray and *The NewsHour with Jim Lehrer*. There were a few giggles, coughs, and sssh's from the next room.

The birthday girl let herself in, car doors slammed behind her, and figures jumped up in front of her, led by Jim, who turned on the lights and yelled, with great enthusiasm, 'Surprise!'

Then Niki and Faith walked in with the food.

The room went dead silent. Daisy opened and closed her mouth, as did several of her friends. One of the men — clueless — said, 'Hey, drinks! Great!' then stopped, bewildered by the empty air surrounding him.

'What's the matter, darling? Are you okay?' Jim asked anxiously. His wife looked at him. Oh, Jim, was written all over her face — and the faces of every woman in the place.

'I'm fine, dear. It was just seeing — I mean, it was just the . . . shock. I think I'll sit down.'

Faith had gone white, then red, and was back to white. She stepped forward with the tray of flutes. 'Champagne?' she asked Daisy.

Daisy started to laugh. 'Might as well, Faith. Might as well.'

★   ★   ★

After that, the party swung into high gear, fueled by plenty of champagne. There was a quality of abandon, risk taking, to it that was unusual for an Aleford event, especially one on a weeknight. The participants could all dine out for months on the experience: 'You actually ate the food!' 'And how did she look?' 'She'd only found the poor fellow that morning!'

Once everyone was seated and the main

284

course served, Faith could stay in the kitchen and let Niki pour wine and water, mostly wine. It wasn't difficult to hear what people were saying, and there were several classic moments, wives not having had an opportunity to brief their spouses.

'Great food. We must get the name of the caterer, Maude. She'd do a bang-up job for Muffy's wedding. Must be booked up pretty far in advance. People probably kill to get her.'

The nervous hilarity increased, and one woman, striving desperately to change the subject, said, 'Doesn't that famous mystery writer Anson Scott live in Aleford? I'm sure I read this someplace. I adore his books, except I can't read them at night.'

Daisy answered, 'He does live here. On the other side of town, but we don't see him much. He keeps to himself, writing all those books, of course. And he travels a great deal, I hear. He looks just like his picture, only more so.'

All the women nodded. The men looked baffled.

'Lived down the hall from me at Eliot House,' a ruddy-faced man with a shock of blond hair turning to silver said, reminiscing. 'An odd character, and we weren't at all surprised the way he turned out.'

The woman who had asked the first question quizzed him excitedly. 'What *was* he like? He's such a mystery man himself, seldom gives interviews.'

'Came to Harvard with a bit of a chip on his shoulder, assumed everyone had gone to prep school. Scholarship student, and I think it bothered him that he didn't have much money. I certainly didn't, either, but there was a lot of it around and some of the fellows liked to make a splash. He didn't get into the club he wanted. I know that was a disappointment. And there was the whole business of his family.'

'What do you mean? What was the matter with his family?'

'It's so long ago. I can't remember exactly, but his mother or grandmother had killed herself when he was a child. Pretty horrible. Ambitious. That I do remember. Made better grades than anyone in the house and was writing even then. The same sort of things — like Poe. He kept a statue of the raven in his room and used to wear a cape. Big man, even then. Comes to reunions, of course, and now there's a scholarship named for him. Life's funny. Suppose there's some more of this duck?'

Faith hastily refilled the serving platter and Niki took it out. Then she sat at the Mortons' kitchen table, lost in thought. Anson Scott's early life had been melodramatic. She imagined him at Harvard's elite Eliot House, watching his wealthy classmates breeze through life while he had to watch every penny. What kind of effect does this have on someone? she wondered. This and the loss of his mother or grandmother? Perhaps his grandmother was the one who'd been in service at Ballou House. Obviously, Scott's parents hadn't made much money either, but had produced a brilliant, and ambitious, boy. His ambitions had been realized. Anson Scott was an extremely wealthy man. Private to the point of reclusiveness, yet he went to reunions. Went to reunions to show them what he'd become. But she was willing to bet he still wasn't in the club.

She'd seen the raven statuette on one of the shelves in his library. Poe had been his inspiration, and in some ways Scott had outdone his mentor in manipulating the reader, creating real fears, psychological horror. Being entombed alive, mistaken for dead and buried — like Poe, Scott regularly used this theme. Faith shuddered. There was no mistake about Jared — or Gwen.

After Gwen's funeral, Faith had tried to get in touch with Paula Pringle to find out who had written the mystery play used at Ballou

House, but she had continually gotten Paula's machine, then not even that. Paula must be away and the machine had filled up was Faith's conclusion. Paula might have written the play herself. She could, or thought she could, do everything else. It was doubtful that any of the mystery-writer guests would have participated, unless paid — as they should be — and Faith thought she would have heard about this at one of the committee meetings. The most likely thing was that Paula had bought a kit.

'Strange,' she said to Niki, who was returning with the empty platter. 'Part of the plot of the mystery game sounds like Anson Scott's life.'

'And parts of a million other people's. I read the thing between courses and it was boilerplate.' She put the cake on a cake plate. 'No fears about strychnine in this bunch. Forget about a lot of leftovers for your hubby.'

Her hubby. Home watching the game. Basketball, football, hockey, whatever. Faith was never sure of the seasons. They seemed to go on simultaneously and forever. Her hubby. She'd found a dead body this morning and had scarcely seen Tom since. She had the distinct feeling that she'd somehow let him down. That by involving herself in finding out about Gwen's death, she'd somehow brought Jared's literally to their doorstep. She shook her head. She was being absurd.

'Open the door,' Niki commanded, 'turn out the lights, and start singing.'

10

Faith was feeling distinctly at loose ends. Despite the accolades the night before, no one had asked for cards and there were no messages of any kind on the machine at work. She'd told Tom at breakfast that they had to face the very real possibility that she'd have to close the business. She could easily afford the rent for some months, but there was Niki's salary to consider — and, more important, Niki's reputation. She was just starting her career. Faith didn't want to jeopardize her assistant's chances. Tom had been sympathetic, but he told her he thought she was being too hasty. He'd been waiting up for her the previous night, with cognac already poured. They'd talked about Jared. About the loss. About the shock of it all. 'I don't know where I am anymore, Faith,' Tom had said at one point. 'And I certainly don't know where I'm going.' She had tried to get him to be more specific. But after that brief declaration, he'd taken her in his arms for what she supposed and hoped was a declaration of another sort. Now in the clear light of day, it was his words that came back to haunt her. Tom, who had always been so sure of what he wanted, from his vocation to the woman he'd married, was sailing on uncharted waters. It terrified her.

She wandered over to the Millers'. Ursula and Pix were sitting at the kitchen table, making pinecone wreaths.

'Faith, dear, how lovely to see you!' Ursula exclaimed. 'Pull up a chair and help. We're making these for the fair.'

Faith had forgotten all about First Parish's Holly Bazaar, the Ladies' Auxiliary's big moneymaker, in mid-November. She had promised baked goods and several baskets of Have Faith's preserves.

'I'm not sure I'm good at this sort of thing,' Faith said dubiously, eyeing the cones, wreath forms, glue guns, and other strange items adorning the table. Crafts of all sorts were second nature to the Rowes, as were bird counts, fern identification, and the ability to get amaryllis bulbs to bloom again.

'You don't have to do a thing.' Pix gave her mother a reproving look. Faith had been through enough lately. 'Just sit with us.' Pix had, of course, been over the day before. As soon as she saw the police leave, she'd arrived with a casserole that Faith hadn't the heart to refuse, and she'd called several times since.

'Nonsense,' Ursula said. 'She can talk while she works. You can sort the cones for us by size.' Mrs Rowe was of the school that believed activity was the cure for all ills.

Faith thought she could do this and started to make piles.

'We voted at the last meeting to donate the proceeds from this year's fair to the Anniversary Campaign, but there was a fair amount of discussion and dissent. Everybody's tired of all the wrangling over what it should be used for — the steeple or the crypt — and I'm sorry the church got into this mess in the first place,' Ursula declared.

'What do you think the money should be used for?' Faith asked. The whole campaign had slipped to the back of her mind recently.

'The crypt just like your husband. Oh, you don't have to say a word. I know what Tom thinks. He's mentioned holding services there often enough, and in any case, it's shocking. The wiring is old and we have no idea what's down there besides boxes of hymnals with pages missing that no one wanted to get rid of.'

'Maybe we'll find a valuable painting, like the Episcopalians in West Newbury. A del Sarto in the closet where the minister hangs his coat. The congregation thought it was ugly and took it down from the choir stall twenty years ago, and there it's been sitting ever since. It sold at one of the auction houses for over a million dollars,' Pix said.

'I don't think we have any del Sartos or anything remotely resembling one in our closets.' Faith had made a thorough exploration of the church as a new bride. Even the crypt. Old hymnals, broken chairs, and stones marking the graves were all she remembered seeing, in addition to a superabundance of spiderwebs. 'Besides, there's some question about the painting being solely the work of del Sarto. It was in the *Times*. Apparently, the auction house knew there was some question about its authenticity, but that wasn't noted in the catalog and not widely known until after the sale. The buyers knew and took their chances.'

'But they may have gotten a fake. A very expensive fake.'

'True, but despite the doubts, the purchasers are insisting they bought the genuine article.'

'I'm surprised at the auction house,' Pix continued, fiercely firing her glue gun. 'There should have been fair warning — 'as is.''

Her mother looked at her. 'From what I've read, the art world is not above such things — and you know very well that unless you go to the preview, you can end up with a pig in a poke even when they give 'fair warning.''

Ursula's words echoed in Faith's head:

'The art world is not above such things.' Bingo. She should have thought of all this sooner. Much sooner. What could Gwen most obviously have had on her employer, a smart girl, well versed in art history, situated right there in the gallery? Selling fake or stolen goods. Thereafter, she either received a cut or was paid to keep her opinions to herself.

'Did you know the Gabriels?' she asked Ursula. 'Millicent told me that Jared's grandparents had a summer house here and that he and Nick used to come when they were little boys.'

'Yes, I knew them well. They were members of King's Chapel, but they attended First Parish when they were in Aleford and were very generous to the church. Even before poor Jared, it's been a family filled with tragedy. You know how his parents went, so close together and neither of them even sixty. His mother, Lucy, never was very strong. They were terribly proud of their son, but I know they wanted a bigger family. It didn't happen and she used to suffer from depression. They should have adopted — Lucy really adored children. Nicholas had always been like a brother to Jared — a good brother — and that helped. He spent a great deal of time with them, because his parents were divorced and his mother lived in Europe. His

294

father tried his best, but he had to work, and of course Nicholas couldn't go running off to Europe, even if his mother had wanted him around, which was not the impression I received. I don't know why his father didn't remarry. Men generally do.'

It was such a typically Ursula thing to say, coming at the end of the story, that Faith couldn't help laughing. She was doing a good job with the pinecones, and if not light at the end of the tunnel, there was now a glimmer. It was horrible to think about, but she was beginning to believe that Nick had murdered Gwen to shut her up once and for all; then somehow Jared must have figured it out and Nick had to kill him, too.

'It's true, Nick and Jared seemed very close,' Faith observed, hoping to hear what more Ursula might say.

'I think they were — although they had completely different personalities. Jared was quiet. I used to think he was always hearing music and preferred listening to what was in his mind than talking much. Nick is very outgoing — and, from what I understand, a very capable businessman. I never thought of him as an art lover. But if that's where the money is these days, that's where he'd be.'

'Nick Gabriel wasn't the kind of little boy who simply had a lemonade stand but would franchise,' Pix interjected.

Ursula nodded in agreement and held up a completed wreath.

'Now, Faith, I'm going to start the next one and you can follow me step by step.'

'Truly, there's nothing I would enjoy more,' Faith lied, 'but I have to get to the market before I pick Amy up.'

'That's all right. Another time.' Ursula was not going to let her off. 'By the way, I understand Daisy Morton got quite a surprise last night.'

'And lived to tell the tale,' Faith said, only half-jokingly.

Ursula, who was not a demonstrative woman, got up and patted Faith on the shoulder. 'People will come around. They don't have much experience with things like this, so they've pulled back. Like a turtle in its shell. We're like that around here, you know. It's a blessing and a curse, depending on the circumstances.'

Faith sincerely hoped this was a time Ursula viewed New England self-protectiveness as a curse, and her next words were reassuring.

'I'm thinking of giving a little party myself, a kind of preholiday get-together. I'll call you with the date. You'll see. Before too long, you'll have more business than you want. When people realize they might have to cook and clean up themselves for their holiday parties, they'll be engaging you.'

It was terribly kind — and terribly wrong. Whom they would be engaging would be other caterers, but Faith appreciated Ursula's vote of confidence and dared to give her a quick hug.

At the door, she turned and said to Pix, 'I almost forgot — what does one wear to a PTA meeting? It's tonight.'

'Something inconspicuous,' Pix answered.

*　*　*

'Sorry, I don't have time to talk. This all sounds delightfully complicated. You just caught me. Someday, I really will leave the apartment and let the phone keep ringing, I keep telling myself. I have a machine, after all. But I don't because it might be someone like you, for instance. Anyway, come see me. Much more fun to talk in person. I'll take you to lunch wherever you want; then we can catch the Eames show at the Cooper-Hewitt.'

'I don't think I can get away. No, it's impossible.'

'Nonsense. You've done it before. Take the early shuttle. But now I must run. Thursday's best for me. Call me when you decide.'

Faith was struck by a powerful longing to go home if only for a few hours. It was like a thunderbolt, what the French call a *coup de foudre*. New York. Autumn in New York. She almost hummed a few bars of the song, smelling the chestnuts street vendors used to roast before the mayor closed them down. She could go to the Chelsea Market. She could go to Barneys. She couldn't go.

She'd go.

'Yes. I mean, I'll come. Where should I meet you?'

'Good girl. Christer's at noon. On West Fifty-fifth. They have a lovely little fireplace and the food is splendid. Scandinavian, but not a boiled potato in sight, or if so, disguised. And I'll do a little investigating about your Undique Gallery. I've heard the name, but I can't remember in what context. See you Thursday, and do try not to turn up any more stiffs in the meantime.'

Faith hung up, wishing that people would stop saying that and wishing even more to comply with their request. Thursday. The day after tomorrow. It was only lunch. Nothing more. Yes, it did involve a plane trip. But it was only lunch.

★   ★   ★

PTA night. She was overdressed. Her tapered black wool pants and soft gray cashmere twin

298

set — clothes she had imagined would blend in with the crowd — stood out among the denim skirts and Dockers chinos like a Bob Mackie frock at a Sunday school picnic. She put her jacket back on, a fawn-colored suede from Paul Stuart. It helped a little, but not much. After every eye in the room trained an X-ray beam on her, the group turned their attention back to the secretary. Janice Mulholland was reading the minutes. She looked bad again — haggard and even thinner. Faith could tell the woman would kill for a cigarette. Janice's hand started to shake and she put the report down on the podium.

Since this was her maiden voyage, Faith had no idea whether tonight's standing-room-only crowd represented the norm or if the turnout was due to the rumors about the principal. There were many more women than men, yet that was to be expected. She wished she hadn't urged Tom to stay home with the kids and get some rest himself. She would have liked company. Arlene MacLean, Ben's friend Lizzie's mom, was seated a few rows ahead and there were some other familiar faces, but no one nearby. She tried to concentrate on what Janice was reading, but it was pretty dull stuff. Apparently, the hot topic at last month's meeting had been Macs versus PCs for the library. Uniformity — the school already had Macs — or diversity. She wasn't the only person not paying attention. There was a low buzz of conversation throughout the room — and not a happy buzz. There was a somber, even sad, look on many faces. George and several teachers, including Julie Black, were in the front row. Faith couldn't see how they looked, but she could guess. Resolute? Resigned? Surely the accusations wouldn't come up tonight. This was a PTA meeting, a place where parents talked about what to do with the cash they raised for the school. A place where invited speakers attempted to decode current educational practices. A place where parents received reassurance that they had done the best-possible thing for their children by assuming mortgages they couldn't afford in order to live in a town with good schools.

They were meeting in the school cafeteria. The tables had been folded up and stacked against the walls, their places taken up by rows of folding chairs. The walls were covered with murals celebrating good table manners, balanced diets, and dental hygiene. A faint odor of macaroni and cheese hung in the air.

'Thank you, Madam Secretary,' the president said. 'All those in favor of accepting the minutes as read, please signify by saying 'aye.''

There was a chorus of ayes.

'All those saying 'nay.''

There was dead silence.

'Hearing none, the minutes are accepted as read. Now, next on the agenda is the treasurer's report.'

Faith was surprised by the size of the PTA coffers — and, as the treasurer pointed out, the current total did not include sales figures for the wrapping paper, since the drive was still going on.

The report was accepted, and the president, a tall, efficient-looking woman with a mop of totally unruly curls, mentioned for the record that special thanks were due to Janice Mulholland for donating her time and talents. Everyone clapped. Everybody seemed to know what Janice had done, apart from what she normally did for the school, which was almost everything. Janice managed a thin-lipped smile and nodded her head graciously at the group.

'What was this for?' Faith asked the woman sitting next to her, who was knitting an incredibly complicated sweater that seemed to involve several dozen different needles and colors of yarn.

'It was in the minutes, but you may have missed it. Janice has volunteered to cover school events for the town paper and for our own Winthrop archives. She's a gifted photographer and has a dark-room of her own at her house. When you leave, look at the pictures of our Halloween parade outside the main office. They're hers.'

Faith thought for sure she would have tuned in if Janice's name had come up during the reading of the minutes, but perhaps not. She had a lot on her mind these days. So Janice Mulholland had a dark-room at home . . .

The meeting moved on at its own petty pace. Tempers flared a bit during a vote on whether to petition the superintendent to increase the size and scope of Winthrop's gifted-and-talented program, but the president handled it by tabling discussion until the next meeting, at which time a study group would report back. Hands were quickly raised and waved: Pick me! Pick me! It really was elementary school. After the names of the volunteers were taken, the meeting proceeded.

Faith was beginning to get sleepy and wished she could believe the coffee urn, which had been a frequent destination all evening, along with the boxes of Munchkins beside it, contained something resembling a decent brew.

Why had she come? To make an appearance. To get to know the terrain. Yes, but also because she thought she'd pick up something about George — vibrations. She'd been calling Janice all day to continue yesterday's conversation and there had been no answer, even after school, when presumably Missy would be there practicing her perfect pitch or working on her soon-to-be bestselling novel. This time, she wanted to talk to Janice with no interruptions — and march her off to Tom or Charley, even George. She would make the woman admit what she had done . . . She jerked her head up. George was approaching the podium.

He looked out at the parents and a hush descended on the room. The woman next to Faith shoved her knitting in a bag at her feet and folded her hands in her lap.

George smiled. It wasn't a happy smile. It wasn't a sad smile. Just a smile. And Faith felt her heart would burst.

'I don't think I have to tell you how much I love this school. You do, too. And it's because of what we share that I've decided to come and talk to you tonight. Trust is an essential ingredient in both raising and educating children and now — '

The ear-splitting siren from the fire alarm pulsated throughout the room. People jumped up, overturning chairs. Above it all, George's calm voice urged everyone to exit from the rear doors of the cafeteria and go to the far end of the playground. Obediently, the parents filed out. Most had remembered to grab their coats, but some soon stood shivering outside. Quite a few simply went to their cars and left. It seemed only a matter of seconds before the fire trucks, ambulance, and police arrived. The revolving red and blue lights intensified the drama of the scene.

A man's voice cut through the night air. 'It can't be a coincidence. You know there's no fire. He was going to confess and resign.'

'Confess what? That's what I'd like to know!' a woman declared angrily. 'All we've heard has been a bunch of filthy rumors. I went to Winthrop when I was in elementary school and now my third child is here. No one's going to convince me that George Hammond is anything but the finest principal in the state of Massachusetts — no, make that the world.' Loud applause greeted her statement, but the man who had spoken walked away with a group of parents to the other side of the swings, staking out turf. Faith suspected that George hadn't been about to confess to anything, yet she was pretty sure he had been about to resign. Now he was with the fire department, taking care of his school. She was glad someone had pulled the alarm. She would have done it herself if she'd thought of it.

There was no time to waste. She had to get Janice to make some kind of statement. Anything to keep George from finishing his remarks. She should have camped out on the woman's doorstep, but Faith had assumed George would tell her and Tom what he was going to do. Maybe it had been a spur-of-the-moment thing. Maybe he'd decided while listening to the minutes. She looked around. The playground was lighted at night to prevent vandalism — it was bright enough to recognize people. And Janice was nowhere in sight.

There was only one thing to do. Go to the woman's house again. And yes, Faith rehearsed, I do know it's a school night.

★ ★ ★

Janice was not glad to see her. She did not invite Faith in. She did not offer coffee. She did not offer anything. She simply stood in her doorway and said, 'Now what is it?'

Faith stepped forward. She felt like an encyclopedia salesman. Janice was forced to move back into the house and Faith was in. She closed the door behind her.

'Well?' Janice folded her arms across her chest. As far as body language went, it was not a good sign. Faith kept her arms at her sides, neutral.

'Janice. We need to finish talking. I'm sure you know that George was probably going to resign tonight. This has gotten way out of control and you seem to be the only person who can do anything to stop this tragic mistake. A mistake that will hurt all our children and the entire community!'

Janice spun around and opened the drawer in her coffee table, fumbling with the pack of cigarettes. As she lighted one, she spoke in angry staccatos. 'It's not enough that I have the police here night and day about Jared Gabriel. And searching my darkroom in the basement. So I take pictures. What's wrong with that? Plenty of people have darkrooms. And you could walk into any house in town and find dangerous chemicals. Then you and this George Hammond thing! What the hell do you people want?' She tapped out some ash. 'Look, get this straight once and for all. George Hammond is not fit to be the principal of our elementary school. Yes, I made those calls. Happy now? As a parent, I have a right and an obligation to complain.'

'But not to make false accusations. If you would only tell the police that you made the calls,' Faith begged. 'That you were stressed about what you thought was going on at school. That you got too emotional. We all know how much you care about your daughter. Sometimes our caring can get in the way — '

Janice had slumped over while Faith was talking, convincing Faith that she was taking the right tack. Except Janice was merely gathering strength.

'You don't know anything about my daughter or what she said, and you don't know what you're talking about!' she screamed.

What her daughter said. It was Missy, Faith realized dully. Not Janice making the accusations, but Missy.

'Did Missy tell you that something had happened at school?' Faith kept her voice low and steady. She was sure the child herself couldn't be sleeping through all this, and she had to get Janice to calm down. Oh God, if Missy had come home and told Janice that the principal had done something to her, no wonder the woman had gone off the deep end. Had the child somehow misinterpreted a gesture on George's part? Without leave and certainly unwelcome, Faith sank into one of Janice's plaid-covered club chairs. It was too much to take in.

'What are you talking about? What's Mrs Fairchild doing here?' It was Missy, awakened, as Faith had feared, and now standing in the doorway, staring straight at her mother. She was a pretty little girl, tall for her age, with straight light brown hair touching her shoulders and large dark brown eyes. Intelligent eyes. Sleepless eyes.

'It's nothing, darling. You go back to bed. Tomorrow's a school day.'

'It's not nothing. I heard you.'

'Go to bed, Missy. This has nothing to do with you.' Janice raised her voice and spoke tersely, but Missy stood her ground, clad in a long-sleeved nightgown with a teddy bear on the front.

'She's always asking me things. She won't stop. Every day when I come home from school or from church after choir rehearsals or from anywhere.' Missy was talking to Faith. 'She always has to know everything.'

'Go to bed immediately, young lady, or you will lose your privileges!'

Missy walked over to Faith. 'I heard you talking to my mother.' There was a pleading tone in her voice.

'Missy, did Mr Hammond — your principal — ever do anything to you or someone you know that made you feel uncomfortable?' Faith didn't know how to phrase the question, but she wanted to get it said before Janice exploded. Missy had gone through Safe Children training at school, so she helped Faith out.

'You mean like bad touching and then

maybe saying to keep it a secret?'

'Yes. Did that ever happen?'

Missy looked at her mother. 'No,' she whispered.

'That's not what you said and you know it! Mrs Fairchild is trying to trick you. She's a friend of the principal's. Don't listen to her!' She ran over and grabbed Missy, pulling her close to her body, as if both she and Missy were shields. Missy arched her back away from her mother.

'She kept asking me all the time. Saying not to be afraid to say something about Mr Hammond or Mr Gabriel. She just wouldn't stop.'

'But nothing ever happened, did it? With either of them?' Faith asked again.

Missy shook her head.

'Get out of my house right now! Do you hear me. I don't care who you are, damn you! Get out of my house!'

Faith left.

★ ★ ★

Janice Mulholland was taken to state police headquarters the next morning for questioning — with her lawyer. Faith had been in an agony of despair after she left the woman's home, but there had been no question about what to do. Tom sat with her when John Dunne and Charley arrived together to hear what Faith had to say.

Afterward, Dunne said, 'We got an anonymous tip that she had a darkroom in her basement — that wasn't you, was it? — and she was considerably more rattled when we went back this morning than she had been yesterday. Made several contradictions.'

'I never called — and if I had, it wouldn't have been anonymously. I only found out about the darkroom tonight at the PTA meeting.'

Dunne raised his brows, creating a truly horrific effect. 'This is what they were talking about at the PTA?'

'Sort of. She's photographing school events and they gave her a round of applause. I hadn't actually taken it in, but the woman next to me explained.'

'That's how I feel at those things,' Dunne remarked.

The notion of John Dunne at a PTA meeting was more than Faith could cope with and she filed it away to consider at another time. Dunne at a school picnic. Dunne at Parents' Night in those little chairs.

'I feel partially responsible,' Tom said. 'I didn't realize how much her husband's desertion had unhinged her. I even thought it was a good thing that she had a child to focus on, someone to bring her out of herself and her depression. She came for counseling a few times, then said she'd come when she needed it. Unfortunately, she didn't — and I didn't follow up.' His admission hung in the air.

Faith hated to see him beat up on himself. 'I don't think pastoral counseling would have helped. Janice needed, and needs, psychological help. She sees danger for Missy — and by extension, herself — everywhere. I think she's really convinced that Missy was abused in some way and that George was responsible.'

'Psych One oh one — or you've been reading those women's magazines,' Dunne said, 'but I happen to agree. She may also have convinced herself that Jared Gabriel was a sexual threat to her child. Somehow, Gwen Lord got his dessert instead — the one with the cyanide from Mulholland's darkroom. Then on Sunday night, Janice finished what she started out to do. The wound was precise and made by someone with a knowledge of anatomy. She was in medical school, remember.' He sounded satisfied. The Aleford pieces were coming together. It was all a little wacky, but they fit. He decided to thank Faith.

'I admit I wasn't happy to see you yesterday, but the way things have worked out, I have to thank you. It would have taken us a lot longer.'

Why didn't she feel better? Faith wondered. John almost never gave her the slightest crumb of acknowledgment, let alone thanks.

'Are you going to arrest her tomorrow?' she asked.

'Early days. We're certainly going to question her, and she's admitted to you that she made those phone calls, so I imagine George Hammond will press charges,' Dunne answered cautiously.

They left and the Fairchilds went to bed.

'Who do you think pulled the fire alarm?' Tom asked sleepily.

Faith felt a little smug. 'That's easy. I knew right away, but everything I tell you is confidential, right? You being a reverend and all. You can't tell another living soul.'

Tom pulled her closer. 'Your secret is safe with me.'

'Our own Mrs Black, of course. Who else?'

But hearing for sure that Janice had been taken in for questioning and that the town had now mustered full force in George Hammond's defense did not provide Faith with the peace — or, to use the current nomenclature, 'closure' — she was seeking. There were too many loose ends.

For one thing, there was Tom.

She was startled to see him come through the back door into the kitchen late in the morning. She was on the phone with Pix, who was passing on Aleford's reaction to the news that Janice Mulholland had started the rumors about George and might be involved in the two recent murders.

'How on earth could people have found out about this so soon? Does Millicent have microphones in all our walls?' Faith asked.

'She certainly learns a lot simply by looking out her window, and she wasn't the only one who saw Charley's car at your house last night. And John Dunne has a pretty distinctive silhouette. Remember, Millicent knows him from the time you rang the bell at the old belfry.'

'As if I'd forget — or she'd ever let me.'

'But it's true — this is swift even for us. The culprit is none other than Janice herself. She called Helen Henry, the PTA president, after you left last night and resigned as secretary. Apparently, she was pretty incoherent, but Helen pieced the story together. Plus, there are only two lawyers in town, and one of them pulled up to Janice's house this morning after Missy left for school.'

'We should have had the whole town in on the case from the beginning.'

'In a way, they always are,' Pix said.

But here was Tom, standing in the kitchen. Faith said good-bye to Pix and hung up the phone.

'Is everything okay?' she asked.

'I was having trouble concentrating. God only knows why,' Tom said sarcastically.

'Sit down and I'll get you something to eat,' Faith offered.

Tom shook his head. 'I don't have time and I'm not hungry.'

There it was again. The man was wasting away.

'Do you think Janice killed Gwen and Jared?' Tom asked. 'I've been turning it over and over in my mind ever since last night. It makes sense. People get pushed to extreme limits when they think their children are in jeopardy.' He ran his hand through his hair, causing a tuft to stick straight up in the back. Faith smoothed it down.

'No, it doesn't feel right to me, yet I don't know who else to suspect.' She did, but Tom had recently spent a great deal of quality time with Nick Gabriel, and she didn't want an explosion like the one that had greeted her suggestion of Gwen as a possible suicide. She continued speaking. 'Janice has certainly not been behaving normally — the phone calls — and she had ready access to cyanide. She was on the scene. And I've been convinced from the beginning that it had to be someone who was right there at the table. Too chancy otherwise. But there's simply no motive. That's been the problem with all this from the beginning. No rhyme nor reason. At the moment, Janice is the most likely suspect. Gwen must have switched desserts with Jared. I do that all the time with you.'

'You do?'

'Except if it's something I really, really like. And even then, I might. It's a female thing.'

'I never noticed.'

'You aren't meant to — and Jared wouldn't have, either, or anybody else at the table. Maybe Paula, and when she comes back, I'll ask her. But you'd have to have seen Janice last night and heard the way she's been talking. Jared was keeping her daughter from a singing career, and she may have believed he was molesting her. The same with George.'

'But she didn't kill George.'

'No, she was going to let the community do that.'

'Maybe she'll confess. I ought to see her, in any case.'

'Yes, you should go see her. She needs you.

And maybe she has confessed already.'

She looked at Tom and saw her own doubt reflected in his eyes.

'Or maybe not.'

★ ★ ★

Faith wasn't quite sure why she didn't tell Tom she was going to New York City for lunch. It wasn't as if she was keeping it a big secret. She told Pix, but then Pix was going to keep the kids until Faith got back late in the afternoon. Thursday was the day Tom spent at the VA hospital and he never got home until after six. She'd be home by then, and if it came up in the conversation, then it would come up.

As soon as everyone left the house, she drove to Logan, listening to the BBC *News Hour* on WBUR with deliberation, eager to keep all other thoughts out of her mind.

At 10:30, she was landing at La Guardia. She hopped in a cab and had almost a whole hour at Bergdorf's before she walked over to the restaurant. It felt more like spring than fall — sunny, breezy, and warm enough to make her wish she'd worn lighter clothes.

Andy was waiting.

He kissed her on both cheeks and took her coat, handing it to the woman in the checkroom. 'Always a sight for sore eyes. Come, let's eat, and you can tell me all about it.'

Faith had lingered a little longer over her toilette this morning and she was aware that the Jill Sander wool skirt and soft ivory silk blouse she'd picked were both flattering and up to New York City standards. She tucked a strand of her honey-colored hair behind her ear. Impulsively, she'd just purchased new earrings at Bergdorf's — deep turquoise enamel disks edged in gold.

Andy. Andy, Andy. They'd met in high school, dated long enough to discover they'd never be in love, and had stayed friends. He was a few years older than she was and had spent some years in Europe before returning to the States to open a gallery in SoHo. He came by it naturally. His mother was an art critic and his father had a gallery on Madison. His brother was a painter and his sister sculpted wood. Faith usually saw Andy whenever she was in the city, but he had only met Tom at the wedding. Andy never traveled to Boston. 'Not really a destination, do you think?' he'd commented when she'd told him of her impending move and marriage. And on Tom's infrequent forays into the city, somehow there was never an occasion to see Andy. Faith knew herself well enough to admit that she liked it this way. The two men had little in common and it was so much more pleasant when worlds did not collide. Andy was the past — the life she'd had growing up and as a single woman in the Big Apple. The life she'd given up.

One of the things about Andy she'd always treasured was his disregard for conventions. He wasn't rude — or mean — but he cut to the chase. The fact that he didn't ask about her children — or her husband — didn't mean he didn't care, but he knew that wasn't why she was there, and so did she.

Faith gave him a quick rundown of the events in Aleford, which did cause him to say she'd be much better off moving back to the city, safer by far. It took them through their appetizers. Andy had the smorgasbord — tastes of herring, gravlax, and other Nordic delicacies beautifully arranged on a large glass plate. Faith was more than happy with her autumnal choice — mushroom soup with chestnut dumplings. They were seated by the fire, which was crackling merrily in the tall stone fireplace, and it was easy to imagine that they would be stepping out of the Scandinavian Adirondack interior into a pine forest rather than into New York traffic. New York traffic. Faith took a sip of the white Burgundy Andy had ordered — a 1997

Pouilly-Fuissé Champsroux. She heard a very faint horn. New York traffic was lovely. There was so much of it. Just like New York people. You were anonymous here. She could walk from one tip of the island to the other and not see a single soul she knew, unlike Aleford, where she couldn't take prints to be developed at Aleford Photo without passing half a dozen familiar faces. She felt suspended in time. A plane had plucked her from her everyday life and, for a brief moment, dropped her into another one altogether. It was exhilarating to know that the Fendi bag she was carrying did not contain a single crayon or granola bar.

'So, you don't think the loony mom did it?' Andy asked.

'She might have, but murders are usually about gain, aren't they? Tangible things, like money, or intangibles, like revenge.'

Their conversation was reminding her of the ones she'd had with the mystery writers.

'I don't know that there is a formula, yet that has always been my impression, yes. If I were to kill, it would most assuredly have to be for something. This *is* what you're implying?'

Faith laughed. 'Yes, and doing it badly. It's just that Janice's 'something' doesn't seem as clear-cut as Nick Gabriel's.'

'I agree. And, by the way, I have found out a bit about your boy, although I don't know how useful it is. Seems to have been successful almost from the beginning. He hit a snag over the John Drewe business, but so did a lot of other people — very reputable people.'

'I don't know about this. What was the John Drewe business?'

'Forgery. Fakes. But with a provenance. Ah, our salmon is here. You'll like this.' Andy actually rubbed his hands together and did so without looking affected.

The waiter cautioned them about the heat and set steaming oak boards with their planked salmon in front of them. The smell of the fish, wood, and accompanying sweet potatoes with bacon and warm vegetable slaw was so delectable that Faith momentarily lost her concentration and became a foodie, pure and simple. After a mouthful confirming the evidence of her senses, she was back.

'How was Nick involved?'

'First of all, Nick Gabriel was not directly involved — or not that I know of. What he did was buy some prints that later turned out not to be by Giacometti and others as signed, but by some poor sap working away in the English countryside who couldn't make it as an artist under his own name but who turned out to be quite good at doing it under someone else's. Drewe was the mastermind, though.'

Faith realized she was eating too quickly. She wanted to savor her food.

'This is fascinating. Even if it doesn't have anything to do with Nick.'

'I didn't say that.' Andy smiled. He had gone silver-gray very early, when he was in college, and instead of making him look older, it had the reverse effect. He was wearing a royal blue collarless shirt and a dark chocolate brown suit. It went well with the decor of the room, and Faith was sure that was no accident.

'Anyway, the difference in this art scheme, as opposed to others throughout the ages, was Drewe's diabolical faking of provenances. He cannibalized catalogs in the Victoria and Albert, the Tate, and other places, inserting his fakes and thus created detailed 'verifiable' records of ownership. You know, with all this new technology, the wonder is that someone didn't beat him to it — duplicating fonts, changing dates, then making photocopies that look like originals. He'd take a catalog apart, insert his information — owners who never existed and so forth — then stitch the binding back together, return it, and, voilà, he now had a genuine Ben Nicholson. It's a terrific mess. This all broke over three years ago and it will be many years before the records are cleaned up — if ever. And many of his wares will float around on the market for the rest of time — fake Braques, Matisses, Dubuffets.'

Faith had cleaned her plate and now took a sip of wine. She was thinking about the conversations Sandy Hoffmann had reported. Gwen would have known all about the fakes. The news would have broken when she first started working at the gallery. What if more had come Undique's way from other sources? What if Nick Gabriel was still making some of his tidy profits from selling false merchandise to his customers?

She thought of a problem. 'But you couldn't sell fakes without the provenance scheme, so it would be hard to sell a fake now, right? Isn't that what you're saying?'

'Lord no! The figure generally quoted is that ten to forty percent of art currently being offered for sale is phony — or so over-restored, it amounts to the same thing. There are all sorts of ways to fake artwork. An artist can even forge himself. Over the course of many years, Dalí signed thousands of blank sheets of paper, which were then used for what were reproductions, not actual prints. While the signature was genuine, the prints weren't. The market was flooded with these.'

Andy was warming to the subject. The waiter cleared, crumbed, and asked if they cared for dessert and coffee.

'Of course we do. Both. Have the apple leaf, Faith. It's served warm with vanilla ice cream and caramel. I'll have the lingonberry sorbet — and lots of those good little cookies you make.'

Faith sighed. She couldn't remember the last time she'd had a meal this good that she hadn't had to cook herself. Rialto in Cambridge last summer with Tom. Jody Adams had done something fabulous with lobster.

'I'm sure cavemen were forging the drawings of the Mastodon Master or whomever in their caves. It's an art as old as Art. Roman practitioners used to churn out lovely pieces by Phidias and Praxiteles — Greeks. More recently, one of my personal favorites is Eric Hebborn, who successfully copied Corot, Augustus John, as well as old masters, and wrote a very entertaining memoir called *Drawn to Trouble*. It's his assertion that there is no such thing as fake art, only false labeling, and it's a point well taken. At his trial for forgery in the late forties, Hans van Meegeren spoke about one of his 'Vermeers,' noting that one day the painting was worth millions of guilders and experts and art lovers came in droves to see it. The next, it was worth nothing and nobody came. Yet the picture hadn't changed. 'What had?' he asked the court.'

Faith made a note to get Hebborn's book. 'We hang reproductions on our walls. I suppose hanging an original Corot by Eric Hebborn is no different, so long as Hebborn's name is on it, too. But no one would buy that piece of art at Corot prices.'

'Exactly. And now, try this on. Your Gwendolyn Lord may have been one of those individuals with an eye. That is a rather rare ability to distinguish between something fine and something ordinary, whether it be a painting, a garment, or a piece of furniture. It also means the individual is adept at spotting fakes. He or she has a sort of internal alarm system that goes off in the presence of a fraud. They know something's wrong. Bernard Berenson had it. He would actually feel an unpleasant sensation in his stomach. Or get slightly dizzy. Say Gwen spots the fake or fakes, confronts Nick, and is persuaded to keep her mouth shut. Then he gets tired of paying out and it's good-bye. His cousin finds out, so he has to go, too.'

This was roughly the scenario Faith had been running through her mind. 'She was trying to get together enough capital to start

324

her own gallery, and she left a surprisingly large estate.'

Andy nodded and took another cookie. 'It might not be so hard to be convinced to keep quiet, money or no. Anyone working in a gallery knows that even when fakes are unmasked, often the buyers refuse to admit they've been duped. They don't want to hear about it — this goes for individuals as well as institutions. I say it's a Picasso and it's a Picasso. Particularly when a large sum of money has been involved.'

'And according to Hebborn, it's simply a Picasso with a misattribution.'

Andy laughed. The waiter poured some more coffee. Faith knew she had to leave soon and catch the plane back to Boston, but it was so much fun to be a grown-up at a time like this. She allowed her cup to be refilled.

'It would certainly explain the words Sandy Hoffmann overheard — 'It was a game and you lost,' and that business about getting blood from a stone.'

'Well.' Andy stretched back in his chair. 'I leave it to you, and do let me know the ending. I hate books that leave you hanging, and it's even worse in real life. Speaking of endings, did you see in this morning's *Times* that all those greedy people who were trying to sublet their apartments for New Year's aren't finding takers, plus those who have might find themselves in trouble with their landlords or co-op and condo boards?'

'I haven't seen the paper yet today, but I've heard that people were asking as much as ten thousand for the week. What are you doing to celebrate? Staying in the city? Since I assume you aren't taking in lodgers yourself.' Andy had a great apartment on Riverside Drive, overlooking the Hudson.

'It's all really Y2Much, as far as I'm concerned, and I haven't thought that far ahead. Probably have some people over, watch the fireworks, go to bed. Or maybe spend it in Paris or Cairo.'

'Difficult choices,' Faith said, teasing him. Andy didn't even want a pet. He once told her he wanted to be able to walk out his door and go anywhere in the world whenever he wanted, or needed to, without thinking about anything more than what adapter to pack for his shaver.

'I have to leave, but I'll tell you quickly about the great First Parish two hundred and fiftieth anniversary debate — steeple versus crypt repair to mark the momentous occasion.'

'You're making this up,' Andy said, signaling for the check.

'I couldn't possibly,' Faith said.

'There's that.' Andy smiled. 'By the way, have I told you how really beautiful you're looking? Happily, you're one of those women who get better-looking as they get older, not that you weren't a dish at sixteen.'

'Oh, go on with you,' Faith said.

It really had been a great lunch.

★ ★ ★

Wedged into a seat in the rear of the plane, she was feeling extremely well fed. Andy had introduced her to Christer Larsson, the Swedish-born chef, on their way out and he'd urged Faith to return after Thanksgiving for the holiday menu and glögg.

The flight attendant had given her the *New York Times*, which she folded subway-style, so she could read the article about the millennial sublets. An ad for a reading and signing by Anson L. Scott at the Black Orchid Bookshop, a mystery bookstore on East Eighty-first Street, caught her eye. It was for Saturday night. So, he was still out of town. That explained why she hadn't heard from him. She'd left a message on his machine the day before, reminding him that he'd told her to come back and talk with him about what the other mystery writers said. She was even more eager now to see Scott. Andy had given her a great deal to think about, and if she could talk about it all with a master plotter, it would definitely help. She'd like to talk to Bill Brown, too — and Tanya O'Malley. Which meant she'd have to see Veronica Brookside, as well. Faith remembered what the writer had said about how small a world the mystery community was. Veronica was bound to find out if she wasn't included. Faith felt a little uneasy about giving her any reason to feel offended, not that Veronica wanted to talk to Faith. But Faith had discovered that the Veronicas of the world had an odd way of popping up inconveniently later in life — and they had long memories.

She wasn't tired, but she closed her eyes and thought about how the afternoon sun in the city had turned the skyscrapers to dazzling silver and gold. Andy could have Paris or Cairo. If it were up to her, she'd spend New Year's in New York.

Then in what seemed like an incredibly short amount of time, the plane began its descent. It hit the tarmac with a thud. She was back.

11

'The whole silly business will be over on Sunday,' Tom said excitedly as he entered the house.

'Why Sunday?' Faith asked, thinking also that *silly* was not the adjective she would have chosen to describe this business. 'What's happened? Is it Janice after all?'

'Not that business. I certainly wouldn't describe murder as silly. The Anniversary Campaign. Steeple versus crypt. *That* business. The vestry met last night and decided that each side could make a ten-minute presentation after the service and then take a vote. You can bet there won't be an empty pew. They're informing the parish by the phone tree.'

'Why the big rush? Not that this isn't great news.'

'Apparently, word of the bickering has leaked out and steeple-versus-crypt jokes are rampant in the greater Boston area. The senior warden overheard several on the train, told with great relish by someone who got off in Concord, and enough very rapidly became enough. Aleford has its image to protect.'

329

'I thought this sort of thing was its image.'

'Now, Faith — ' Tom admonished.

'Let's just hope there are more crypts than steeples,' she said, interrupting. 'I wonder if there'll be banners? 'Vote for above, not below'? 'All rests upon a mighty foundation'?'

'I get the point,' her husband conceded.

It was only as she was dropping off to sleep several hours later that she recalled she had completely forgotten to mention she had had lunch in New York.

★ ★ ★

'So now you think it's Nick Gabriel?' Niki asked. 'It makes sense. Maybe he's harbored a secret hatred for his cousin all these years, pretending to be close. Maybe he was jealous of him. I mean, the guy did seem to have it all — money and the dame.'

'Except they're both dead now.'

'True. But even aside from possibly peddling hot or phony art, there's a motive. With Janice, all you've got is the crazed-mom angle, not that I don't buy it. I read the papers — and remember what Anthony Perkins said in *Psycho*: 'A boy's best friend is his mother.' Make that 'girl's' and 'hers' and you've got Janice. Having the darkroom right there seems mighty convenient. But then,

Nick would be in and out of artists' studios all the time and could easily palm some cyanide from one of the photographers the gallery represents.'

Faith had asked Niki to come over to talk. Niki had said she'd be happy to but that she reserved the right not to listen to anything she didn't want to hear. So far, any and all attempts on Faith's part to discuss the future of the business, and Niki's future, in particular, had met with not-so-subtle resistance. Niki had insistently steered the conversation toward other topics.

'Look, forget about the murders. You have got to listen to what I have to say, and I never agreed to your terms. We're going into the holidays without any work. There's no money coming in, and we have to face facts.'

'We do too have a booking. You heard it yourself on the machine. Ursula is having a party.'

'We can't really count that,' Faith objected.

'Of course we can. We're going to charge her, and we have an obligation to stay in business until then.'

Faith sighed. 'It's not the money. You know that. We're okay for a while. But what kind of a job are you going to get with me for a reference and all this following you around like a bad smell?'

'Hey, I resent that. Now look, boss, I appreciate what you're trying to do, but, number one, I think you are reacting way too fast, and, number two, I wouldn't want to work anyplace that didn't think a recommendation from you wasn't peachy keen. Which leads to number three — namely, I don't want to work anyplace else. Have Faith suits my lifestyle, and when you aren't trying to do what you think is the right thing, you're fun to work for.'

Niki went to the refrigerator and started pulling out eggs and butter. 'Now I want to try that new recipe you found for those almost-flourless individual chocolate cakes.'

'You're hopeless,' Faith said.

Niki whirled around. 'No, *you're* hopeless. You're supposed to be saying to hell with them and riding it out.'

And I would have a few years ago, Faith realized with a start. Was living in Aleford, in the parish, making her lose her nerve? The notion was extremely depressing — and scary.

She reached for the Valrhona dark chocolate. 'You're absolutely right. We'll go out of business when we're good and ready.'

Niki laughed. 'Glad you're back.'

'Brave words,' Faith said.

By the next morning, she was beginning to

think some enforced time off might not be such a bad thing. It would certainly make the holidays easier; plus, here it was a Saturday and she didn't have to rush off to a job. She had actually been able to make something tasty for their lunch, a new, and absurdly simple, coq au vin recipe that was simmering away on the stove top. Tom was working on his sermon, and Faith was raking leaves with the kids in the backyard, creating huge piles for them to jump in. Pix had walked over, remarking on how much she missed the smell of burning leaves now that Aleford had banned open fires.

'Maybe you could sprinkle some on top of your fireplace logs,' Faith suggested.

'It won't be the same indoors,' Pix said.

Not having participated in this suburban rite, Faith found it hard to share her nostalgia, but Tom, coming out to stretch his legs, immediately agreed, and the two had a jolly time talking bonfires.

When he left to go back indoors, Pix, gazing after him, said, 'Poor Tom. He looks tired. I'm glad that at least this crypt/steeple matter will be out of the way when we vote tomorrow.'

It was one thing when Millicent Revere McKinley said 'Poor Tom' and quite another when Pix did. Faith leaned on her rake, then ran after Pix, who was returning to her own leaves.

'Wait! Do you think Danny could baby-sit tonight so Tom and I could maybe go to the movies, get something to eat?'

'Great idea, and if he can't for some reason, I'll come myself.' Pix said this so enthusiastically that Faith felt as if she were being offered the last seat in the lifeboat. Obviously, Pix thought there was a lot at stake here. And there really wasn't — of course. Just a night out.

'I'll go right in and ask him. We can catch an early show.'

Faith ran in the back door and into Tom's study, stopping short when she saw that he wasn't madly typing away, as usual on Saturdays, but staring at the keyboard, his face in his hands.

'Honey?' she called. Startled, he sat up straight and clicked the mouse. The flying toasters screen saver gave way to lines of text.

She leaned over the back of his chair and put her arms around him. 'How would you like a hot date tonight? We've got a sitter and can go anywhere we want. Movies, dinner, motel.' Her words felt forced and she already knew what his answer would be.

'I'll take a rain check, okay? I don't really feel like going out tonight.'

It was a little after three o'clock when the phone rang. Amy was asleep and Faith had just put Ben down to nap, as well, after finding him with his eyes closed next to his father, who was watching a Celtics game. Ben didn't protest, and she hoped he wasn't coming down with something. Tom was half-asleep himself. We're all tired, Faith thought as she went to get the phone. It was bound to be about tomorrow's vote; most of them had been so far, and she intended to tell whoever it was that the Reverend Thomas Fairchild could not be disturbed. Let them assume he was praying. She couldn't use working on his sermon, as an excuse. First Parish would not be particularly sympathetic to leaving something so important to the last minute. But it wasn't someone from the church. It was Anson Scott.

'Faith, my good — and talented — lady. I received your plea for help on my answering machine and dare to hope that you might have a moment anon. Admittedly, greediness is almost as strong a motive as base curiosity. I'm sure you have something in your cookie jar to bring me.'

'But aren't you in New York? Don't you have a reading at a mystery bookstore tonight? The Black Orchid, I think it was called. It was in the *Times*.'

'*Last* night. That particular obligation has been met. Dear people, the owners, Bonnie and Joe.' He sounded slightly annoyed, and Faith wondered if the turnout had been low. She had thought the ad said Saturday, yet she had been concentrating on other things during her flight back from the Big Apple. 'So, my dear, let's meet.'

Faith was reluctant to leave. They might not be going out, but she and Tom would at least have time together at home.

'Tonight's not good for me. How about tomorrow afternoon or evening?'

'No can do. I have merely the most minuscule of windows before I must away to more of my adoring public. If not tonight, how about now?'

Why not now? It was, in fact, a perfect time. Everyone was asleep, or nearly so, and she could slip away for an hour or two. She really wanted to run her latest theories by Scott and then call John Dunne.

'Yes, that would work. I can be at your house in fifteen minutes or so.'

'Margery has gone to her sister's in Ashtabula — really, that is where her sister lives, so much fun to say — and the house is rather shut up. I'm simply camping here, poised between flights.'

'There's always the Minuteman Café, good muffins, but very public.'

'Too public. I'd rather not sign any more books or paper napkins, whatever. Hand gets rather cramped, you know.'

Faith was staring out the window. He could come to the parsonage, but she wasn't sure she wanted Tom to know she was talking to the mystery writer. Especially not at the moment when things between them were — well, what were they? She felt profoundly depressed. She looked at the church's steeple. Even from here, she could see it needed work. Paint was peeling on one side. The church. Perfect. She had a key. No one would bother them. They could use one of the older children's Sunday school classrooms. Somehow, she couldn't picture Anson in the rocking chair in the day-care center, and it would be Goldilocks all over again with one of the small chairs.

Anson thought the church was a fine idea and they arranged to meet. Faith promised cookies. She'd baked some more oatmeal lace ones the previous day.

She hung up the phone, filled a bag with cookies and a thermos with milk. She didn't want to take the time to brew coffee. Scott might be amused by this throwback to childhood, and she'd heard that milk and cookies were appearing as a dessert item at some of New York's trendiest restaurants; the milk was even being served in small containers with straws.

The game was still going strong and she went in to tell Tom she was going out for a while, to the library. As she formulated the fib, she thought about the last week and felt 'sick with secrets,' as the old saying went. She was relieved to find she didn't have to say anything. Tom was slumped over, dead to the world, and snoring slightly. She scrawled a hasty note — 'Had to go out for a while; back soon' — and left it on the kitchen table.

She was early. Scott had said he'd need a half hour. She left the back door open for him and walked into the sanctuary, past the church offices. Missy's wrapping-paper display was still up. Maybe Janice *had* killed both Gwen and Jared. And if she had, Faith better be looking over her shoulder. After the other night, the woman certainly had no love for her. Janice and Missy. Perverted mother love. She thought about the Texas cheerleader case. The facts had seemed so unbelievable that they'd stayed in Faith's mind. Wanda — again, a name you didn't forget — had plotted to kill both the girl she thought had kept her daughter from the squad and the girl's mother, who she believed had engineered the whole thing. In the end, Wanda settled on just the mother, because hiring a hitman to kill both was too expensive, and anyway, the girl would be so distraught that she'd likely drop cheerleading. Was this so different from Janice? Janice believed Jared was responsible for thwarting Missy's musical career, that he didn't recognize Missy's true talents. Maybe she'd hoped he'd quit when Gwen died. Maybe she'd believed he, like the principal, was a sexual threat to Missy. And what better way to punish him than to first kill his girlfriend and then kill him after telling him about it? Were Janice and Wanda soulmates?

The door to the crypt was open. Faith smiled. She was surprised there wasn't a whole tour group of parishioners checking it out before finalizing their vote. They must have come in yesterday when the church was open. They couldn't very well climb the steeple. But the crypt was something else. She went over to close the door and decided to take a look around while she waited. It had been years since she'd been there. She stepped down and her pocketbook strap caught on the handle of the door, pulling it shut. Annoyed, she straightened her bag and turned the knob to open the door. It was the crypt, after all.

She now realized why it had been left ajar. It didn't open. The knob didn't budge, no matter how hard she turned it. She groped for the light switch and received the second blow. There was no power in the crypt, or, rather, what had been was presently kaput. Instantly abandoning all pretense of objectivity, she vowed to call the entire parish tonight to inform them of these facts. The crypt was a death trap and its repair was critical to the well-being of the church. It wasn't as if the steeple was falling down on their heads.

Her bag contained any number of possible aids, including a Swiss army knife. She could try to slide it between the door and the frame, releasing the catch. She also had a little penlight to help. After several frustrating attempts, she was forced to concede that the church was simply too well built — or the wood had swelled over the years. There was no way she could get the knife blade into the tiny crack. She sat down on the top stair. When Anson didn't find her by the back door, would he leave after a while, look around for her, or call home? The last two might bring help. She should start pounding on the door soon in the hopes that he would hear. And Tom would search for her, wouldn't he? Of course he would. In any case, the worst that could happen would be that she'd have to spend the night in the crypt.

Spend the night in the crypt!

It was a prospect straight from one of Scott's books.

She stood up and pounded on the door, yelling, 'Help, I'm locked in the crypt!' a few times for good measure.

Scott's books. She shuddered as the memories of some of the more sensational plots came flooding back. Inexplicably, the memory of the ad she'd seen in the paper came back, too. She could visualize it. Saturday, November 6. 'Spend Saturday night with the master of crime.' She was positive. Why would he lie?

She stopped pounding. She kept very quiet.

The master of crime. Suddenly, she knew who had killed Gwen and who had killed Jared. And who might very well be intending to kill her, too. Right now.

When the footsteps came, she retreated down the stairs, stumbling over a pile of framed religious prints at the bottom. One slid to the floor, the glass shattering. The footsteps stopped. She flashed her light, searching for a place to hide. The crypt didn't offer much cover. There were, as she'd recalled earlier, boxes of hymnals, chairs in various states of disrepair, some coatracks, and a great many memorial stones, some flat on the floor, some set into the side walls. The best she could do was crouch behind one of the supporting columns. She did so immediately. She was still clutching the thermos and bag of cookies. The thermos was a heavy metal one. She dropped her pocketbook and the cookies and held the thermos in both hands as a club. Hope flickered as she prayed the door would prove as impenetrable from the outside as it had from the inside.

Anson L. Scott. Why?

Bill Brown's voice came back to her. 'Murderers are crazy.' Leopold and Loeb. And Veronica's: 'Place can be another character, you know.' They'd all said that murderers are accomplished actors. Tanya had suggested a sexual thrill, and Anson himself had summed it all up, saying that murderers are conceited. They believe they can fool the world.

Hubris. Anson L. Scott. It was all there, all the time. From Ballou House, the setting, to the mutilated squirrel, to Halloween night — to now.

And Faith herself had suggested the meeting place.

'Ah.' Hearing his voice panicked her so much, she thought she might pass out. She tightened her grip on the thermos. She'd have the element of surprise. 'A faulty door. And, silly girl, you've locked yourself in. I'll get you out in a jiffy, dear lady,' he called. 'Thank goodness I heard your calls for aid. Nasty place to spend the night. Fortunately, I have my picks with me. Trained with the best — although presently he's doing six to ten at Walpole — for a book I wrote some years ago.'

He sounded absolutely normal. Normal for Anson L. Scott. Could she be wrong? She would feel silly indeed if she knocked him out cold and he wasn't the murderer after all. That it was Janice — or Nick. But Nick wouldn't kill Jared. Ursula had said they were like brothers, the good kind of brothers, close. And Janice — the night of October 23, Janice had been in the wrong place at the wrong time.

She saw the beam of a powerful flashlight on the stairs. The door was open — and he was coming down. 'No lights. This suggests penury rather than thrift on the church's part, but I always carry my trusty torch in my greatcoat.' He sounded positively jovial.

'Faith, where are you? Playing hide-and-seek?' When the silence of the grave was all that greeted his query, good humor swiftly vanished, and there was no mistaking the menace in his voice. 'Answer me!' Not finding her right on the other side of the door had immediately given him the clue he needed. 'Now, lovely Mrs Fairchild, I know you're down here. No need to be frightened. It's only me.' He laughed theatrically. A Vincent Price laugh.

The stairs creaked under his weight and Faith wished in vain he'd go through one, injuring himself. Of all the things in the crypt to be in good shape . . .

'Come out, come out wherever you are,' he called mockingly, letting the flashlight beam play against the walls.

'I see you,' he chortled, and walked directly toward her. She didn't move. She'd known the narrow column wouldn't hide her for long, but she'd make him come to her.

'Let me see. What little trick do you have up your sleeve? Not a gun. Ministers' wives are seldom armed in these parts. You would have been carrying a purse, and, aside from the goodies for me, it probably contains any number of lethal implements. A nail file — good when aimed at an eye. A pocketknife. Go for the jugular with that. Especially in my case. Too much avoirdupois over my heart. How about pepper spray? That would be annoying. Except in Aleford, you have to get permission from the police to carry it, and I can't see good old dim-witted Charley agreeing to a need for it on our safe streets.'

Anson L. Scott was enjoying himself. He was so close she could smell the faint musk of his aftershave.

She screamed. There had never been the remotest chance. Scott had blinded her with the strong beam of light and wrenched the thermos from her hands. He kicked it to one side and drew a knife with a long, thin blade from his coat pocket. He held it in the light, close to his face, smiling. It was a nightmare.

'It's all been such fun and you have played your part admirably. I am going to miss you. So you had a thermos. How thoughtful. Coffee — or maybe milk — to go with the baked goods,' he said, pulling her in front of the column and pushing her against it. He was wearing soft leather gloves.

'My husband knows I'm meeting you here. You can't possibly think you're going to get away with this.'

'Not an accomplished liar, dear thing. Not like *moi*. Of course I have ascertained that your husband has no idea as to your whereabouts or with whom. That's why I needed a bit of time. A call or two to make. I explained to him that I was checking my messages while on my book tour and would get in touch with you when I was back in

Aleford. He told me the Celtics game — I am rather a fan, too — was so boring, he'd fallen asleep and that you had slipped off he knew not where.'

'When you don't show up for your reading, it will come out that you weren't in New York. Plus, you must have been seen coming into the church. And your car is in the parking lot. Not too many other people in Aleford, or anywhere else, drive cream-colored Rolls-Royces.'

'I mustn't laugh. You are such an amateur, though, it's difficult not to break into peals of merriment. First, I *am* in New York. Working in my room at the Carlyle, not to be disturbed for anything save immediate threat of peril. They know me and my ways. No one will knock on the door or ring the phone until I give the word. And when I return after the appearance at the Black Orchid, there will be a whole new crew at the desk, who will assume I left earlier. My car is in my garage and the rental, something American that looks like every other car on the road, is parked in the Shop and Save lot with others of its ilk. Easy to slip through the woods behind the church to and from the lot, you know. It gets dark so nice and early now. My favorite time of year. And even if I am noted on the shuttle, there's nothing to connect me to all of this. I barely know you. No one would think to suspect me and check the airlines.'

He was right. He'd appear at the bookstore in time and no one would know he'd spent the day in Aleford. Just as no one had known she'd spent Thursday in New York. There was something ironic in all this, but it wasn't something she wanted to think about at the moment.

'And now here we are, the crypt. I couldn't have picked a better spot myself. The book will be fabulous. My crowning achievement.' He gestured expansively with the knife.

'You're writing a book about all this? It's all been so you can write a book!' She was indignant. Who knows? Perhaps his sales figures *were* slipping, but that was no reason to murder two — make that three — people.

He looked at his watch. 'We have a few minutes to spare — and it's the least I can do after you've brought me a treat.' He pointed the light at the bag on the floor. She immediately kicked it against the wall, where it came to rest, appropriately enough, beneath Hiram Slaughter's marker. Sometimes life is truly stranger than fiction, she reminded herself.

'Temper, temper. But no mind. I can retrieve it later. Now, I was about to tell you a tale. The abridged version, sadly. It all started last summer when my agent was calling with a great many dire predictions. He tends to be excitable. I knew the book that's out currently would lay his fears to rest, but he started me thinking about my legacy. Certainly people will remember *Blood Root* and *Fool's Poison* for a long, long time. But I decided to write a book that would live forever, unlike we poor human beings. I would commit the perfect crime, write my account, and leave instructions for it to be published after my unfortunate demise. I would leave not only an immortal book but also an audacious act.'

The whole thing was unbelievable and inexplicable. 'Why did you select Gwen and Jared as victims? What had they ever done to you?'

'Absolutely nothing. That was the joy of it all. I knew my story would find me, so I waited. When the invitation to the event at Ballou House came, I had my setting. My grandmother, who raised me after my poor mother killed herself, had worked there. I'm afraid her employers were not very enlightened, and as a girl, she was forced to suffer many physical hardships and even worse psychological indignities. Mother was born out of wedlock and, in the family tradition, so was I, except Mother couldn't stand the stigma and left this earth. Granny was made of tougher metal and determined that I should make something of myself. And so I have. I even tried to buy Ballou House, a monstrous ark — don't know what I would have done with it — because I knew it would have pleased her. But I digress. My book is a work in progress. You, for instance, have selected this scene. Throughout, I've simply been following the course of events, with only an occasional intervention. I poisoned one of the desserts when they were on the counter in the kitchen. No one was about. I knew from the paper what you would be serving, and cyanide was a nice old-fashioned touch. All those lovely British village mysteries redolent with the odor of bitter almonds. Little did I dream that Lady Luck would place me at the same table as the victim. It was too delicious. And such an abundance of suspects. There was your husband, fawning all over the girl — sorry, Faith, but these things must be said. Her fiancé, who may have wanted out of the relationship. His cousin, who employed her at the gallery and, I recalled, had been selling prints of dubious provenance not so long ago. There could be something there. I ruled out Ursula Rowe. Too intelligent, and she might figure it all out. Her daughter was no threat to me, but a bit too colorless. All those good works. Of course, they could mask some nice pathology, but I wasn't interested. I *was* tempted by Paula Pringle. She'd been calling incessantly and presuming a relationship where none existed. She is really quite horrible, but she was leaving town, and that didn't fit in with my plans. I knew suspicion would inevitably fall upon the caterer, and I'm afraid I have been murmuring a word here and there about your business — reminding people about that other 'mishap' when you were catering the movie shoot. Such fun having them here, even though they were filming a dreary old Hawthorne and not me.'

Faith was furious. 'So that's why everyone's been canceling!'

'You give me too much credit and Aleford not enough. Most of them acted solely on their own. You know how rumors spread in this town. Like the one about the reverend and the deceased.'

Faith was so choked with rage, she couldn't speak.

'Again, just one or two words. I'm afraid Margery is an inveterate gossip.'

She certainly didn't look the part, Faith thought bitterly. Poor Tom.

'Yet once more, fate stepped in and gave me the perfect suspect. Someone capable of murder. A veritable time bomb. Janice

Mulholland. I'm quite a good listener, you know, and all that was necessary was to ask an occasional question and make sympathetic noises. Janice's life became an open book, including her vendetta against the principal. Again, I was able to fan the flames a bit that evening. It was all there waiting.'

'So *you* framed Janice. *You* put the receipt for the wrapping paper in Jared's briefcase.'

'I had to direct the police to her darkroom, don't you know.' He was adopting a kind of Bertie Wooster/Jeeves tone. 'She's quite insane when it comes to her daughter. Completely gaga. Actually gave me the form. I noticed as I came in just now that rather serendipitously she's got a table full of them here at the church. Wonderful red herrings.'

Faith felt a ringing in her ears. Her head seemed about to explode. It was an Anson L. Scott book come to life — and he himself was the quintessential murderer. An amoral sociopathic psychopath. Murder — the ultimate expression of narcissism.

'All this time when you've been on your book tour, you've been coming back to town.'

He nodded. 'I believe it was D.C. when young Jared was killed.'

'And was that really necessary! You'd already committed your crime!' Faith blurted out.

'You must not read much mystery fiction, Faith,' he said reproachfully. 'You always have to have a second body — and in my books, rather more than that. Gwen was chapter one. So obligingly in costume. Marvelous details. That lovely beaded turquoise dress she wore, covered with her so very bright red blood. My words have never flowed as easily across the page.'

Faith gagged.

'Oh dear, I've upset you. Never mind. The end is near.'

Faith straightened up. She had to keep him talking.

'So, it was you who left that squirrel on my doorstep — and followed me home that night.'

He grinned, and as he answered, Faith heard a very, very faint creak. Someone was coming down the stairs.

'Just fooling with you. Again, details. The pleasure of my craft is in the details. Readers love those little touches. I wonder if there might be some way I could get the recipe for those scrumptious muffins you brought when you came to my house. Manna from heaven — the food and your arrival. It was all falling right into my lap. I could print the recipe in the book. You'd be leaving a little something, too.'

'No, thank you,' Faith said frostily.

'No need to take offense.'

Faith didn't, especially since she could see a dim shape inching slowly toward them from the other end of the crypt. It was so dark, she couldn't make out whether it was a man or a woman. Not tall enough for Tom. But whoever it was, it was help.

She started talking frantically, loudly.

'I don't understand why you have to kill me. This has all been a figment of your imagination. I don't believe a word of it. That's what I would say to the police or anyone else. You certainly had me fooled for a moment, but now why don't we go upstairs and have the milk and cookies.'

'Delightful, delightful. Would that I could. But I must bid you adieu. And this won't hurt but a moment. Jared didn't feel a thing, I believe. If there's one thing I know, it's how to kill people. Again, one of those happy accidents. I saw him on his way to his car — apparently after playing in church — asked him for a lift home, killed him, then deposited him on your lawn later. Now hold still.' He pinned her against the column with one hand, forcing the flashlight painfully hard against her neck, and lifted the other hand to strike.

Faith screamed, an inarticulate gurgling,

and tried to push him away.

The shadowy figure took a giant step forward and brought one of the huge First Parish altar candlesticks squarely down on the mystery writer's head. It was an ecclesiastical mace and the man dropped like a stone.

'Let's get out of here. Places like this give me the creeps. I need a cigarette.' It was Janice Mulholland, the woman herself.

★　★　★

Faith called 911; then she called John Dunne at state police headquarters and Tom. Finally, she got a cup from the church kitchen for Janice to use as an ashtray and said, 'How in God's name did you just happen to come along?'

'It had nothing to do with God — or maybe it does — but I got a call from someone from the church saying that they were meeting here to interview candidates for music director and that it was the expressed wish of the committee that I withdraw my daughter from the choir to make the job easier for the new person. They dragged up that old business about Missy tripping the soloist last year on purpose, when everyone who was there could see the girl was a klutz and fell over her own feet. Whoever it was — I didn't catch the name — said I was welcome to express my opinion at the end of the meeting, which would be about five o'clock, and not to come before then or I wouldn't be heard at all.'

Actors. Murderers are marvelous actors.

'The more I thought about it, the more pissed off I got. I mean, who do you people think you are?'

Faith felt called upon to remind Janice that it had been Anson, that there really wasn't any meeting, and that, in any case, she wouldn't have been there.

'Right. I know this. Sorry. Just thinking about it makes me mad all over again. He certainly knew the right buttons to push.'

He certainly did. Only, thankfully, this time he pushed a little too hard. He'd planned on being long gone by the time Janice showed up.

'Anyway, I came over and the church was empty. I couldn't figure out where they were meeting. Then I figured maybe they were showing the candidates the organ and the choir loft, so I went into the sanctuary, but that was empty, too. I was going to leave, when I heard Anson Scott's voice. I recognized it right away. It was coming through the heat register in the floor.

I thought that was odd. He's not a member of the church, and why would he be in the crypt? I thought maybe he was researching a book, and I was going to go down to say hello, when I heard my name, so naturally I lay down and put my ear to the grate. I couldn't believe it! At first, I was going to call the police and let them handle it, but I was afraid he might kill you while I was away, so I grabbed one of the candlesticks — they weigh a ton — and went down the stairs. The rest you know.'

The sirens in the distance were getting closer.

'The rest I know,' said Faith, throwing her arms around the PTA secretary.

'Chair the book fair in the spring?' Janice asked, never one to let an opportunity pass.

Everything has a price, Faith thought, yet this was one she would happily pay. 'Anything you want.'

★   ★   ★

By the time Faith got home from the police station, the casserole brigade had been out in full force. Patsy and Pix were still holding the fort.

'Millicent dropped by and brought you this.' Patsy held a package of freeze-dried beef stew by one corner, as if it might be contaminated. 'She said you should save it for later and you'd know what that meant.'

'Unfortunately, I do.' Faith's throat hurt and every molecule in her body called out for Tylenol and sleep, but she was so happy to be alive, sitting on the couch, that she forced herself to stay awake. Tom had arrived at the church with the kids — Amy sockless and shoeless — and he hadn't left her side since.

'Fortunately, while you've been gone, I've cooked some smothered pork chops, collards, and rice,' Patsy said.

'I knew this house smelled better than when I left,' Tom said. 'I'm starving.' He looked at his wife. 'Go eat,' she said, thrilled that his appetite was back. 'I'll have some tomorrow. But you should all eat now. It does smell fantastic.' She'd had Patsy's smothered pork chops before — onions, peppers, rich brown gravy, and meat so tender, it dropped off the bone.

They returned with heaped plates and a big bowl of Crème Crémaillère ice cream for Faith.

Before everyone got settled, Faith stood up and said, 'The first person who says 'I told you so' doesn't get dessert, but please help me move this couch back where it was. We'll be lighting fires soon and it's ridiculous not

357

to sit in front of the fireplace — besides, I've had my fill of looking at headstones.'

★   ★   ★

Faith was sitting in church, counting her blessings, or trying to count them, so she could avoid thinking about her intimate acquaintance with the area just below her feet. It was the time set aside for announcements. The senior warden got to her feet and said, 'In light of recent events, the vestry has decided to forgo today's meeting to decide the use to which our Anniversary Campaign fund-raising be put. It has become evident that the appalling condition of the crypt demands our immediate attention.' Faith was stunned. The senior warden had been one of the most militant and outspoken steeple advocates. 'The campaign will concentrate on a project to put in new wiring, clean the memorial stones, and, in general, make it possible for us to use the crypt for services when appropriate. If there are any objections, individuals may make them known to myself or the junior warden, but this is our decision.' She faced Faith directly. 'We would now like to offer a prayer of thanksgiving for the deliverance of our minister's wife.' Feeling slightly like a parcel and with a passing wish that she had been named, not labeled, Faith was nonetheless extraordinarily touched and surprised. The faces of the congregation *did* look thankful and a few eyes were brimming, most notably Pix's. Tom was beaming at her from the pulpit and they exchanged a glance. Yes, these people could drive you crazy, but you had to love them.

* * *

Several hours later, walking at Drumlin Farm, Faith told Tom how she'd felt.

'Exactly. This is how I feel most of the time, too, except at long meetings. Anyway, I'm glad the steeple/crypt thing has been resolved. I wasn't looking forward to more acrimony. The whole thing has gone on much too long. Of course,' he said swiftly, 'I would have liked it to have been resolved in a different manner.'

'Me, too.'

They were on a nature walk led by an earnest guide from the Audubon Society. Faith couldn't remember whether it was about seed dispersal or identifying animal droppings. They had been on so many of these that she didn't pay much attention to the topic except when they came for sugaring off in the spring. Ben had scampered on ahead. Amy was in the Gerry Pack on Tom's back. Her little head, with its wispy corn-silk hair, rested against his shoulder blade. She was talking to herself.

The drumlin, a high ridge left by the glacier, was ahead of them and they were soon at the top. Rural Lincoln, which happily existed in a kind of eco-time warp in a corner of the sprawling western suburbs, lay at their feet. The nature group was at one end, examining milkweed pods or deer pellets.

Faith looked at her husband. 'We still have to talk,' she said softly. 'It doesn't have to be now, but sometime.'

For a moment, Tom didn't reply; then he said, 'She was having panic attacks about getting married. She'd had trouble with depression before and was afraid of saddling Jared with her problems. She came to me a few times, but she rejected all my suggestions — that they come see me together or that she get some psychological help. She used to go through very bad periods where voices would tell her things — get married; don't get married. I advised she put the wedding off, but she wouldn't hear of that, either. I had the feeling it wasn't just her engagement that was bothering her, but something else, as well. She mentioned how guilty she felt quite often, and I don't think it was simply about misleading Jared. The last time I saw her — that night — she told me everything was fine. That talking to me had 'cured' her. But I didn't believe it. The way she was acting, it was as if she had to convince me.'

Faith took her husband's hand.

'When she died, I felt worse than I've ever felt in my life. That somehow it was my fault. I felt my faith slipping away — both of them. It's been horrible. I've been horrible.'

'No,' she said. 'Just human.'

He managed a smile. 'But ministers aren't supposed to be human.'

'You don't believe that.'

'No, I don't, but you know what I mean. We're supposed to be above emotion.'

And temptation, Faith added silently, thinking of how heart-breakingly attractive Gwendolyn Lord in great distress must have been.

'Then the whole thing broke with George Hammond and finally Jared's murder. I went off the deep end myself. I just couldn't put things in perspective. I've started going to see Max; it's helped.' Max was older than Tom, the rabbi at Aleford's synagogue.

It was hard to get her arm around Tom's waist with the backpack, but Faith managed and pulled him close.

They'd be continuing this conversation for the rest of their lives, but there was one thing she had to tell him right away.

'I went to the city on Thursday to have lunch with Andy.'

'I know,' Tom said. 'Your boarding pass was in the trash. I hope he took you someplace good.'

Ben came running up. 'You have to see this! It's called jewel-weed. As soon as you touch it, it kind of explodes and shoots its seeds into the air.' He grabbed Faith's hand. 'Come on, Mom! Come on, Dad! You're missing everything!'

Oh no we're not, Faith thought, and let herself be pulled across the wide-open field.

Epilogue

Millicent Revere McKinley sat in front of her tiny black-and-white television surrounded by her Y2K compliant storehouse of goods. She had been up before dawn, as usual, and watched with growing annoyance as the New Year came without incident, starting in Kiribati in the Western Pacific. Of course, it was an uninhabited atoll and there weren't any microchips in the conch shells that celebrants from the inhabited part of the Gilbert Islands blew to signal the start of the new millennium. Her hopes had risen at reports of ticketing problems on some buses in Australia and computers crashing in rural Japan, only to be dashed by the lack of any substantive glitches as the earth turned. When the Greenwich Mean Time New Year arrived, shortly after 7:00 P.M. EST, she was resigned enough to enjoy the sight of Big Ben illuminated by fireworks. She even gave a passing thought to purchasing a color television. Throughout the day, she'd had a nagging feeling that the celebrations she was witnessing might be losing something in black and white.

She had never watched so much television in her life, leaving only to stretch, take bathroom breaks, and open a can of some kind of non-perishable food. At midnight, Aleford time, she toasted the 2 million revelers in New York's Times Square with Poland Spring water and wondered how they went about counting so many people. And how would they clean up three tons of confetti? Well, it was not her problem. She switched off the television and made her way through the provisions to bed.

It had been quite a year. Especially this fall. She was glad George Hammond's name had been cleared. He was a good man. Maybe too good. He wasn't pressing charges against that crazy woman, Janice Mulholland, so long as she agreed to get help. He wouldn't even let her resign from the PTA. But she had done real harm, and even the letter she wrote to the paper and the announcement she made at the next PTA meeting wouldn't completely quell those rumors. There would always be a shadow cast on George's name. It might be slight, but it would be there. Supposedly, she had gone off the deep end after her marriage broke up. Marriage. Millicent never regretted her decision not to get involved in that particular institution. Men were all right in their place, but she couldn't have abided having one around all the time.

Then there were the murders. She wasn't surprised it was that mystery writer. She'd heard authors would do anything to sell books, and this one just took it to the limit. He was writing away in prison, she'd heard. Wouldn't do poor Jared or that girl any good. She'd always liked Jared. Faith Fairchild had come by with some muffins and a pretty cyclamen plant the day after Christmas. Millicent wasn't sure how to take her 'coals to Newcastle' comment about the food, but it was nice to have something homemade. Millicent had never been much of a cook. Too much trouble to go to for one person, even herself. Faith still had a few too many New York ways for Millicent's taste, but they'd had a good talk about what had happened. Faith said she'd been on the wrong track at first because she'd been looking for a motive when there wasn't one. Millicent had disagreed. Vanity, pure and simple. Pride goeth before a fall. It was one of the maxims by which Millicent lived.

She was sleepy. It had been an exciting day, even though nothing had happened. She wasn't worried about what people would say now that Y2K had proven to be Y2Bad. How did they know what might have happened if all the governments, banks, businesses, and everybody else hadn't been prepared? She'd give a lot of her supplies to the Boston Food Bank. But not yet. Not until after February 29. It was leap year.

There was still hope.

We do hope that you have enjoyed reading this large print book.

Did you know that all of our titles are available for purchase?

We publish a wide range of high quality large print books including:
**Romances, Mysteries, Classics
General Fiction
Non Fiction and Westerns**

Special interest titles available in large print are:
**The Little Oxford Dictionary
Music Book
Song Book
Hymn Book
Service Book**

Also available from us courtesy of Oxford University Press:
**Young Readers' Dictionary
(large print edition)
Young Readers' Thesaurus
(large print edition)**

For further information or a free brochure, please contact us at:
**Ulverscroft Large Print Books Ltd.,
The Green, Bradgate Road, Anstey,
Leicester, LE7 7FU, England.
Tel:** (00 44) **0116 236 4325
Fax:** (00 44) **0116 234 0205**

Other titles published by
The House of Ulverscroft:

THE BODY IN THE MARSH

Katherine Hall Page

Faith Fairchild's husband, the Reverend Thomas Fairchild, learns that nursery school teacher Lora Deane has received threatening phone calls. And she's not the only resident of Aleford, Massachusetts, who is being terrorized. Some local environmentalists, protesting about the proposed housing development that will destroy Beecher's Bog, have become targets of a vicious campaign of intimidation — reason enough for Faith to launch into some clandestine sleuthing. But when a body turns up in the charred ruins of a suspicious house fire, Faith is suddenly investigating a murder — and in serious danger of getting bogged down in a very lethal mess indeed!

THE BODY IN THE BONFIRE

Katherine Hall Page

Caterer and sleuth Faith Fairchild goes undercover at Mansfield Academy, after learning about anonymous racist attacks against senior Daryl Martin. However, her inquiries are undermined as somebody tampers with the ingredients for a cookery demonstration when she attempts to teach Cooking for Idiots. Then the incinerated remains of Faith's prime suspect are discovered. It's not mischief but murder! The headmaster's wife, the teacher, the loner, and the hacker are all connected — but how? Faith frantically struggles to make sense of it — knowing the killer is tracking her every move. It's a race to save Mansfield and her own life.

THE BODY IN THE SNOWDRIFT

Katherine Hall Page

Faith Fairchild's father-in-law celebrates his seventieth birthday by taking the entire family for a week-long stay at the Pine Slopes ski resort. All starts well until Faith discovers a body on a cross-country trail, and Pine Slopes' star chef vanishes without a trace. One catastrophe follows another: a malicious prank, a break-in at the Fairchilds' condo and the sabotage of one of the chairlifts. There is also a mysterious woman living in the woods — and Faith's nephew Scott, and Ophelia Stafford, are up to something . . . Family secrets abound as Faith struggles to salvage the reunion . . . and save her own life.

THE BODY IN THE BIG APPLE

Katherine Hall Page

Young and single in New York in the 1980s, Faith Sibley's catering enterprise is a success. But she assumes an unexpected new role when she runs into old friend Emma Stanstead at an uptown party: *Sleuth*! An anonymous blackmailer is threatening to expose certain secrets of socialite Emma's past — thereby destroying her reputation and her husband's political career — and Faith leaps into the fray. Determined to unmask an extortionist, Faith is led into the low life of the bustling Big Apple. But a murder suddenly makes Faith realize that it's not just her friend's good name that is in peril . . .

THE BODY IN THE BOOKCASE

Katherine Hall Page

Faith Fairchild lives in a quaint Massachusetts town. A minister's wife, Faith is a caterer-detective. Working at full stretch with a demanding bride-to-be, she faces tragedy when she discovers the body of her elderly friend Sarah Winslow, who had apparently surprised burglars ransacking her house. Then the Fairchilds themselves are targeted — the parsonage is stripped of their most precious possessions. When Faith takes action, scouring pawnshops, and auctions, she finds some of their stolen property, but then she is drawn onto a dangerous path of corruption in New England's antiques business — a path that leads Faith straight to a killer!